'Soula Emmanuel's prose
deliciously funny, profoun
devastating read. An extra
intelligent and emotionally
Danielle McLaughlin

'*Wild Geese* is heartfelt, thought-provoking and beautifully crafted. Soula Emmanuel is a phenomenal talent.' **Laura Kay**

'Phoebe Forde, an Irish trans woman living in Scandinavia, illustrates with insight, candor and wit, the chrysalis of loneliness, in which she, and others perhaps, find themselves living. I am reminded that some women still have to leave Ireland for the chance to become themselves. *Wild Geese* is an intimate and deeply affecting portrait. Destined to be a classic of migrant literature.' **Carmel Mc Mahon**

First published in 2023 by
Footnote Press

This edition published in 2024 by Footnote Press

www.footnotepress.com

Footnote Press Limited
4th Floor, Victoria House, Bloomsbury Square, London WC1B 4DA

Distributed by Bonnier Books UK, a division of Bonnier Books
Sveavägen 56, Stockholm, Sweden

First printing
3 5 7 9 10 8 6 4 2

A CIP catalogue record for this book is available from the British Library.

ISBN (paperback): 978-1-804-44016-2
ISBN (ebook): 978-1-804-44015-5

Printed and bound in Great Britain
by Clays Ltd, Elcograf S.p.A.

FSC www.fsc.org
MIX
Paper | Supporting responsible forestry
FSC® C018072

Wild Geese

Soula Emmanuel

FOOTNOTE

Ten thousand nine hundred and ninety-two

Thursday

16:12 There is a daub of grass shaded by the university library, tufted with sapling trees held up by planks of wood. It is home to a scatter of hedgehogs, who come and go like apparitions, to whom I retain a pious devotion. After three and a half years in the city, I have a deeper kinship with them than I have with anyone else. They are allies more than friends – comrades, even. It is a comfort to imagine learning from them to back-and-forth unseen, to arm my flesh against the enduring dangers.

Their Swedish name is *igelkott*: the Old Norse *ígull*, meaning sea urchin, plus *kottr*, meaning cat. I found the etymology in an online dictionary once, and it's lingered in my memory, the way the poor divil straddles marine and feline. Evidence of man's talent for misassignment – an intrepid Viking, perhaps, on hearing a phantom purr, presumed the obvious and grabbed the wrong end of the ontological stick.

At home, *igelkott* is *gráinneog* – 'detestable little thing' – a moniker of almost un-Irish frankness. The hedgehog is a cross-culturally maligned and misunderstood creature: it may have an abundance of pricks but we're in no state to pass remarks.

16:19 The streets are kissed with grey and the air shivers with traces of fog. A caustic, mottled sky cloaks the college town: Lund, an ancient, adamant place through which I move now like a breath released.

Drifting over mud-sodden footpaths hemmed by naked birches, weighed down by the spoils of the day: a rattling lunchbox, a veteran laptop and dozens of annotated printouts about Liberian wastewater. They had a civil war in Liberia and it did for their sanitation, among other things. As an indirect consequence I am halfway through a doctorate that my life has outgrown.

Most people come to the faculty because they want to save the world. I came to save myself, and, having done so, begin to wonder if the planet can wait. I labour over a homeopathy of human existence: dysentery and Ebola and mass death reduced to beats in a paper soap opera.

There is no succour in it: the lanyarded rope-throwers, the curiously funded internships in Geneva and New York, cut-glass people who speak briskly but say little, and corporate loveliness exercises by now reduced to arguing for their right to carry on failing. Sustainable, sustainable: the talk of it is anything but – we are honour-guarding conveyor belts at the platitude factory in the hope that we will one day get to pan for the raw material ourselves.

My routine is a garden above a sinkhole. Most of it has fallen away, yet still I tend to the jagged edges, for want of better; for want of something to want.

But nature compensates for these arrears of nurture. A carpet of Siberian squills in front of the library portends warmer days, dappled with the layered blue of midsummer twilight. The building itself is as much tourist trap as book depository – ivy clinging to its front changes colour with the seasons, and the Harvardian red bricks are now weeks from dissolving behind a pelt of late-spring green.

16:25 For once, my route is straight: past the observatory, the botanical garden, the fur-lined army of hand-held children returning from day care, the anarchic open-window swell of a brass band's rehearsal. No detours, no embellishments. The city and I have an amicable understanding – we have nothing left to say.

The old town hums in the shadow of the *domkyrka*: two chalky towers like great slabs of frosted ice. They look translucent against the smouldering clouds, the better to diffuse God's grace. The cathedral is surrounded by the young family it has mothered, in spite of itself: sushi bars, ice-cream parlours and falafel joints – long-ago houses in which modernity has grown quietly like a mass of mushrooms.

These streets are crooked with memory, of rock-hard wooden chairs and half-clean glasses, of music: loud, and people: louder, and me: saying nothing at all.

I was less a late bloomer than a late sprouter – I didn't know what it meant to be a child until I grew up and left home. College towns are apt to arrest development, and there is a blitheness to this place, to the gaudy boiler suits and liquid picnics, ultimate frisbee and endless whizzing bicycles.

On days like this, though, Lund is self-contained. It hoards its own warmth. It is red bricks and yellow paint, brown and orange roof tiles, old wooden window frames, sky-blue and prolific green. It says: you need us more than we need you. It says: you will not outlast us.

It plays both ways, font and crypt. But, now, it and I live equally as ruins: old rotten into new, born into old, so that everything is ageless.

16:39 A small place on Sankt Petri kyrkogata, opposite the statue of Carl Linnaeus. Another repurposed old house, with a chalk board outside saying, *You are what you eat, so eat something sweet*, and low ceilings inside, ill-fitting.

The bite of early evening mingles with high-powered steam and the chime of plates and cups. The queue in front moves with the briskness of a warehouse floor. My order is a cortado – a dairy-heavy thing, new-fangled, to me at least. Spanish.

Cold green eyes prevail behind the counter – uneasy, then glazed as if by a confectioner. I'm asked if I want a cake but I demur, a firm *nej*, careful not to spoil myself. There are hissing sounds from machinery.

A second glance from the barista.

A third. He is efficient but not efficient enough.

I peer into my phone as I wait.

Until again I am on the move, threading myself through rush-hour pedestrians, paper cup in hand, warm as forgiveness. Past the supermarket beggars, past the sludging wheels of the city buses, past an art shop with a Warholian portrait of Olof Palme in the window, boyish hair and mannish nose. Cobbles dither beneath me, but I am resolute.

A person is no more than a contrivance of lessons, and, with enough new ones, I became someone else entirely. I used to fear solitude, and the way it left me putting out fires, but here I stoked them, and filled myself to the lip with sweet thick blackening air.

It was once a secret, a double life that in time became singular and various. Like love, like sickness – utterly human, I suppose, I reckon.

16:52 There is a tremor of chatter and artificial light and I feel myself the epicentre. It's stuttered movement and standing room only, so Malmö is less an urbation than a form of purgatory.

Central, Triangeln, Hyllie – underground stations, placeless places. Rubbish bins and condensation, spotless platforms, a bilingual sign saying: *Ballongförbud. No balloons*. In my hand, a half-empty coffee cup, smear of nude lipstick on the lid, another day's armour partly discarded.

Through newly built tunnels, not rattling but skating. Sharp-green emergency-exit lights repeat every second or so. The inside of the carriage is replicated on all sides, trapped infinitely, gradually losing distinction.

No one told me how jealously I'd need to guard myself. That I do it at all is proof enough it's worthwhile.

I no longer live for the city, or the university. Lund was too small for me. It knew me too well. Its streets and shops and shared kitchens were painted with faces.

It is a very old story: a won war and a lost peace.

To stay would require me to talk, so I have replaced one form of dissemblance with another. There's a reason the butterfly moves quicker after the chrysalis: she has secrets to keep. Now, all I have left of my larval city is a loveless doctoral thesis and half-spoiled vestiges of what I used to be. I have moved on, just like everyone else.

Once jolted above ground, out of Hyllie, out of Malmö, there is urban wilderness, nothing but these streaking carriages and the adjacent motorway surrounded by grassy wasteland. Bare vegetation besets this expanse like body hair.

The whole area is flat as an ultimatum. These horizons are aggressive in their endlessness.

The train inclines delicately as it curves towards the coast, scant shards of setting sun cutting through the carriage, devouring me, leaving me blind – alone with all I have lost, and all I have gained.

My name is Phoebe.

I am now over the water.

A bridge younger than me, diagonal girders undulating like the writhing of a sea creature. A train that was once a ferry – but that is someone else's history. It is a truism to say things change and we adjust, that the past only controls us if we let it. Years from now, I will have discarded these impatient days. I will be remade again, older hands and lighter lifting.

Outside the window, Malmö drifts away, its evening flicker coughing into life.

Then I spot him, pretending to read his folded copy of *Aftonbladet*. He looks up – over his newspaper, under his bonfire eyebrows – at me. My only reference for these glances is the smile of strangers once received with ignorant enthusiasm. I want to grin at him, to acknowledge his contact, human being to human being – but I am not a child anymore.

I lower my gaze and try instead to focus on a raucous conversation in Arabic in progress elsewhere in the carriage, the two men's words comfortably alien and impersonal, negating the effort of understanding.

I pull the coffee cup towards my lips a final time, but it is already empty.

18:26 'Shut up!' I cry, fishwifely. 'Okay, okay!'

It's a generous all-clear, or a selfish clear-off. She starts yapping the moment the key scratches the lock. I don't know why – it's part of a fascination with doors. My best guess is that they spark in her a notion etched somewhere in the frontal cortex, and so, every evening, she finds herself sat beneath the bluish aurora light of an idle television, bitten by transient fear. But neglect amounts to a death of spirit, and she is right to fear it. She is a wise and perceptive dog, with a rake of Maslovian anxieties.

'Hello, my dear,' I call out, but now she says nothing because her mouth is full.

I flick a light switch, and, once I'm visible behind the sitting-room door, she click-clacks along the wooden floor of the hall with a red rubber bone in her teeth – the same thing she did the first time I met her, on this spot, a year and a half ago. I've come to interpret it as a calling card, one placed eagerly at my feet like an offering of alms.

She runs her head between my hands with pack-bond eagerness. She gives an excited dry sneeze.

Dolly is a ten-year-old bichon frise. Her fur smells like bran flakes and her breath smells like rotting flesh. Most of the time she's a languid, trip-over dog, a little cat of a dog, though in her usual stance, splayed sideways on the floor, she looks more like a baby polar bear. She came with the flat and has a greater claim to its ownership than I do.

An animal's role, its alternating corner in the drama triangle of domestic life, is of much greater significance than its name, or even its species. To me, Dolly is inhabited by the ghost of an older woman: an anxious wandering soul, whittled by grief and injury, reborn as an apartment-friendly dog – the sort of being for whom *pet* is a term of endearment and not a subject status.

Ours is a relationship of calm through mutual attention: *there you are again, Phoebe*. We only truly exist to the extent that we furnish each other's eyeballs.

And that is what I need: to be seen but not remembered. I am, in a manner of speaking, an adolescent now, an adolescent again, and I know from experience that the best legacy I can bequeath my twice-adult self is as limited a record of my hormonal indiscretions as possible. So, I spend my throwaway years with Dolly, who can be trusted not to betray them.

18:33 The sitting room is not a room – it is a parsimonious quota of space. A custard-coloured sofa, a television, someone else's trinkets. A lamp with an adjustable arm, which stands permanently crooked next to the balcony door, lanky and restless like a Tim Burton creation. It is, at times, like living in a furniture showroom, which is also not a room.

This non-room smells of fresh laundry and that, to me, is the smell of home. Not of an Irish home – boiled ham and furniture polish – but of the kind I have willed into being through middle-aisle scented candles. Home-making is a craft of deception: the art of retuning garish colours so they seem to match.

There is a wooden block print on the wall to the right of the TV. It says: *spend time with people who make you happy* – a tidy square of white influencer calligraphy on a baby-blue background. It's also not mine. When I first moved to Copenhagen, I considered taking it down and discarding it, feeling its message unwelcome, but relented because, by living alone, I am indeed surrounding myself only with those who put me at ease. Seen a particular way, *spend time with people who make you happy* is less an invitation than a warning, and that's how I came to agree with it.

It is its own triumph, to escape the regime of other people and find here a slackness that is all my own. Taken in a certain gossamer light, this space becomes proof of success, corroboration of an asserted personhood.

A woman without a past can be anyone she wants.

18:47 The peppers must be cut small and thin – more surface and less interior aids the absorption of heat. They are stripped of their structure, reduced to jagged streaks of colour. Bit by bit, swish-pop, swish-pop against the wooden board.

Then the same for the meat, made to suffer, but for good purpose. Animal remnants, it hardly matters which animal, reduced to anonymous hunks. I take ownership of them by depriving them of their individuality, becoming godlike, in a way.

The flame is encouraged until as intense as possible, until it is aquamarine, until it resembles upward streams of cool liquid subject to their own law of physics. There is a contented sigh from my labour.

I used to spend so much of my time living in pasts and futures, real and imagined, that the idea of dwelling in the present was fearful. More than that, it felt like death, as though I risked being swallowed up by the intolerable systolic convulsions of my own body. Then, when I ate at all, I was eating to forget.

But now there is a reward for my attentiveness: the flavours interlacing, intact but permanently remade, the sensations on my mouth, soft to less-soft, fragments dissolving on contact, built up to be broken down again, dust into dust into dust.

19:12 Frederiksberg is quiet and tree-lined, once the home of artists and the moneyed class, now filling slowly with professionals and students. It is a place of parks and boulevards, cafés and townhouses.

Sometimes I conjure for myself an alternate life, in Nørrebro, or somewhere equally fashionable, where I might work at a world-renowned restaurant and have a patchwork quilt of stylish friends. Where I'd be both hot and cool: K-holes in Vesterbro when the wind blows, bong-hits in Christiania when the sun shines. But every time those visions come, they fade just as quickly.

I am thirty years old and living in postscript already, not on the edge but over it, a happenstance life on a tranquil margin. It is a gatecrasher's quiet. I cannot explain what a thrill it is just to be here.

The apartment I rent is on the third floor of a building constructed in the 1930s, a suburban funkis block with stone cladding and large windows, facing out onto a narrow street lined with more of the same. It has scratches on its doorframes and dust in appropriate places. It is a lived-in space for an out-spaced life.

People existed here while Denmark was under Nazi occupation. Beneath layers of paint and wood there must still be traces, scribbles and finger prints, so I am still surrounded by them, blessed with a situation in history – and, really, all spaces are shared, because they ring with the workaday echoes of the now-departed.

Looking out the balcony door, across a lamp-lit courtyard – little more than a car park, a chain-fenced football pitch and a playground next to the goods yard of a small supermarket – I can see a couple, a straight couple, sitting at a window-side table in another flat. Attractive, maybe, but I can't tell from so far away. Hybrid human-silhouettes, half themselves and half the property of the evening – focused on each other, unaware of my presence.

Dolly walks over and stands against me, digging her front paws into the fabric of my leggings. She is demanding. She makes her presence felt. Small dogs know they are small. I read an article about it. They are aware of their powerlessness and develop a spiky personality to compensate.

I lift her up and swing her around and we collapse in a heap over the side of the sofa, onto a scratchy purple throw. She lets out a protracted exhale as she lands. We end up sat together, her on my lap with eyes darting and tongue unsteady. I reach up and pull out a hair tie. Her white fur spirals outwards in curls fit to conduct electricity, but my hair falls in waves, forgivingly, over what is left of my shoulders. The two of us combine like chemical clouds.

The dog sprawls on my lap and I see the warts on her underside. I've researched them: they're not dangerous. She has about a dozen of them across her body; the most recent of which I observed developing from nothing over six months last year. They resemble a constellation, the kind a person might wish on if wearied of the sky and its empty perpetuity.

Then Dolly is up and gone, alerted by someone at the door. Four knocks, neatly spaced, and she is howling again.

I pick her up to keep her quiet, assuring her it is probably a neighbour with a missing cat, or a Nespresso machine for sale, or a flyer for a Jazzercise class. Her heart pounds against my hand as we go. It moves quickly, gently, as if to caress me, as if she thinks I am the one whose fears need comforting.

Then I find Grace Keaney in front of me, and it seems I am.

19:19 She still has the ring, a winking life buoy adrift of her left nostril. Taller than I remember – or perhaps I am shorter. Yet now her hair comes only to her shoulders, not half the chestnut swish I remember. It is blonde, dirty with dark streaks, like seaweed washed up on white-gold sand, apparently at random.

I know Grace Keaney, but I don't know the woman in front of me. She sums to almost nothing as she tilts officiously out of the corridor, eager in contemplation of my current face. We are like forgotten relatives, linked in theory by an absent cousin thrice-removed or a great-grand-auntie, but with no direct relationship; at once strangers and blood-bonded.

I hear the lift slithering shut, the growling insistence of the edifice around us.

She gives a service-sector grin, and I force out some teeth in response. I put the dog on the floor and without notice Grace throws herself around me, so I receive the dry, anxious chill of her nylon coat sleeves.

Dolly's watchdog calls moor me to the moment: *you-you-you* every half-second.

There is a hesitancy between Grace and me, a swollen moment, and then she speaks, in tones familiar to the point of chimera. 'Phoebe Forde! It's so wonderful to see you again. You remember me, right? I haven't come at a bad time, have I? Someone let me in downstairs.'

'Grace,' I say. 'Of course. I thought you lived in London?'

She laughs like a friend. 'I left London a while back. No, I'm just here for the weekend, thought I'd come by so we could catch up a bit.' She says this as if following up on an offhand invitation of mine, but the last time I saw her we clutched on an agreement to stop catching up, and that was seven years ago.

I realise with a sharpness that this is the first time she has ever called me Phoebe. It is uncanny, the unselfing of the actualised, like my words are caught beneath her tongue.

I ask her how long it has been, half-rhetorically, and she answers correctly: a sign that this ambush, or whatever it is, has been diligently prepared. The dog's Norse temperament has never jibed with small talk, so I have no recourse but an unwilling tactical retreat.

'Come in, come in. She'll calm down if you're inside,' I say, closing the door as Grace manoeuvres past me. 'Her name's Dolly. After Dolly Parton.'

'Dolly Parton?'

'Yeah, I think it's the platinum curls. That and her fondness for warbling. It wasn't my idea, but I sort of get it.'

Grace bends her knees, rubs the crown of the dog's head and coos honey at her. 'Jolene would be no match for you, would she, Dolly?'

I try to hurry the encounter along in the manner of a French oral exam, stammering through the procedurals of a regulation rendezvous in the hope of disembarking promptly at *au revoir*. 'Here, let me take your coat. You'll need to leave your shoes over there,' I say, pointing to a tidy corner next to the front door.

'My shoes?' Grace says, gooing at me like I've asked her to disrobe lock and stock.

'It's a Scandinavian thing, one of their rules. Something to do with not getting melted snow on the floor. That's the old wives' tale I heard, anyway.'

'But it's not snowing. And we're not Scandinavian.'

'Culture doesn't have to make sense, Grace. It's invented by people. You know what they're like.'

Having left her sneakers in a heap next to the wall, Grace hands me her jacket, still cold. The coat hooks are already occupied, so I put it in the spare room, where it joins my landlord's belongings, these things with which I am less than comfortably cohabited.

By the time I get back to the hall, she is gone, and Dolly with her. They are perched on the couch, the dog on Grace's lap, the same spot where I was not two minutes ago.

There is something indelicate about all this, but it is happening, it has happened; as it etches into me, I am irretrievable, unable to remember a time without it. Normality obliterated and refashioned into normality: ex-girlfriend and bichon frise on the sofa together, like always.

But that's Grace: a woman to whom done-things are discretionary indulgence. She's always had the mobility and tact of a Fisher Price telephone. Indeed, having already broken the first commandment of Nordic social life – never show up without scheduling in advance – what difference does it make what she does with her shoes?

19:27 'Have you just flown in?' I ask, balanced against the sitting-room doorframe like an old shovel.

'Yeah, I got here this afternoon. It's nicer here than in Dublin. It was pissing down at home.'

'So Dublin is home again?'

'Kind of. It's where I live again.'

My face drops slightly as I begin clambering into the unavoidable. 'Grace?'

She pauses, then looks up, as if to offer a final opportunity to prove myself more entertaining than Dolly.

'How do you know where I live?' I try to ask the question in a calm, we're-all-friends-here sort of manner, to indicate that I have no problem with her being unbound by convention – aren't we all! – but that the sanctity of my flat is a more solemn arrangement than most.

Grace laughs, seemingly at nothing. 'Don't worry, don't worry. I'll explain. Your thirtieth was last month, right? The twenty-second?'

I nod. The twenty-second of the second. This ambush has been *very* well prepared.

'So, at the beginning of February I got in touch with Michelle on Instagram. You know Michelle.'

'My sister, yes.'

'Yeah, and I told her I wanted to send you a card – just, you know, wishing you well with, like, everything. I told her to keep it a secret because I wanted it to be a surprise, but, in the end, I didn't send the card and decided to come over instead.' She pauses. 'You know Michelle has a baby now? He's so cute!'

Grace spits frothy words at me, so I end up affecting a verbal Ginger Rogers, dancing backwards to the point. 'So you . . . just decided to fly over and visit me?'

'Well, I was in the city anyway and thought I'd swing by, like. It's cheaper to go on holidays at this time of year. Summer is a no-go for me. Too expensive, and I can't get the annual leave. I'd looked up a website and it said Copenhagen was number two for city breaks. I couldn't afford number one. Venice would break the bank.'

I stand up straight and ease the stiffness out of my shoulders. 'I appreciate your sacrifice. You know, people used to emigrate and they'd never see their friends and family again. Remember the song? "Won't you remember me," not "won't you come over whenever the mood takes you."' I exhale. 'Sorry, sorry. I'm not being fair. What else are you planning to do on this completely spontaneous trip to Copenhagen?'

'I've never been here before,' Grace says, 'so I'd like to see everything, you know?' She sits back into the couch, holding the dog like a panting hostage. 'Listen, it's all right, Phoebe. I thought it would be nice for us to see each other again and you'd know a thing or two about the place, but if you don't want to see me, I'll go. It's grand, don't worry about it.' She speaks without engaging the pretence she's about to get up, inert on the sofa like a pile of ironing.

But she's also just called me Phoebe again, so I relent. 'Sorry,' I say, 'it's a bit odd, though, you know?'

'I know, I know. I mean, I don't usually show up at my exes' houses. But you were always hard to reach, you know? I didn't want to look for you and hear nothing.'

'You mean you didn't want to have to worry about my boundaries.'

'Stop,' she says. 'I just don't have any other exes who turned out like you.'

'Dog owners?'

'You know what I mean. You can't blame me for being interested.'

I appreciate Grace's directness. She hasn't said the word, but after ten minutes she's closer than some get in an entire academic year.

'You're making me sound like a tourist attraction,' I say, 'or the site of some horrible disaster. But this *does* explain why Michelle kept texting me about birthday cards. I was like, "You're only three years older than me, you know people don't send cards anymore," but she wouldn't shut up about it.' I let out a vaudeville sigh. 'Right, you can stay for a bit, ogle me for future reference. As long as you don't start going on about how I wasn't like other guys.'

'But you *weren't* like other guys!' Grace hoots, springing her right arm upwards and startling the dog.

'Yeah, I know. Oh, have you eaten? I could put something together for you, if you like.'

'No, it's fine, thanks. I ate a couple of hours ago.'

'Are you sure?'

Grace beams at me and her nose ring flares. 'Yes, Mammy, I'm sure.'

I smile. 'Is wine okay?'

'Wine is always okay.'

Wine, at this point, is a straightforward necessity.

19:45 The locket dangles next to Grace's sauvignon blanc as she leans to pluck her glass from the coffee table. It is a modest silver oval – ellipses don't distract the way hearts do. I'd forgotten about it, though in truth it never really left me.

Years ago, she told me the locket contained an image of her father, who died before I knew her. I'm taken by the incongruence of it and her top – a blue cottony number emblazoned with a smiling cartoon sheep. I see something in her now I couldn't have put words to when we were younger, that she possesses one of life's necessities: the gift of seeing in grief its slow-glowing branches of joy.

Dolly sits next to Grace on the couch, with me on a dining chair opposite.

'I'm doing a PhD at the moment,' I say, 'studying urban water and gender in sub-Saharan Africa. In Lund, where I did the master's.'

'Wow,' Grace replies. 'That's . . . interesting. Very interesting, actually.' Her fascination seems to warm up like an old television. 'And you get to go over the bridge every day. I saw it from the plane when I was landing.'

'I was probably on the bridge when you saw it. Going over is the highlight of my day,' I say, with a laugh. 'No, the PhD is all right, but I don't know what I'll do with it afterwards. I'm a bit tired of the whole field already, and I'm not even halfway through the thing.'

She smiles, revealing a wayward incisor that had also slipped my memory. 'Sure, no one knows what they're going to do with a PhD. Nature of the beast. You're not the first PhD student I've met who fell out of love with their topic. Anyway, it sounds like you've done really well for yourself. Well done, girl.' She says these words like they are a poem she has learned to the syllable.

I nod at her, slowly, open-eyed, conferring full marks for effort, and cross my legs. 'And what are you up to?' I ask, with an excruciating regality I only notice after I've spoken.

'I'm working for ThinkClass, a new yoke set up a couple of years ago that operates mental health services.'

'Counselling?'

'Yeah, mostly. I do admin work, appointments and fees, that sort of thing. When people ask, I say my job is to cheer depressed people up just enough that they remember to pay.'

'Well, you're helping people, sort of. That sounds fulfilling.'

Grace leans forward and speaks through a curled, mocking lip, 'Don't forget: it's okay to not be okay.'

I laugh. 'I haven't been okay since I was about ten years old.'

'I know, right. The job is fine, it's not back-breaking stuff but the money is shite. Charities – they're all at it. The grunt workers get peanuts and the directors make off like bandits. The CEO is on two hundred grand. There was an article about her in the *Examiner*. I don't know, I just want to do something that means I can get out of bed in the morning and feel like I'm making the world a better place.'

'But?'

'But this just doesn't pay enough. I'm sharing a flat in Inchicore with my friend Shahnaz. Do you remember Naz?'

I don't, but nod anyway.

'Naz is basically my renting wife. We've agreed to go down with the ship when the time comes, sleeping bags side by side, you know what I mean.'

After so long away from Ireland, I can't be entirely sure that's a joke – then I look at her and it seems neither can she.

'The landlord is saying the rent will go up in September,' she continues, 'so we probably won't be able to stay there after that, unless I get a massive raise in the meantime.'

'Why did you leave London, if things are so bad in Ireland? Was it Brexit?'

She takes a sip of wine. 'Yeah, Brexit mostly. I mean, things are bad everywhere.' She pauses and looks to the decorated walls. 'Everywhere except here.'

I squinch my eyes. 'I don't know what you mean by that.'

'This place looks like an escape from the outside world. It's nice.'

'Well, there's a lot to escape from.'

Grace smirks. 'And you've lost your accent.'

'What?'

'You sound like the Swedish Chef now. Bork bork bork.'

'That is *not* true.'

'I'm just buzzing with you,' she says, winking at Dolly like the bichon is an accomplice. Grace turns and looks at me with dreamy eyes. 'Dolly and Phoebe. Like Thelma and Louise.'

'We drive each other off the edge all right,' I say, staring daggers at Dolly, but she's too interested in Grace to pay attention to me. While I find myself attempting to curate Grace's thoughts, the dog merely sprawls on the sofa and imbibes them, which is probably the wiser approach.

Grace puts her glass on the table, atop a pristine copy of the *Economist* I stole from the faculty. 'Here, tell me,' she says, tucking her hair behind her ears, 'where did the name come from?'

'I said already. Dolly Parton.'

She laughs and shakes her head. 'Not her name, yours.'

'Oh, right.' I take a lengthy slug of wine. 'I didn't really pick Phoebe, as it were. It's not like I picked it off a list, I mean. I didn't have a book of baby names. It was *always* going to be Phoebe. This is going to sound really weird—'

Grace claps her hands on her thighs. 'Now we're talking.'

'I could get you some popcorn if you like.'

She apologises and I linger for a moment, long enough to see the peril in what I'm about to say but not long enough to craft a lie to replace it. 'See, when I was little there was a girl in my school called Phoebe. She was gorgeous and popular and smart and I wanted to be her so badly – though I didn't see it like that at the time. I just thought I had an earth-shattering crush on her. It hurt me to look at her,' I say, and I flinch, unsure whether I am being dramatic or protective. 'When I was a little older, thirteen or so, the boys I knew would make comments about her, about what they wanted to do to her, and I couldn't stand it. They didn't understand how wonderful she was the way I did. They didn't get it at all. I wanted to run away with her and be her best friend.' My words hang in the air like the wilting of a paper lantern threatening to burst into flame.

'Were you, like, friends with this girl?' Grace asks.

'No, no, not at all. It was just one of those things. It was about me more than her. I was projecting my feelings onto a stranger. I suppose you'd call it a parasocial relationship. But the name stuck with me, and now it's my name. It was always my name, in a way.'

Grace eyes her glass, too far away to be reached for without drawing attention, and so she reverts to me. 'That's really interesting. And a bit sad.'

I shrug and say nothing. This is the first time I've told the Phoebe story to anyone. I've skipped through deep meaningful conversations and tissue-box therapy sessions and pornographic psych assessments for the best part of twenty years without ever blurting it. I never thought it was sad. It was instead a source of something silent, *terra nullius*, within me – a thing I might have called 'shame' if I'd had the courage to name it.

But the story collects something in the retelling. Perhaps my name is my locket: a kernel of regret carried always, silently, wielded with a sparkling defiance.

20:28 Dolly is dozing next to Grace. We've been sitting for an hour in the conversational arrivals' lounge. When I think about what we're doing, the words *jet-à-tête* comes to mind, and I laugh at the silliness of my own mind. Grace asks me what I find funny, and I just say: everything.

We cannot catch up in one sitting. The distance is too great, and, the closer we get, the more the unsaid mists onto the horizon. The question of why recurs like a spring shower, which rinses but never cleans – it hasn't been answered, and I know it won't be tonight.

Grace remembers for me when we were last in contact. We stayed Facebook friends after the break-up, and it was there that she and hundreds of others saw my big announcement in 2016. Grace says she sent me a congratulatory message, and I tell her I'll take her word for it.

'It looked like the whole thing went pretty well,' she says, smiling.

'It did, more or less. I was deluged with messages. I needed that support at the time, but I look back on it now and, well, maybe I'm a bit cynical about it.'

'Oh?'

'The people who congratulated me then aren't following up to see if I'm okay now, are they?'

'One of them is,' she says, giving a sheepish wave.

'Touché. I don't know. It's just hard to tell if people are being supportive for you or for themselves after a while. If they just want to be *seen* to be a nice person. It reminds me of a joke headline I saw online: "Trans Person Crosses Street to Avoid Overly Supportive Liberals". There's a lot of truth to that. It's a kind of objectification.'

She laughs. 'That's pretty cynical, yeah.'

'Yeah, but in my experience once all the fair-weather types are out of the way the only people left talking to you are dudes with usernames like *iloveshemales123* asking for dick pics. At least those guys are honest about their intentions.' I pause. 'Actually, I tell a lie. First they tell me they don't approve of children getting surgery, then they ask for dick pics.'

Grace looks at me with perplexity, like the right-hand side of her mouth is trying to escape to the vicinity of her cheekbone. 'But you wouldn't send them dick pics, right?'

'No, no, of course I wouldn't.'

'Because . . . ' she says, shifting her head diagonally ' . . . you can't?'

'I could . . . hypothetically,' I say, feeling like I'm pulling the legs off a spider and deciding to myself that that's not a metaphor for anything else.

'Oh, you could?' she says. 'Right, right.'

'Hypothetically.'

'Hypothetically, yeah, gotcha.' Grace looks to the dog for backup.

In the end I decide to put us out of our shared misery. 'Grace, if you're asking if I've had *the* surgery, the answer is no. But it's pretty rude to come to someone's house and interrogate them about that sort of thing. I mean, how would you feel if I asked you about your last gynaecologist's appointment?'

She looks at me blankly.

'Most people would be upset by that,' I say.

'Fine, all right. Yeah, okay, I'm sorry.'

I study the bowl of stale potpourri in the middle of the coffee table. 'Apology accepted. I'm on a waiting list. It's a long waiting list.'

21:06 It's a bit like an auspicious first date: as it becomes obvious we'll meet again, the present fades a little while I linger, prematurely, on the future, in a way that both dulls and heightens the thrill.

There's no need for grandiose farewells, just the promise of more to come. I'm not a believer in permanence, and tonight I feel quite vindicated in that.

'So how long are you here for?' I ask, as Grace puts her shoes back on.

'Flight home is Monday lunchtime. I know you've work tomorrow but I'm here all weekend, so if you want to meet up for a drink, or something, let me know.' Then she stands up straight, an untied sneaker on one foot and only a sock on the other, and for a moment she looks like Dolly, sniffing something in the air. 'Do you hear that?'

'Hear what?'

'Listen.'

I make myself as silent as possible, and hear high-pitched singing and an insistent bassline coming from another apartment. '"Funkytown,"' I note aloud.

'It is, isn't it?'

'Well, that's a sign of what a funky weekend you'll have.'

She laughs, and I appreciate the charity.

We exchange phone numbers, her jacket is returned to her, and she makes for the door over the noise of a reawakened Dolly.

'Before I go,' Grace says, 'I know you don't like to hear this, but I'm really proud of you.'

'Thanks,' I say. We embrace.

'And,' she continues, 'I was thinking. You remember how you said you were always Phoebe, since you were a child? Does that mean you were when we were together?'

'Well . . . yeah, I was, I guess. There was certainly stuff going on in my head at the time.'

She puts her hand on my shoulder as if to measure the weight it carries. 'I wish you'd told me.'

'Thanks. I never would have, but thanks.'

Grace moves cautiously towards the lift, her head three glasses lighter than she was when she arrived. Then she whips her gaze back to me. 'You can see why I'd be interested in you.'

I smile. 'Yeah. See you again, Grace.'

21:42 Two glasses are perched on the kitchen counter, both with lipstick marks, but I can't tell who owned which. It takes some thorough inspection to establish that one smear is slightly heavier and almost imperceptibly darker than the other. That one must have belonged to Grace.

I pick the glass up and stare into it, like it's a mirror, dirty and inhabited, as the best ones are. It is the only tangible evidence she was here.

She used to say 'cool beans'. Someone would say something and she'd respond, 'Yeah, yeah, cool beans.' I didn't know what it meant, but apparently it's the same as 'cool'; just like in a cooked breakfast, the beans are superfluous. One of her friends told me that was a new thing she was saying, but I didn't stick around long enough to find out if it lasted.

When I first met her, I was a dilute twenty-two. Our eight months together are out of place set against the chronology of my early twenties, like a respectable existence punctuated by a short prison stay. We were at an age of thunderous movement, the backdrops of life shuffling with excitement and prospect, and, in the end, Grace moved too quickly for me; she was just another thing I chased with a certain futility when I was younger.

For a time, though, I was in thrall to her. Not merely in the palm of her hand but tucked behind a fingernail like fortunate dirt. She was every inch a human being, and, as such, she was everything I wasn't. She carried waist-length hair around with her and it swayed pleasingly as she spoke, like a banner into which she could channel excess kinetic energy. She had tattoos – scary, oversized artistic ones, ones that required commitment, or recklessness, or both.

She had sex with both men and women. I know because she told me, and goodness knows it was two more than I'd been having sex with.

She once recounted an incident from a few months before we met: she was riding a guy in his shower – and when I say a guy, I mean a fifty-year-old man who worked at a betting shop and was in the midst of a custody battle over two tweens – and he had a heart attack. 'He went red,' Grace said, 'and then he went.' She assured me he survived, and I assured her his survival was all I cared about. It was a mild cardiac incident, and I wondered if she took that as a personal affront, being, as she was, the sort of person who might well have aspired to a body count.

She had history, where I just had time.

Grace and I had the kind of relationship that might have made other women jealous – I appeared happy to exist in her shadow. We always went where she wanted: bad comedy sets, bad poetry recitals, bad concerts by posh, sweaty men who subsequently developed a reputation for grooming schoolgirls.

I was content to make room for her, to be a worthy and dutiful addendum to someone else's life. There was something refreshing, perhaps even feminist about my turmoil. How good I was, how *nice* I was – I was so nice, it was almost unbelievable. I was the perfect man.

But, now, something has led her into temptation and delivered her to my doorstep.

I pick up my own glass and plunge the two of them into the sink. Spiky heat rolls over the back of my hand and the sudded water stings my cuticles, but, here we are, cleaner now. It is a useful skill, getting accustomed to the shock of the new.

22:19 Someone else's clothes: a grey New York Yankees T-shirt. The print of the logo is cheaply made, and, after so many years, the left arm of the great Y has all but faded away. I know nothing about baseball and have never been to New York.

My nightwear belongs to him. Though he was no better travelled than I am, he feigned a worldliness, a comfort with places he'd never get to see because I determined never to let him.

I rest with surprising ease in his porous companionship. If I had a boyfriend I might sleep in his T-shirts – if I had an ex-boyfriend, maybe I would do the same. And, really, he is like an ex-boyfriend, or an ex-husband. He made off with so much of me, but I retain small parts of him, ornamentally.

It is a victor's peace that exists between us: total, but eventual, and not without wreckage.

Dolly cannot sleep alone. She lies at the end of my bed, eyes closed so that she resembles less a dog than a disembodied tumult of pale curls surrounding a proud nose. In these moments, she looks like an impressionist painting of herself, a canine idea no longer occupied by the real thing.

I take it as a gift, the beauty she leaves behind when she relinquishes the world at night. But it doesn't last. In the dark, she interrupts my own beautification with vehement little kicks that dig into my thigh and sometimes stingingly against my left breast. I suppose that too is the boyfriend experience.

Grace and I met while out socialising. That was the story we told, anyway: eyes across the bar – which bar, can't remember; too lidlessly in love.

What actually happened was that I was eating fast food for one, managing exam stress through bodily punishment, a lashing of fries, and she peeled off from a group of friends and talked to me. 'I'm Grace,' she said, invigilating my plastic tray, my short receipt. Had I been really clever I'd have replied, 'And you don't have any,' but I was repeating my exams, so I just said, 'Oh.'

It was six p.m. on a Tuesday. It seemed entirely possible that no one had ever met their soulmate at six p.m. on a Tuesday before, so why wouldn't I be the first? And there was a screeny romance in the setting's lack of allure: not the best restaurant on Grafton Street, not even the best Burger King on Grafton Street.

At the time, I was a committed disassociator, sat blankly in the corner of a cavernous existence; I still can't hear the old name without an echo attached. I used the internet to throw myself into fantasy. Movie stars, glamour, Clara Bow and her painted, unspeaking lips. Anna Karina – I wanted to be Anna Karina, claiming ownership over a bank of the Seine, even if I didn't know it. I wanted to be beautiful. I wanted the power of it; I believed, wrongly, that I had no power.

Was that a crime? Was I under the misapprehension that it was? I can't even say. I carried these desires like a stone weight – but, in hindsight, what I was doing wasn't shameful, or even particularly strange. It is the most normal thing in the world, to want.

In the final analysis, I was spiritually unemolumated. I was whatever the opposite of verklempt is. I was a fucking idiot.

The worst thing about looking back is seeing all that wasteful embarrassment surrounding you like the polystyrene foam of early adulthood, weightless and toxic. Wanting to go back and explain that you'll always be like this, so you might as well make the best of it. You are both more and less interesting than you think. Your sadness is not a virtue. Stop wanting to be someone else and resolve to be your own febrile self.

We were Ireland's human surplus: built up, overvalued in hindsight, scattered like unpainted houses. The people were steaming and the politicians were also steaming. That was the backdrop: rage, incredulity, and different busking men sharing the same Mic Christopher song on the streets every evening.

When Grace and I first met, I was at university. *The* university – the small-pond big-fish in the city centre. I was entering my final year of PPES, a degree whose impact on me was so limited that I can scarcely remember what the initials stood for. *Philosophy Plus Extra Subjects. Posh People Everywhere, Sigh.*

Grace was doing communications at DIT on Aungier Street. I don't recall her saying anything about it.

We went places. The zoo was too cruel for her; the National Concert Hall too overstimulating for me – so galleries were a frequent default. One of our early dates was at the Museum of Modern Art in Kilmainham. Grace walked around the grounds looking at well-dressed people and muttering that there was no recession in their house. She understood perfectly well that there were reverse-binocular people around her on whom real life never intruded – she just never seemed to realise she was dating one.

After, we went for drinks at an unkempt bar in the Liberties. The place was gurgling with anticipation because Shamrock Rovers were playing in the Europa League that evening. We were the only people in the pub who weren't getting the Luas to Tallaght Stadium afterwards. We didn't know where we were going.

We drank pints of cider and ate veggie burgers, appalling ones with sweetcorn in them. She made silly jokes about people she knew, and I laughed even though I didn't know them. She told me a Seán O'Casey quote, about laughter being wine for the soul. She said she'd seen it Sharpied onto a pub table once – I assumed it was really a pub toilet but first impressions require a certain verbal constipation. We exchanged stupid wisdom and got drunk in multiple ways.

Normally, I'd say there's no use dwelling on the past, but, as I lie here, I hope more than expect that it has all stood to me – that it is the residue, the plain failures, that really define a life. For all that the carpenter gazes proudly at her handiwork, it is the sawdust she breathes in and takes away.

And there is joy in seeing portents of the present in memory. It is like looking at a photograph of a familiar street in alien historical monochrome and recognising the same old rooves and the sweep of the roads – knowing with certainty that these things exceed you, and will probably outlast you. It is a kind of immortality.

22:47 He's hanging out of a bottle of something. Black Magic, it's called – dark, liqueur-ish. My cousin in Toronto. Hands akimbo like he's doing gang signals, like he didn't used to watch ear-splitting Scottish children's programmes while I babysat him, like he's not from a plaintive little housing estate off the Navan Road. He's grown into a problematic little habit.

Perhaps Grace is doing the same thing right now. Not drinking – scrolling. Scrambling her mind and observing what emerges. The endless procession of other people's grainy ultrasound pictures, other people's holidays to Marrakech, other people's devastating hip bones; all of it contributes to clearing intellectual blockages, like valves of the mind – ensuring thoughts do not gum themselves, and are instead carried along by the relentless march of nothing and no one. And what is intelligence, really, but the dextrous navigation of all the world's stupidity?

Or maybe she is thinking of the beginning, or the end. She was the one who broke things off – that almost goes without saying. I wasn't particularly offended. It wasn't mean of her, but mean-reverting, Grace fading back into apathy, becoming the same as everyone else. There was an unassailable logic to her decision – indeed, it was as rational as anything I'd ever seen her do. Her, to me: a series of anecdotes; me, to her: a teachable moment. That was it: fit, fitting and final.

I thought it felt like yesterday, the way everything gone for good does. But now it's here, around me, I'm acutely aware of how long ago it actually was. Nothing creates psychic distance quite like physical proximity.

There's an effusive post by my brother, Liam. In the picture, he's kissing a girl on the cheek with his eyes closed while she stares into the camera like Mona Lisa. He's got that side-fade haircut all men in their twenties have. She's wearing copious amounts of blusher either side of a snubby nose, and the dark roots of her hair are showing. The caption calls her an angel.

Her name is Fleur. At first, I think it's the same girl I met at Michelle's wedding, but that was Fiadh. Not to be confused with Lia, who was the love of Liam's life for a period roughly coterminous with the deaths of Bowie and Prince. Liam and Lia – we all thought he was taking the piss. It's a wonder I've survived a life surrounded by such indigent heterosexuality.

Maybe Grace is bringing news. I am mortally offended by the way she is holding back – reduced to the status of a questioning child, why though, why though, in my own home.

I keep laughing to myself and I don't know why.

Who is she? Who am I to her?

Perhaps I am doomed to have sillier and sillier identity crises until I am dead: the one label that accepts no backchat. Paralysis by analysis begetting paralysis the old-fashioned way.

But I keep thinking. I think: contentment is not the root of nostalgia. She wouldn't be here if she was happy. She hasn't come to gloat. That much is obvious.

One of the German supermarkets has a special offer on Greek food. Half-price olives. I'm pretty sure the ones in the picture are made of plastic, but they're dripping water in a manner both laboured and curiously erotic. In small text at the bottom, it says **product of Montenegro.*

And then she comes up in my recommendations. I sit ajolt. But of course, of course. I added her number to my contacts two hours ago. That's why she's there.

Profile picture: her and a glass of wine. White. Al fresco. Somewhere warm.

I press on her like she is a lump, hoping for something benign.

grace_linguini: This account is private. Follow this account to see their photos and videos.

Her bio contains a sun emoji, and nothing else.

The dog is sound asleep, venting strained, snorty exhales. Her body rises and falls programmatically.

23:05 Ana Kralj is five foot nine and has die-straight brown hair that surges in the manner of a watery chocolate fountain from a freckled, egg-shaped head. She told me she moved to Scandinavia because she was too tall for the men at home.

I met her through my master's. Croatian: somewhere near Split. University creates the oddest bonds, to say nothing of emigration, and she and I came together over our status as peripheral Catholics surrounded by affluent Protestants. The Germans, the Dutch, the Norwegians: they got grants from their countries to study abroad. Our boot-arse homelands were just happy to see us off.

She still lives in Lund, and works in Malmö. Her office has tropical plants and decent coffee. I don't know what her job entails – presumably she sits at a desk and sends emails, like everyone else. The company has a babyish, disyllabic name: Foofum, or Weewoop. The Øresund region is full of these mysterious enterprises, who all operate through English, because they are eager to enter the international market for whatever it is they do.

Ana was the first person in Lund to find out about me. Shortly before the autumn term of 2016, at her old student room, drinking tangy loose-leaf tea out of a pot shaped like a Dalahäst. There were silences. There always are.

You learn so much about a person by the way they respond to the distantly monumental. There is the question of whether or not to feign nonchalance – to pretend that on some level you already knew, and are merely having the blindingly obvious confirmed. And then there are the you-go-girls, the you're-so-strongs, hand-crafted bromides forced into your mouth like unfamiliar medicaments for a disease you didn't know you had.

Most people aren't hostile, but few can hide the extent of their over-interest.

Ana's response vindicated my decision to tell her first. 'Transgender people are so interesting. It's a fantastic thing to do,' she said, with the tone of someone accepting a large charitable donation.

She talked of a documentary she had once seen, about a woman who went to Serbia for surgery. Her name was Ljupka, which means peace and love. 'She was beautiful,' Ana said, and, in the moment, maybe, tentatively, I thought I was in a state of something approaching pre-beauty.

'Do you really want to have these?' she then asked, holding her breasts, as if I had asked for a lend. 'You can have them.

It's no fun carrying them around all day.' Then she cackled. 'You're going to hate the underwire! Oh my god, you're going to hate it.'

Conversations with her always took on the mechanics of a food fight. Silence couldn't get a word in. Things stuck and congealed in a satisfying way. There was no judgement and no bullshit. She reminded me that I am special, but not so special that she couldn't figure me out.

We don't talk as much these days. She and I are in different parts of Lund at different times of day. We maintain a digital line of communication through news articles, memes and gossip about the exploits of our former classmates.

From time to time, we trade jokes about our old professors, now my colleagues. We speculate about their late-night extracurriculars: who does what to whom, and with what, and in which room of the *sommarstuga*. I send her titbits about them gleaned through access to the staff quarters, and, in practice, compiling this information and transmitting it to her is probably the most productive and societally relevant part of my doctoral studies.

My phone screen displays a heraldic green blob next to her name. Ana is online.

Me: *Hallå hallå! I have some weird and interesting news*
Ana: *oooh*
Me: *Weird and interesting to me, at least. My ex from Ireland came to visit earlier this evening. I haven't seen her in seven years. She just turned up*
Ana: *she just showed up out of nowhere?*
Me: *Yep*
Ana: *wow. your life is full of surprises*
Me: *I don't know why she's here*
I don't ask for this kind of drama lol
Ana: *it's like something from a film*

it's romantic <3
Me: *I don't know if I want to be in a film. Especially a romantic one.*
Give me some advice. I don't care if it's bad, anything will do
Ana: *what do you mean? how long is she in cph for?*
Me: *Until Monday*
Ana: *do you still like her?*
Me: *I don't know*
Ana: *it sounds like you do like her ;)*
and people don't visit people they don't like. talk to her!
Me: *You fly home every Christmas even though you don't like your parents :)*
Ana: *very funny. DO IT AND TELL ME EVERYTHING*
Me: *She'll be gone on Monday though*
Ana: *even better! you have nothing to lose!*

She's right: I might never meet Grace again. I can see Monday from here.

I am like an ant that has inhaled a spore that is eating its brain. I now have no choice but to climb to the top of the dandelion and wait to be devoured.

Another message appears. Ana has sent me a link to an article about the first-ever Balkan Trans and Intersex Pride march, happening in Zagreb this weekend. She translates the slogan for me: *My Body Is My Temple*. I don't read the piece, but react to it with a thumbs-up.

I put my phone on silent and leave it on the bedside locker. Then I pick it up again and write a message to Grace. In utilising the phone, I am rejecting it. It has done all it can for me, and now I must go on without it.

I decide to leave the nuts and bolts until the morning. Before I turn off the light, I set an alarm, early enough to allow me time to call in sick for work.

Ten thousand nine hundred and ninety-three

Friday

10:17 I thought I'd be there first, but she's on our agreed spot when I arrive. Grace stands in front of Magasin du Nord, the grand department store, leaning against a digital display board – an advert for discount mortgage rates, which morphs into one for a chicken burger meal deal. She is a victorious pinprick amid the pitter-patter of the late-morning commute – those around her have places they must get to by ten-thirty, but she is already in situ.

The morning is crisp and cloudless. Any warmth stowed in these streets will have long ago risen skywards in search of the sun.

It is a simple task, picking out an Irish person in an international crowd: a sort of reverse *Where's Wally?*, in which a wretched Hiberno is surrounded by wallies drinking sparkling water and wearing clothes that actually fit. Grace carries in her bearing the bewilderment of a startled housefly looking for a window.

I stand in sly acknowledgement of the power I have when I look at her and she cannot look at me. I am tempted for a moment to leave her there, to embark on a different day.

But then she spots me, and her confidence returns. As I approach, she waves and says, 'G'morning, chicken!'

We hug again. Her hair is frizzed, almost antiseptically so. It seems to splay around her head in search of form.

She considers my face carefully. 'Attack of the velvet scrunchie.'

'Oh,' I say, laughing and touching my hair. 'I just picked this up randomly this morning. How are you? Did you sleep all right?'

'Not really. What's the story with the pillows here?'

'The square ones?'

She nods with a grimace. 'I woke up with a pain in my neck.'

'They're not built for big Irish heads. I had to bring pillows from home.'

'You were always very sensible. So,' she says, putting her hand on my back, 'where are we off to?'

I tell her our first stop is the Little Mermaid – a perfect start to our day, because it's a copper-bottomed disappointment. A tiny statue, half an hour from anything, permanently beset by chattering peripatetics huddled eight-deep at the shoreline. You walk until you're out of breath, you see it, you walk back; you never bother with it again.

And I might be tricking her the way she used to trick me.

Three days before Christmas 2011, Grace turned up to my parents' house dressed as a sexy Santa. We had relatives over from a dignified part of Tipperary. Grace had bare thighs and a flimsy beard and a cushion up her top simulating Santa's belly, so it was more disturbing than flirtatious – a little bit Krampus, a little bit *Mean Girls*.

The reception from my family was a pudding mix of tuts, whoops and snorts. Grace sang 'Santa Baby', a cappella, which was just confusing – 'are you not supposed to be Santa yourself?' a second cousin asked, making a selection from a tin of fancy biscuits.

She gave me a present in front of everyone: a Chris Hemsworth calendar. 'Your letter mentioned how much you loved his biceps in *Thor*,' she said, in a ho-ho-ho voice. It disappeared within hours of being gifted, an act of larceny for which my mother was the only suspect.

And so, the city and its attractions are a dish of cold-served revenge.

The Little Mermaid statue is a life-jacket demonstration, and that always comes at the beginning. It is an obligation – you'd be in trouble if you didn't bother with it. It offers more in the way of accountability than aesthetics. If Grace gushes about how marvellous the little lady is, I'll know she's lying and catch her buttering me up.

'I'm not surprised you want to bring me to the mermaid,' Grace says.

'Why's that?'

'You always loved the sea. You were like Captain Birdseye, or something. We'd walk along Clontarf Strand and you'd look out over it. Sometimes Bull Island as well. I always wondered what you were thinking about. I assumed you weren't thinking about me.'

'I can't remember what I was thinking about.'

She grins. 'I know you better than you think. Even if we've never gone on holidays together before.'

'Well, that wasn't my fault. That was because you didn't have the money.'

'Oh my god, that is *such* a lie!' she says, outrage iced with a beaming smile. 'I was hustling at the Carphone Warehouse while you were sipping Pimm's with your Trinity wanker friends.'

'I didn't have friends, wanker or otherwise.'

'You didn't want to go on holidays with me. I was up for it, but you were like, "Stall the ball, Pope John Paul, it's too soon for me."'

'I definitely didn't say anything about Pope John Paul.'

'I know you, Phoebe Forde. I *know* you,' she says, and she points at me and stifles a grin, like an actor in an outtake.

I recall what they say about history and victors, and surrender without a fight. Grace has come to reunite me with my secrets; now my liking the Little Mermaid is not merely a fact, but one commensurate with my personality. She reminds me what I was like, and what she was like. Dealing with Grace was like playing in sand – her fine detail gave an illusion of control while she glibly endlessed around me. There was a multiplicity, a hint she could take any shape possible, a romantic fluidity to her that served to conceal the used condoms (figurative) and stray bottle caps (not always).

The smell of fumes and footsteps hangs in still tart air. Bitter sunlight is magnified by legions of parked bicycles on either side of the streets. We seem to have the place to ourselves.

A weekend break is a split in the routine of routine. As we move north, past closed restaurants and office blocks and shops still waiting for customers, I am separate from the usual with Grace, and completely safe, scattered on the flatness of her vowels and freshened by the sharpness of her presence.

Every time we reach a historical building, anything with ornate windows or gilded lettering over the façade, Grace asks me what is inside. Most of the time I don't know, so after a while I start making things up. *This is the place where they test Lego to see which ones will be most painful to step on. This is the factory where Mads Mikkelsen was designed and assembled.*

She smiles, but doesn't laugh. She might be tired from the pillows.

10:44 At the end of Amaliegade, I point out a small landmark. 'That's the Yellow Palace. Where the penultimate Empress of Russia was born. Not joking, this time. She was from here originally. She survived Lenin and the gang and spent her old age back in Denmark.'

Though it is certainly yellow, the building is more townhouse than palace, with a wrought-iron balcony over a large black door. There's a white van parked in front, thwarting any photographs we might take. As Grace and I talk, a group of joggers with disciplined hair chug past, chatting loudly in Danish.

'You haven't changed at all,' Grace says, smirking. 'You're still into Russian royalty.'

'No,' I say, easing out a gentle laugh. 'I suppose not.'

'I remember you read a story about some lad in America who found a Fabergé egg in his basement. You were like, "Isn't it great, isn't it great." You kept asking me if I thought it was beautiful. I thought it looked like it was made of chocolate.'

'God, yeah. I always dreamt of finding something, something life-changing.'

'That was such a funny thing for a young lad to be interested in. No offence.'

I wobble my head. 'None taken.'

'It was your little online obsession. I should have copped on there and then.'

'Well, I didn't, so I don't blame you. It was mostly the last Tsar and his family. Something about decadence and inevitable doom appealed to me.'

'And power.'

'Yeah, power. All of it. I suppose I needed a Rasputin to come and sort me out.'

'He was Russia's greatest love machine,' she says, laughing. 'Anyway, we were all embarrassing back then. I was a cringe factory, remember?'

I smile. 'You? Never. I think my dream job was to be one of those women with big hair and pastel-coloured blouses who does documentaries about the British royal family. Walking around a stately home shouting, "Queen Victoria's bloomers weren't all they seemed!" into a camera.'

'I could see you doing that.'

'I think I'd have been very happy doing that.' And we're both laughing, and we're about to turn around and walk on. 'But it wasn't just that,' I say. 'I think I envied people in history. Imagine not knowing about the Holocaust, like. Imagine dying before it happened and never knowing about it. An easier life. Not knowing what people are capable of.'

'Not really. What if you died of measles?' She pauses. 'Or in childbirth?'

'Fair. I don't know, sometimes I think about what it would have been like if I'd been born two hundred years earlier and just worked the soil my whole life. I'd be unhappy, yeah, but I'd never have heard the word transgender so I wouldn't know any better. I wouldn't know anything about anything. I'd just be a sad person somewhere. I'd marry some woman from two fields over and we'd have children and then I'd be dead. I wouldn't have to worry about anything. I think I'd like that.'

Grace looks at me with a meditative expression. 'You want to be a bimbo.'

I glance ahead, to the statue in the courtyard in front of us – a man on horseback, another of history's bird-bothered winners. Then I look at Grace. 'Yeah. I want to be a bimbo.' I give a knowing smile. 'I sometimes think about the last Empress of Russia. Not the one who was born here, the one after her. The Empire came down because of her failure to produce a healthy male. Try as I might, I couldn't do that either. I wish I hadn't had to try.'

'Do you do astrology?'

'No. Should I?'

'Absolutely. It makes me feel connected to the universe. When I feel a bit fragile, it helps me understand myself. I feel like I make sense.'

'I don't think I want a connection to the universe. I want the universe to leave me alone.'

'You're such a Pisces. You're sensitive.'

'I'm cantankerous.'

'Yeah, that too. And you're a Virgo moon. You're organised.'

'And dogs howl at me.'

She places her hands on my cheeks and I can feel their coldness. 'Don't be so cynical,' she says, in a baby voice. 'There's a lot of wisdom in this stuff. I wouldn't have come here if the stars hadn't told me it was the right thing to do.'

'Really? Do you really believe that?'

'I don't know. It's nice. When you're watching a good film, you don't pick holes in the plot. I wish I'd brought my stuff over with me now.'

I smile, mostly out of relief that she didn't. 'What sign are you?'

'Taurus. Stubborn and extravagant.'

'The bull. Does that make me the china shop?'

'If you want,' she says, smiling. 'But sun in Pisces, moon in Virgo. You want to help others. I can see that. You want a role.'

'I used to have a role and I didn't like it. That's why I related to royalty. Because they lived in this fake world. They were born into it. A gilded cage. They had to give themselves up for power.'

'They were probably crying into their jewels.'

'You know what I mean. I felt trapped.'

'Yeah. Still, it's funny. And if you ever need a spiritual guru, you know who to call.' Then she starts singing Boney M, and I join her, chirruping about cats and Russian queens.

We fall about and she lets out a laugh like she's gargling her enjoyment. It is a sound I haven't heard in years. A middle-aged man in a raincoat walking towards Amalienborg glances at us and smiles to himself.

Shortly after, we head off in the same direction, into the courtyard of the palace. There is only a smattering of sightseers: raincoat hoods, backpacks, furled umbrellas and bottled water. An array of spoken languages creates the air of a summit meeting. The horseback statue is surrounded by what appear to be four separate stately houses, sandy yellow in colour, but I tell Grace that they're connected by tunnels. The green copper dome of Frederik's Church looms over everything, like a sun rising in the west.

One man in a red uniform and a bearskin hat moves across the cobbles with theatrical slowness. His face is expressionless and he moves as if programmed. He's not really a guard. He protects nothing. He is semi-static furniture for other people's memories, existing in trace in photographs, on screens, and now in our day, too.

11:16 By now, virtually the only people around us are tourists, moving to and from the mermaid. For me, it's a familiar onslaught of overpriced tourist bistros, overpriced tourist bike rentals – and restrooms, presumably for tourists, which, mercifully, are free.

Expectation is aggravated by the sound of footsteps, outdoor shoes on concrete. Besides the odd seagull, it is the only thing that can be heard. It is both cyclical and discordant – sometimes the steps accidentally fall into rhythm, like a collective heartbeat, which quickly dissipates.

Then we reach it: a spot of unmistakable presence, Babel-like, a crowd saying, 'Here it is' in every conceivable dialect, then, 'Is that it?'

This is the sixth or seventh time I've been here and, by now, I regard the mermaid as a backdrop to the assembled rabble of map-holders and selfie-takers. The real star of the show is the ability of the thing to draw people from far and wide. Hype, even overhype, is itself a wonder, a kind of art. It is communication exceeding language. It makes the world feel smaller.

If the purpose of a fairy tale is allegorical, to express plural and ulterior meaning, then perhaps the statue is an allegory of allegory, dispersed conclusions collapsing to a point, right here, in front of us – weathered proof that we have all, bespokely, done the reading.

A woman in a hijab gives a peace sign in front of the mermaid, standing barely out of the water, while a man in cream slacks takes her picture on a smartphone.

We stay on the path overlooking the crowd, not wishing to get our feet wet.

'It's certainly popular,' Grace says. 'She's a big draw.'

'A big draw for something so small. It's like this all the time. It's lit up at night so people are always here.'

'Have you read the book?'

'I saw the film when I was little. With the Rastafarian crab.'

She laughs. 'That doesn't count. It's full of erasure.'

'Erasure?'

'Hans Christian Andersen was very gay. Or bisexual, maybe. He wrote the book as a love letter to a fella he wanted to impress. I read it years ago, when I was still in school. The little mermaid gives up her speech so she can marry the prince. She loses her only way of expressing herself so she can fit in. And then the prince rejects her for some princess anyway. It's a metaphor.' As Grace speaks, I realise there is a woman over her shoulder half-listening to her.

'The prince rejects her? Bastard,' I say, hamming up my part.

'I know. And the movie leaves that out. The book is really dark. Sorry for spoiling it.'

I raise an eyebrow. 'And it goes to show: you can't trust royalty.'

Grace takes out her phone for a picture. 'Exactly!' she says, while pressing the screen for focus. 'It's like you said, they live for their roles. It's a tragic story for the prince too. He's doomed by his own privilege. Hans Christian Andersen's friend married a woman. He was devastated by that.' She presses the screen again and it flickers.

'What do you think of it?' I ask. 'The mermaid.'

'It's a bucket-list job, isn't it? I can't even see her tail because of all the people. It's basically just a statue of a woman in the nip.'

We stand there, saying nothing, looking at the nip woman with serene lackwit smiles on our faces. We observe the popularity of this silent figure, dozens swarming around her, like a damp agar plate in which we are all being cultured.

Grace turns to me. 'I'm glad you didn't give up your voice. I hope you know that.'

'Yeah. Yeah. You too.'

I look at Grace again but now she is taking another picture – this time with her hand in front of the camera lens, so the statue looks to be between her thumb and forefinger. A scatter-plot of bobbing human heads spoils the illusion, but she doesn't seem to care.

And I recall what I once read: that people are most likely to fall in love with someone who reminds them of a person they used to know. Sometimes a familiar sanctuary appears in another's face. A smile is a reminder of giddy, carefree joy; a looping ear evokes the great young world and its promise of adventure; a scatter of freckles is fresh proof of the existence of a time, muted but ill-forgotten, when you did not have to be afraid.

11:47 We make our way back to the city along the waterfront. Though the cobbled path is relatively quiet, the tranquil water of the channel is alive with activity, with small boats moving through and naval ships parked Sphinx-like in wait.

There are more statues along this route, though they attract no crowds. A davit, a stone column, a replica of Michelangelo's *David*. The buildings on this side are old, with red bricks and small windows. Across the water is the new city opera house, round with bulging glass, like a life buoy on its side.

'I remember you trying to convince those American tourists you were Mary McAleese's daughter,' I say to Grace.

We walk past the fountain at Amalieparken, still skeletal, empty of water as the city emerges slowly from winter.

'I really thought they'd buy it,' she says.

'The president's daughter going on a public tour of the president's house?'

Grace raises a hand, visible out of the corner of my eye. 'Do you not think I have a Kennedy vibe?'

'Drunk and cursed? Yeah, maybe.'

'Well, you can get fucked. Anyway, I don't think a Kennedy would have the smarts to steal a shaker of salt from the State Dining Room at Áras an Uachtaráin.'

'I think JFK might have taken a couple. De Valera was blind, like.'

We sit down on one of the benches beside the fountain. 'That was what impressed me about you,' I continue, 'the way you just *did* things. You weren't caught up in yourself like I was. I wouldn't in a million years have gone over and talked to someone like you did to me. I still wouldn't.'

Grace looks out at the water and the people moving by in dribs and drabs. She looks like she isn't listening to me at all. 'It's funny,' she says, 'what I liked about you was that you didn't need to show off. You were just . . . you. I thought you were very secure in yourself. Shows how wrong I can be.'

'I was very secure. The way people in padded cells are very secure.'

'You were so weird.'

'Thanks, Grace.'

'You were. You always left the pub early. Always gone by eleven. Everyone knows the best conversations happen late. That's when we start talking about James Joyce's love letters and how sexy Richard Boyd Barrett is. But you always wanted to go, and then I had to go. It was like having a baby.'

I say nothing.

Grace laughs to herself. 'But it's okay, like. You know I'm not judging you. You were gas. I once texted you and asked you what you were up to and you said you'd been listening to Des'ree's "Life" for forty-five minutes.'

I let out a sigh of embarrassment. 'I thought I was too much of an oddball for you. I always presumed you'd be the one to leave Ireland behind, go off and do great things. Meet people who were more interesting than me. I thought I'd be stuck at home for ever. I assumed that, whatever happened, you'd be all right.' I pause. 'Sorry.'

'For what?'

'For thinking you're not all right. Because you're here.'

'I am all right. Don't worry about me. I'm made of titanium and fucking bee-stings. And I've got my health. My physical health, at least.'

'What happened in London?' I ask. 'It seems like somewhere you'd belong. Somewhere exciting and a bit out-there.'

'London is terrible. It's too busy. Copenhagen – no offence – but Copenhagen is Ballykissangel compared to London.'

'Yeah. I know.'

'The Central Line gave me a stress headache, and the less said about the Tories the better. The food was great, though. Give me London food without everything else and I'd be a very happy bunny. All I ate was jerk chicken and halloumi kebabs. But I used to smile at people and they'd scowl at me, for no reason, so I'd end up scowling back at them. I felt like

I got nastier while I was there. And, in the end, I was on my own, without a job and things were going to shite in England, so I left, and now I'm still on my own, with a bad job and things are going to shite in Ireland.'

'Were you always on your own?'

'No, but I ended up that way. That was the universe's way of telling me it was time to get out of there. I didn't even need astrology.'

'Was it not nice to move away? A learning experience?'

'I mean, yeah, of course. I was there nearly five years. I learned a lot.'

As Grace speaks, we hear geese in formation above us, impertinent and uncaring. The sound of their squalls is distorted by distance so it resembles the corrugated wheeze of an old alarm clock. They are a white irrelevance set against the supercilious blue beyond them.

Grace looks skyward, and the midday brightness bathes her face. She seems to cast not merely her gaze but her entire being towards the birds. 'Look at them go,' she says. 'So free.'

12:29 The old townhouse restaurants at Nyhavn are a fissure of colour between the water and the city, crowned by a symphony of footsteps and seabird mewling, joined now and then by the urgent ruffling of canvas canopies against the air. On our left, music plays through speakers: 'Islands in the Stream', 'Rolling in the Deep'. On our right, a tour boat moves through the canal, resembling a submersible emerging from below.

It is a spot for people-watching. We survey the early-to-lunchers, already at their tables outside. In front of them, DSLR cameras are perched like crown jewels, garlands of hardened, proficient travellers commanding strict itineraries. Off-season tourists are an elite unto themselves. They make the best of a boreal streetscape in which the coffee kiosks are closed, the ice-cream shops are open, and the Christmas mulled-wine stands are long gone.

At the tables, some fidget for loose tobacco in bags. Others carry out grave discussions. We pass one group where a man speaks confidently about human rights, though I don't know which in particular have exercised him. There are no heaters for the alfresco diners – further evidence of their commitment to the bit – but in most places small blankets are provided to allow patrons to keep warm. Grace and I, lacking their experience or the wherewithal to fake it, decide to take a chance finding a spot indoors.

We end up in one of the herring-and-Tuborg places along the canal. The inside is gloomily lit, by way of contrast to the primary colouring outside – but it's a room-temperature room, and that's what matters to us.

Two men at a table hold a boisterous-sounding conversation, all *ja ja ja absolut fuldstændig* with laughs and the odd raspy cough, while a young couple at another, who don't speak but look foreign, leer at their phones. We sit at a table for two in the far corner of the room. A woman in a black apron gives us two menus, and I pass one to Grace and point to the lunch section. 'You should try smørrebrød while you're here. It's a local delicacy.'

'What?'

'It's an open sandwich with herring and other stuff. Seriously, it's really nice.'

'And what's it called?'

'Smørrebrød.'

'Again?'

I glare at her gently, like a weary parent feigning annoyance at an insolent but loveable child.

She gives a look of divilment. 'I just like hearing you say it.'

We probe the menu, trilingual, with English and German: pickled herring, salmon, capers, raw onions, horseradish.

The server comes back with a touchscreen device, and I order sandwiches for the two of us in rote-learned Danish. I also ask for two glasses of white wine.

'I had no idea you spoke so many languages,' Grace says, with a hint of mockery.

'My Swedish is better than my Danish. Swedish is easier and sounds better. It's all long vowels and funny whistling noises. Danish sounds like a drunk man chewing tinfoil.'

'It didn't sound bad when you spoke it.'

'Here, now, let me regale you with my Swedish: *alla känner apan, men apan känner ingen*.'

'Lovely stuff,' Grace says. 'What does that mean?'

'Everyone knows the monkey, but the monkey knows no one.'

'The poor monkey.'

'It's a proverb I saw once. It's basically about how people who stand out become very recognisable, but no one around them really knows them.'

'My friend Agnieszka has a saying – not my circus, not my monkeys. That's Polish.'

I look ponderously at her. 'See, I'm not sure I get that one. The story of my life has been me slowly realising that these *are*, in fact, my monkeys. I don't think I've ever been in a situation where the monkeys weren't mine.'

The server brings over two glasses.

'At least the monkeys don't have typewriters,' I say, craned over an arm, as the wine is placed between us.

12:48 Grace is right: she does have her health. The lottery of memory throws up that point. My recollection is like a spider's web: diaphanous, more air than thread, but the fibres, where they persist, are stronger than I might expect.

Her voice doesn't croak like it used to. The vocal fry has cooled to a simmer. Words like 'night' and 'place' no longer have a jagged, rope-bridge feel. She wasn't sickly back then, the way some young women are – wan and emaciated, a gin-powered cadaver – it's fair to say she was always just a little bit feverish. She was cold. A buzz-killing cold, the kind that got in the way. She carried a sniffle around with her the way a fancier woman might handbag a Chihuahua. As someone who sought always to make an impression, it made sense that she wished to be slightly infectious.

I remember things and trouble myself slotting them into a schema. The way she'd droop from a chair like third-world scaffolding. Autumn leaves, she liked autumn leaves. She liked autumn leaves and the word 'gooch'.

I want to stitch her back together, like a garment, or a wound – to piece-by-piece her from nothing more than memories and the content of my current vision. I am eager to imagine her whole and complete, but she doesn't owe me straightforwardness any more than the other way around.

She keeps glancing at the top of my head, every twenty seconds or so. Idle, no malice in it, but persistent. I don't know what it is. For a moment, I wonder if a bird has had its way with me. But of course, it's the scrunchie. It's the entire ensemble.

The more she observes it, the more acidly aware I am of how high on my head this ponytail is. With each flicker of her eyes it seems to creep over my skull like Shakespearean forest. How proud it must look, how bumptiously it must catch the window light.

Grace eats the minutes while we wait for something more substantial. She talks about campy cyborgs, a film we once saw, black and white and slightly noir. I don't remember it.

12:57 The smørrebrød, like so much food here, tastes of the sea – bitter and bracing, loitering in the nose. Its purpose is to inform the world that the locals have mastered nature and its various flavours, that they eat for sensory pleasure and not to satisfy a primal urge. I tell Grace that around here even the sweets are dipped in salt, and no one eats for the sake of it.

'Denmark, on the whole,' I say, 'is a bit like Ireland with the corners taken off. It's Ireland with bike lanes and better healthcare. The Swedes think of the Danes as fast-talking, exuberant and not very trustworthy. So they're basically the Catholics of Scandinavia.'

'And what are the Swedes like?' she asks.

'The Swedes are more of an island nation than the Irish. A very peculiar people.'

'How do you mean?'

'See, like, Danes have a cultural chauvinism to them. They banned the burka and they're horrible to refugees. They're bang-average European in that way. Whereas the Swedes flex their patriotic muscle by insisting, regardless of the evidence, that their country is the best-run in the world. In Sweden they have egalitarianism on steroids. Everyone is watching everyone. When a country's self-image is built on equality, it becomes a way to silence dissent. People who stand out get squashed down like Whack-a-Moles. Sweden is like a country run by a tidy town committee.'

'Very dystopian. I don't know how you managed. It must have been rough for you,' Grace says, laughing.

'I'm serious. You know me, I've always been suspicious of esprit de corps. I've had friends deported from Sweden, I've seen the shit they had to put up with, the petty bureaucracy. It's horrible. People think authoritarianism is when you have too many laws, but it's actually when the laws are vague and enforced selectively. That's Sweden. The rules are secret and you have to guess what they want. Everything has to be *lagom*. What does *lagom* mean? Nobody knows.'

'No wonder you're having a drink with lunch.'

'Oh, Christ, *that's* another thing,' I say, in my element now. 'In Sweden the supermarkets don't sell drink. You have to go to the off-licences, which are state-owned. *Systembolaget.* It sounds like a stomach complaint. They're open regular office hours, ten to six Monday to Friday, plus Saturday mornings. But people only go on Friday evenings and Saturdays, when it's thronged. They could go on a Tuesday evening, after work, when it's quiet, to stock up, but they don't.'

'Why not?'

'Because that would be against the rules,' I say, manoeuvring my hands to draw an invisible line that may not be crossed. 'My first landlord in Sweden explained it to me – and he would know, because he was a raging alcoholic.'

'Love it. Love it. Love that Sweden has smacked you sideways. What kind of drunk was he, angry or friendly? He didn't cry, did he?'

I let out a noise like a slowly deflating balloon. 'His name was Lasse. I lived in the spare room of his house. In a village called Vigglöv, which is about half an hour from Lund on the bus. Have you ever read Henning Mankell?'

'No.'

'No, me neither. But apparently, Vigglöv is right out of his books. It has a population of about five thousand, but it felt emptier. The place was dead quiet. You could hear yourself go mad. And the land around was all flat farmland and forest, so you could hide a body easily enough. If you wanted to.'

'Good to know.'

'So, picture me, August of 2015, closeted princess of the Howth Road, eager to start my master's, living off three years' worth of savings, fresh off the plane, and I end up in this lad's house in the armpit of nowhere. Lasse was in his forties, I think, but he looked older. Greying beard, denim jackets.

He smoked forty a day. He looked like patient zero for a new venereal disease.'

Grace laughs.

'Apparently,' I continue, 'he had kids, but I never saw them. He was a student of archaeology, that's what he told me, but he never went on excavations or anything. He just pottered around in his house shoes all day. He spent his student grants at the off-licence. He was happy enough to be seen at *Systembolaget* at eleven a.m. on a Tuesday. They probably knew him there.'

'He probably had a loyalty card.'

'Yeah. The woman at the checkout saw him and was like, "*Hejsan*, Lasse, vee haff your favourite: ninety-nine per cent proof aquavit made with nail polish remover."'

Grace smiles at my Swedish accent.

'So,' I say, 'the combination of smoking and drunk-sleeping meant that he coughed through the night.'

'If I were you, I'd have killed what's-his-name by now.'

'Lasse.'

'Whatever.'

'I didn't kill him, but I bought cheap earplugs that made the inside of my ear scabby.'

'Lovely.' She pushes her empty plate away from her.

'I don't know, I didn't want to be mean. Addiction is a disease, you know?'

'You're not a doctor.'

'No, but I didn't want to punish him for something out of his control.'

'You didn't want to get down off the cross.'

I labour before responding. 'Yeah, there was a bit of that. I prefer to think I was more forgiving of people back then. Other people, I mean. Lasse once told me over pizza that he voted for the Sweden Democrats.'

'Is that bad?'

'Yeah, they're fash.'

She sighs. 'All right, all right, unless you murdered this lad, I'm not sure I want to hear the end of this story.' She laughs to herself. 'I wonder what he'd think of you now.'

'He'd probably be inspired by the bravery of my journey, much like everyone else. Now, I should say, there *was* a crime.'

'Wood-chipper?'

'Nah, it was he who did the deed. One Sunday I went to the Ikea museum in Älmhult.'

'How was that?'

I give a so-so hand gesture. 'When I got back, he'd emptied my bottle of Albariño. He left it in the fridge, so I could find it. He wasn't a clever thief.'

'In the *fridge*? I'm sorry, if that happened to me, this guy would be dead now. D-E-D, dead. Food for worms.'

I give an exaggerated shrug. 'It was good to have some challenges to start with. It forced me to think about what I wanted to get out of life. I moved out not long after that. You know, if things were too easy, you'd never question anything.'

'Well done.'

'For what?'

She shakes her head slowly. 'For turning this stupid little thing into a story with a moral.'

13:38 We swap yarns like explorers trading spices, making pacified colonies of our pasts, flat miniature worlds on which lessers may be organised like toy soldiers. It doesn't even matter if what we're saying is true – what matters is that it is ours. The scuttlebutt dividend is the nearest thing to capital we have.

The walk to Tivoli is about twenty minutes, but as we move past banks and bookshops, past men trilling alveolar whistles and women frogmarching children in rubber boots, our minds are elsewhere.

Grace talks about one of her old housemates. 'I wouldn't have thought the roadkill in north London was any good,' she says, 'I imagine it's fairly chewy, but Chris loved it. He said it was more ethical to eat food sourced locally. Sometimes he'd go out on these trips into the countryside with his friends. They'd go out to Hertfordshire in a van, like they were in *Scooby-Doo* or something, and come back with all sorts. Badgers, squirrels. The rest of us decided we had to push Chris out of the house share after a few months. It just wasn't working out.'

'Because of the roadkill? Bit harsh.'

'No, because he didn't brush his teeth and they were rotten.'

'Oh.'

'That was another thing he didn't believe in. Maybe he had a vendetta against fluoride, I don't know. He always looked like he was chewing walnuts.'

'Jesus,' I say, and on the ground I see an empty cigarette box depicting what looks like an exploded tongue.

'He said he knew his teeth were going to fall out, but when they did he'd make wooden falsies for himself.'

In a curious way, I'm a bit like Chris, this guy I've just heard about and will almost certainly never meet. He put an intolerable psychic burden on Grace, and for that he was confronted and ejected, forcibly egressed, fucked off with extreme prejudice. At least his teeth were visible – whatever was rotten within me must have taken longer to perceive.

At times I feel like I'm debriefing at the gates of Heaven, recounting my life to God Herself – capital G and capital H – hoping for clemency.

'Just think,' I say, 'there's probably an unfortunate straight woman out there who thinks she can change that guy.'

'Yeah, but she's a dentist.'

We both laugh, heading towards Knippelsbro, another bridge over canals that soothe the streets, sharing ourselves not merely with each other but with the city as a whole, walking past men in workman's trousers, a guy sat by the window of a shop playing air guitar on the body of his bicycle.

If we were in Dublin right now, the climate would be so heavy, so dreary with memory and the possibility of chance encounters, that we wouldn't be able to talk like this. It is like we have sprouted listening ears just for today. The purpose of any reunion is the sharing of these sediment stories. Grace and I are not engaged in a homecoming, but a theregoing, comparing our experiences of being wind-bidden, trying to prove we are more than the place that made us.

We have both lived a life to pieces. Now we are tasked with making a self from half the remnants and a friend from the other half, from the ones that got away.

Grace puts her hand in front of me. 'Phoebe, mind!'

'Shit.' A herd of bicycles move by, left to right, fizzing like desert snakes. The pedestrian light remains a stern red.

I lean towards her. 'There's another lesson about life in Copenhagen. You need to have your wits about you. The cyclists own the place.'

'A city owned by cyclists is better than one owned by Johnny Ronan.'

'Who's Johnny Ronan?'

She ruffles my hair like I'm a child. 'Oh, Phoebe, you're so lucky. You sweet, innocent bimbo-bambino. I hate you so much.'

We are pipped across by the traffic lights.

13:52 'They didn't read my email properly,' I say, 'so they got a nasty surprise when I went to the viewing. They tried to be okay with it, but, well, you know how it is.'

'I don't know how it is,' Grace says.

'It was uncomfortable. Looking for somewhere to live is like auditioning at the best of times, and that wasn't the best of times. I'd only been out for a year.'

'And then, what, someone swooped in and saved the day?'

'Yeah. Literally, yes. I got a message from a woman called Camilla, a professor at the University of Copenhagen. I met her at a seminar in Lund towards the end of my master's, one of those round-table discussions where everyone sits and looks at Twitter. They had free pizza to lure in starving doctoral students. I can't even remember what it was about. Something something microfinance. Camilla was the first trans woman I ever met in an academic setting. A gentle tall woman with white-blonde hair. I know it's corny to say, but she looked like a Viking. We went for coffee after, and agreed to stay in touch. I didn't think we actually would. But then she offered me the use of her flat, for a nominal rent, and in exchange for taking care of Dolly.'

We walk past the front of Christiansborg, the parliament building, a palace that appears grey in wet weather and a rich sandy brown in the sun, so it is a truly representative chamber, a brazen panderer with a mirror-like quality. A man is protesting outside the great portal entrance. I'm not close enough to read the writing, but the word *ISLAM* is in large print.

'Camilla was moving to the University of Maryland,' I continue. 'Teaching business to young Americans. Like teaching lobsters to boil water. But it saved my arse, and that's how I ended up in Frederiksberg.'

'Do you keep in touch with her?'

'Yeah, she gives out to the dog over video chat every so often, and she comes over twice a year to see her kids. They live with her ex-wife, in a small town on the coast.'

'So you have a guardian angel, and her name is Camilla. Thank Christ one of these stories has a proper happy ending.'

'Sort of. She'll be back in three years. Then I don't know.'

'Don't worry about the future,' she says, while a steady breeze nudges her hair canalwards. 'Anyway, I like hearing about how you got where you are today. I hope that's okay.'

'Why wouldn't it be?'

'I don't know if you like talking about the past.'

'I like talking to someone. To you, I mean. The subject doesn't really matter.'

She smiles at me. 'Cool. Good. I'm glad.'

And she hugs me, conspicuously, by a white painted railing. It comes as a defibrillator-shock, how much these last few years I've needed to feel the contact of another against me. I feel interrupted by myself. To be a woman is to be public property, that's what people say – and here I am, in hock. It is a source of faint anger that I am still this vulnerable, still nursing a pool of need, a holdout, untouched in every sense. I have been waiting and waiting for the time to be right, but, really, any moment would have done, because connection itself is an act of postponement, its purpose to make the present pass wonderfully.

A woman walking in a mac gawps at us. I make a face at her over Grace's shoulder.

14:16 Tivoli haunches in the dead-centre of Copenhagen. Its stately gate, drizzled in light, is the first thing to be seen on leaving the main city railway station. Other capitals make a serious first impression: a frosted office block, a bank, maybe a university. Here, instead, lies an amusement park, gaudy yet endearingly earnest, with rollercoasters and lobster restaurants and its own symphony orchestra.

It is a nick-of-time intervention, a quieting set of jangling keys. 'Time to have some fun after all that chatter, honey,' Grace says, as we stand in a queue, modest but chilly.

It is not merely fun, but organised and disciplined fun. Copenhagen is belt-clipped with a strenuousness and rigour that speaks to me. The city is salty, like the song says: sodium and chlorine, purifying, a neat and tidy chemical compound.

Dublin, by contrast, is the pungent output of a biological process. It is fermented, yeasty, unrequiring of light and unlikely to get it.

The entry fee is expensive, but as she taps her PIN into a card machine, I assure Grace that the park's finances are propped up by the eccentrics and overgrown children who buy season tickets at a discount. Our visit is an opportunity to ogle them and feel superior.

And maybe it's a cliché. Maybe everything we're doing is a cliché. But the oxygen of a strange city is not its art or its architecture, but the way it reveals whole new ways of living. Clichés come pre-appreciated, and, as such, they remove one task from the work of enrichment.

Through the park, the city demonstrates its fealty to the things that make life worthwhile. Walking-shoe days. Human voices raised to new heights. The heavy smell of cinnamon and popcorn butter. (Cliché! Cliché! Cliché!)

Our ticket barcodes receive an approving beep and we are channelled onto a narrow lane modelled on a mediaeval village, the bucolic touched with the bubonic. The houses look like they might be made of gingerbread. The music is inane and chirpy, the kind that must long ago have tunnelled its way into the nightmares of staff. It rattles the small bones in our ears like whistle-pips. It loosens our fingernails. It trims our nose hair.

'This is mad. Isn't this mad?' Grace says, again and again.

14:39 Grace spots a stand: a wooden-shack funfair fancy at which a teddy bear may be won upon conquering an undoubtedly rigged game. She approaches it with a shot putter's confidence, a stride of pride – a consequence of the lunch wine.

She interrogates the attendant, a man with cropped ginger hair and what can only be described as a pregnant head, the approximate shape and colour of a butternut squash. 'So, what do you have to do?' she asks, carrying on like she is attempting to bend the odds by force of personality.

I see the man glance downwards, and imagine him considering for a moment pressing some form of emergency button to get rid of her.

'You throw a dart at the balloon and then you win a prize,' he says, gesturing towards an assemblage of dolphin plushes to his left.

I try to come up with a joke for the moment: *they're good but they're no Blåhaj*, but everything that crosses my mind just sounds mean-spirited. Then I put my hand on her forearm. 'If you win, you'll have to fit that yoke in your hand luggage. You know what the airlines are like.'

'If I win, you can have it. I'll give it to Dolly.'

'It's twenty crowns. Cash only,' the man says.

Grace glances at me and whispers, 'How much is that?'

'Too much, but we're here now.'

She rummages. 'Danish money is so pretty,' she says. 'Look at the hearts.'

She hands the man a coin and is presented with five darts. They are yellow, with plastic fins, like the ones in a well-upholstered pub. The balloons are about five feet away, but the game's contrivance is that they are only half-filled with water, so a powerful direct hit is needed to burst one.

She flings dart after dart, each of them hitting the back wall of the stand and falling to the ground without coming close to a target. Her confidence wilts into something approaching vengefulness, incredulous eyes and sweeping statements. 'I have to get it this time,' she says, before her third attempt, which is also unsuccessful.

I ask her if I can have a go. Grace gives me her two remaining darts. 'Go for it,' she says, placing her hand over mine like she is divesting herself.

I have no particular technique. I just chuck it, and pop: there goes a pink balloon, slightly left of the centre of the board.

Grace lets out a shriek, leaps on me and kisses me on the cheek. 'I knew you'd do it. You're a local. I knew you'd know better than me.'

I am so unused to being reacted to like this – the sensation stirs and stirs within me, like I am one step behind reality, watching its fresh footsteps, in need of catching up. The man hands Grace the dolphin. He speaks, but I am not listening.

Then Grace scowls at him. 'Just so you know, *she's* my friend.'

I'm a she and I'm her friend. Statements of fact, but I don't know what Grace is responding to. What did he think I was? A he-friend? A he-something?

The man stands back slightly. 'Oh . . . okay. Sorry.'

I steer Grace away from the stand, backing into the wandering crowd. We end up standing between a litter bin and a four-foot-long cardboard cut-out of a hot dog surrounded by marquee lights. Grace looks at me indignantly. 'If that happens again, I'll wallop someone.'

'Please don't wallop anyone on my account. It's fine, really.'

'It's *not* fine.'

'It's my life, Grace. If I yelled at everyone who called me the wrong thing, my face would be on the internet in no time. It's not worth it. And besides, don't they say "she" is the cat's mother?'

Grace looks at me, then downwards, as though calculating exactly how much respect she has lost.

15:03 She has tucked her dolphin between her ankles at the front of the car, assured by staff it is not too valuable to travel, and it's probably filthy now, collecting dusty souvenirs of its own. 'You know the song?' Grace asks, '"Life Is a Rollercoaster"?' I do know the song. I was eleven when it came out. Not a great age. An age when life resembles less a rollercoaster than a malfunctioning lift, or a wheelless suitcase, or

Off we go.

I close my eyes.

I recite the alphabet silently.

M follows L follows K follows J.

I am sagging through a jungle of consonants.

Others accrete vowels – As and Os and the occasional disgruntled U.

Hock-spat noises, here and there but mostly there, like an argument in proooogress around me.

The soooooooooooouuuuuuuuund hits my ear like an apology, hurried and whining, sincere but self-interested.

Sounds without words, without meaning, without the capacity to

Without the capacity. Tiny little French jam jar sounds.

Up and up, up-and-up, twisting and turning, honest hurtling, adrenaline flowing like truth, veritas and its vino.

Colours slow dance across my grief-black view. I see a place both darker and more lightful than this, within my confines.

Words were emptier once. The world was larger, too large for me, so large that it was clearly meant for someone else – like the economy, fantastically huge and impossible to understand, filled with people dressed like sofas. I belted through it like it was a pair of trousers. I dangled my small-person's legs over it. It was an embarrassment of space and time.

Scarcely a minute later, shunt, exhale, *hahaha woo!*, and we leave the car like a pair of agitated snow globes.

'You can see the whole city from up there,' Grace says. 'I could see your flat.'

We go to the preview screens and observe the snapshot of ourselves, with no stated intention of buying. Grace is windswept and smiling behind an encroaching tongue.

I am also there, a picture of enjoyment.

15:54 A sinister animation of a plasticine-faced cartoon family precedes the ride, informing us through the medium of juddering computer graphics that we must use our laser pointer to shoot at diamonds along the way.

'What do we get if we win?' Grace says, to no one in particular.

'I don't know,' I say. 'Called a bloke again?'

We have a four-person car to ourselves. The contraption, front-heavy, tremors forward at wake-up pace before lurching into the water, splashing us both on the legs and doing untold damage to Grace's toy and its resale value.

We gain speed as we make our way to the inside of what appears to be an underground mine. The place is dark and the air is damp and cold. The only sound is that of our cart moving forward: rhythmic splashes and the going-on clank of metal on metal.

Grace puts her hand on my leg and wobbles her head as if to say, *Isn't this all very exciting?* and her hair flutters back and forth over her face.

Rides like this thrive on the element of surprise – but the element of surprise, like zinc and uranium, is in finite supply. Small children carry the element of surprise in vast seams, which is why they come over so endearingly triggered by peek-a-boo and bathroom hand dryers and the fact of their own mortality. As we get older, the surprise stock dwindles as suppositions harden and are increasingly impossible to thwart. That is maturity: the process by which expectation is wiped clean like an incriminating hard drive. I am an old soul, a status sublime, one I have glided into: I no longer have an authentic emotional reaction to anything.

Moving forward, there is the tinny piercing sneeze of flute music through an old speaker.

After a few seconds sloshing through, it becomes clear that the diamonds are actually blue lights – if we shoot at them, they turn red and flash. But we are much too enamoured of the pew-pew-pew sound of the laser to care where it is pointed, and by now reckon we are probably well behind the more competitive nuclear families.

Grace taps the rhythm of the music on her leg, then puts her hand on mine again. 'Oh god, Phoebe, look.'

And there it is: a mechanical dragon with eyelashes like sunflower stalks. A dragon in drag. A train-of-thought-stealing sight, all lips and cheek, hair cascading. She emits steam and makes hissing noises, yet the vista resembles less a furnace than a department store perfume sample being sprayed across us.

Her name is Poppy.

This dragon has done the work. She has won at gender and I get no more than an honourable mention. Papier-mâché, chewed paper – isn't gender always chewed paper? Gender coupons ripped to shreds by a gender self-service checkout.

Grace laughs and starts talking into my ear. 'You're like the glamorous dragon, and I'm one of the little sloth things collecting diamonds for you.'

'Please don't compare me to a glamorous dragon,' I say, and suddenly it is present, in trace amounts, a few drops here and there: the element of surprise. I think, sat in the cart, about how strange the world is, how all sides can be blind sides – and how Judith Butler would have a field day.

'Why?' Grace says. 'Are you going to snort fire at me?'

'If only.'

Then she puts her hand on the back of mine, but our attention is quickly confiscated by the looming prospect of a wall of water, and a two-metre drop.

Grace turns on me, giving my arm a thump. 'Ah, you bitch, you didn't tell me about this.'

'I didn't know!'

We grab hold of each other as we go over, an unknowing jumble that resurfaces without too much damage, though the dolphin is a write-off.

16:46 We buy churros and sit on the grass in front of the bandstand. The sky is pink and peeling. There is a Friday-night rock show scheduled for later and a man on the stage flits between instruments, testing them. The roof of the bandstand spells out the word TIVOLI in a style that looks oppressively recreational, like it bespeaks the entertainment at a fascist holiday camp.

A small crowd of people have already assembled on the grass, braving the conditions by drinking beer out of clear plastic cups.

'I hope you're happy, Phoebe,' Grace says, crossing her arms theatrically. 'I've come all this way and I'm probably going to go home with a cold.'

I stick my tongue out at her.

'It's been an experience,' she says, pulling a grain of churro sugar out of her scarf. 'Thanks.'

'I've had worse days at Tivoli.'

'Is that a joke or have you actually had worse days?'

'I came here with my parents during my first semester in Lund, about three years ago. My dad got distracted by a slot machine and had to be left to his own devices for an hour and a half.'

She gives an open-mouthed smile. 'I wouldn't have thought your dad was a Tivoli kind of man.'

'I think that was his way of saying he wasn't.'

We laugh.

'Wait,' she says, spitting out crumbs. 'Did your parents ever get to meet the alcoholic landlord? That would have been a good cross-over episode of your life.'

'Yeah. They thought he was a great lad. Very friendly.'

She gives a sigh, which fades into a smile. 'Your parents are drips.'

'Where do you think I got it from?'

'How are they?' she asks.

'Oh, fine. You know, fine. Mam still gossiping at the credit union. Dad still the big cheese at the supermarket. Monsieur le Grand Camembert. Making sure the salami is presentable – then nine holes at St Anne's every Saturday, like clockwork. I'm sure in both cases their colleagues can't wait until they retire. How's your mam?'

'All good. She makes jewellery now. Babs's Bracelets. She did a class, she loves it, says being creative keeps her young. Botox for the brain, she calls it. She sells her wares out of the back of her car on Sunday mornings. Little earner.'

The last time I saw Barbara Keaney, she was sitting in the back garden of her house drinking tea from a mug that came free with a tabloid newspaper and had Stephen Cluxton's face on it. She wore a shocking pink beret and tinted sunglasses, like she'd just been doing the entertainment at a paramilitary funeral. She raised a single finger at me by way of a wave. Perhaps she knew Grace was about to dump me, and was counting down the weeks.

'She's getting herself some tax-free income,' I say. 'Nice.'

'She'd lamp you if she heard you saying that. And have your parents adjusted to everything? You know, with you?'

I flatten out my face, as if to imply that the question is so foolish I have chosen not to answer it.

'Is that a yes?' she says.

'They're okay with it. They haven't cut me off or anything. But I'm here and they're there. I don't talk to them that much.'

'Oh. Okay.' I can see her mind at work, trying to establish who detached from whom, like she is sweeping for mines, keeping an eye out for freshly moved earth. She finds nothing, but that doesn't mean there's nothing there. 'You must have a community over here, though,' she says.

The man on the stage attempts 'Smoke on the Water'. Someone on the grass, closer to the stage than we are, shouts something, but I cannot hear what.

'I have friends back in Lund,' I say. 'I visit them sometimes.'

'But trans people, there must be loads of them around here. With it being so liberal.'

'Yeah, I went to a support group a few times, but it wasn't really for me. There were teenagers there with their parents and stuff. They seemed more complete than I was. It was . . . I don't know, it felt weird.'

'Fair enough.'

'I suppose everyone is different and everyone has to do things differently. I hate to use the word "journey" but everyone is on a different journey. Being trans isn't really an identity, you know? It's more like a path you get shunted onto by fate. You have to hide for a while. Sometimes five years, sometimes twenty-five years, sometimes almost your whole life. How much hiding you do sort of ends up defining you. There are thirty-year-olds who've been out since they were kids and there are thirty-year-olds who've been out five minutes. I wouldn't necessarily relate to either.'

'That's a shame,' she says, and I suppose she's learning something: that even a life lived unconventionally is still mostly filler. What's seldom is merely seldom. She inspects the stub of her churro, the airy dough, as if looking for inspiration. 'You'd benefit from having people around you,' she says. 'Do you know many Irish here?'

I laugh. 'Nah. What would I do with them, watch the Six Nations?'

'I wouldn't have managed in London without knowing a few Irish people. You need that connection, don't you? When you bump into someone and you can place their accent, and they can place yours. You'd be like "Galway?" and they'd say "Loughrea" and even though you've never been to Loughrea, you'd be fast friends,' she says, pushing her fingers together to illustrate. 'I loved being Irish abroad. One Christmas, I remember watching the *Toy Show* in some hall in Kilburn and having the time of my life. The prosecco was flowing. Take a drink every time Ryan Tubridy has a costume change – you're completely gone after twenty minutes. I wouldn't even watch the *Toy Show* at home.'

'Maybe you went abroad to work on your inner child.'

'I think my inner child eats glue.'

We laugh. Grace belongs nowhere, and that almost allows her to stake a claim on everyone she sees. I want to walk her streets – not the familiar ones in Dublin, but in London – to walk by the cafés she went to, the houses she drank in, the sites of her tree-branch life experiences. It seems that every so often, she yields a little, allows what lies beneath to be revealed, but never quite enough, and the cat-and-mouse goes on.

What must it have meant to her, to leave home and return, like an unread message in a bottle? To abandon a new self and resume the discomfort of an old one? It's true enough that growth is rarely linear, but when does non-linear growth become a non-growth linear: two steps back, three steps back, forward only a memory?

'What did you do for your thirtieth?' she asks, as she plays with the paper napkin, now empty.

'Well . . . it's only a day, isn't it? There was a phone call to home, but otherwise it was just a regular Friday.'

Grace looks at me.

I lean back. 'I don't usually go out on Fridays. It was fine. It was quiet.'

'So, you didn't do anything?' She lets out a sigh. 'Ah, Phoebe. No. No, no, no. I'm not having that.'

17:34 It's funny – the more you look at someone the less sense they make. *He's highly strung. She's just a bitch. They're just like that, they can't help it.* People are always just like that and it could take a lifetime or two or three to establish exactly what *that* is. In the end, everyone is judged and sentenced in the way they are seen by others, and perhaps that is to be feared, as I have always feared it. There is violence inherent in perception. There is death and decay. The ordeal of being known is mortifying in the original, putrescent sense of the term.

Grace is taking me away. She has a youthfulness about her, yet seems so much older than me. I am timeless, like an unmoving pond, and she like an ancient city; both run down in different ways. She says it is not an intervention unless I want it to be. Next to her, I might as well be a hamster rolling in a ball. We no longer graze the pavements like a pair of untied shoelaces. Our footsteps have intimations and the waning light has intimations, too.

17:46 The evening begins to whisper itself. A secretive gloom creeps over us, rendering the streets half-mystery under seams of LED lamps. We allow the nervous energy of the pavements, the cold, and the unwinding workweek to sweep around us.

At one point, Grace spots a bicycle on a rack. There is a sign inside the frame, between the pedals and beneath the seat, saying: *Reduce your carbon footprint.* The sign is green, but in this light it looks brownish. The back wheel of the bike is bent and unusable. Grace says it's a metaphor. I say: a metaphor for what?

We end up in a small restaurant in the crowded footprint of city hall. The sign over the door reads: *Bar og et lille køkken*, which I find cute. It reminds me of toy kitchens with miniature food, plastic cherries disappearing on contact with a doll's unmoving mouth.

We decide that, in the same way a bakery might emit the smell of fresh bread to entice customers, eateries in the city have contrived a way of giving off heat to lure people in, and it is no less effective for appearing deliberate.

The special on the board outside is fish curry, abominable enough in concept that it is best avoided in execution – but it's too early to eat, anyway. The place is thick with people in smart-casual clothes, the after-work set, chattering loudly. There is a mood of busy festivity. The weekend is here, where they left it, where they agreed it should be. Grace goes to the bar and orders two glasses of white wine.

We sit at a table with a candle between us, next to a window behind which hurried cyclists and pedestrians move in silhouette.

Grace sips as though trying to stave off the effects of the day's alcohol by taking only a little more, then speaks carefully, venturing to ensure that her words come out exactly as intended. 'Can I say something to you? And please don't take this the wrong way.'

I regard the blue of the tablecloth, its silky finish, almost reflective but not quite. 'Say away.'

'I just . . . I think when I came over, I expected you to be . . . I think "stronger" is the word I'm looking for. I guess I had this idea of you in my head. That you'd overcome all these obstacles, that you were living your authentic life now—'

'And you're a bit disappointed by the reality of me?'

'I didn't say that. I thought I'd be intimidated by you. I thought you'd be accomplished and powerful and . . . '

'Inspiring?'

Grace glances towards the window and sighs. 'I don't know. I don't want to hurt your feelings.'

'Reality doesn't always live up to the hype,' I say, laying a hand either side of the candle and my glass like I'm liaising with the hereafter. 'I guess it's easier to let people think I'm braver than I am. That way they can imagine that the person they used to know and worry about is off living a happy life somewhere. Then they'll leave me alone.'

'Ouch. Was that about me?'

'No. Well, maybe. A bit. It was about everyone. I sometimes think if I could climb inside the head of every person I pass on the street, then I wouldn't be so afraid of them. But that's impossible, so I keep my distance.' I pause, and then laugh to myself. 'Only my dog sees me as I really am.'

'I've missed how thoughtful and weird you are,' she says, smiling.

'You can't escape thoughtful and weird,' I say, 'no matter how hard you try.'

17:58 Ice cubes crack sharply in a jug of water placed between us. Neither of us asked for it; it was put there by a member of staff, like a conversation piece. When the woman set it down, she said nothing, just a snippy hum, self-praise for a job adequately done. A flicker of candlelight appears warped behind an empty glass left with me, also unrequested.

'Did you know the Baltic Sea used to be a lake?' I ask.

Grace gives a bemused, dilligaf look, as though trying to stuff the words back into my mouth.

'Seriously,' I continue. 'It was.'

She shifts her head sideways. 'I believe you. I mean, why wouldn't I? I just don't know why you're telling me.'

'Everything from here to St Petersburg was one big lake.'

'Right.'

'Because of the Ice Age, the sea levels were lower, so the Baltic was cut off from the ocean. Completely isolated.'

'Oh no, I hope the Baltic didn't get lonely,' she says, and then she smirks with recognition. 'Stuck on its own.'

'But then,' I say, 'about ten thousand years ago, the polar ice caps were melting, as they do, and the sea levels rose, as they also do, and the narrow strip of land between Sweden and Denmark, which is now the Øresund, the coast of this city, flooded with sea water. Like Niagara Falls, right here, in Copenhagen. Except there was no Copenhagen.'

'And then the Baltic wasn't lonely anymore.'

I nod. 'Suddenly it was open to the world in a way it hadn't been for a very long time.'

She laughs softly. 'Very exciting.'

'But also scary!' I say, through wide and smiling eyes. 'The lake was freshwater, so it wasn't used to being exposed to the sea. All that salt, you know?'

'But it got used to it.'

'Yeah, over thousands of years, it slowly became saltwater. You're right – it adjusted. But it took time.'

'You'll get saltier too.'

'I don't want to.'

Grace pours herself some water, spilling slightly melted ice cubes into her glass. 'No,' she says. 'But you will.'

18:17 Periodically the talking in the restaurant subsides and I hear music playing through a small speaker. Italian arias, from the fifties, I think, with all the vivacity and birdsong warbling that followed the end of the war; major-key notes twisting and turning like the corpse of their old leader. I don't understand the words, though – only *destino*, which is presumably what it sounds like.

Grace looks at her wine glass, running her finger along the base as if checking for dust. 'Phoebe, I have an invitation for you.'

'Go on.'

'It's my thirtieth next month and I have a little thing planned at a restaurant in town.'

'Which town?'

'You know which town,' she says, with a lopsided smile. 'You can come along if you want.'

'Come along to my ex's thirtieth birthday do in another country?'

'Yeah, yeah. As of now, you're invited. You should know a few people at it, and if you don't it'll give you a chance to be Phoebe with different people anyway. To get out of your . . . to get out of your apartment for a bit.' She gives a nudging smirk. 'And I'll be there.'

'I can be Phoebe by myself,' I say, feeling the skin of my back churn against the seat.

'I know, I know. I . . . I just think you deserve better than that.'

What I deserve is an academic question. But I conclude that what's really bothering me is being put on the spot, so I yield, if only a little. She agrees to let me think about it.

'You'll only know if you're ready by trying,' she says. It's a statement of the obvious, but over time I suspect I've lost touch with the obvious, so it's useful to have someone around who retains an acquaintance.

'You're right. That's the kind of mentality that drives someone to visit their ex in a foreign country out of the blue, isn't it? I'm starting to understand you.'

She laughs. 'Maybe.'

I wonder if I've hit a nerve, and then if I've let her down. 'Grace, if you'd known things were like this, would you still have come over?'

She smiles and lifts her hand, as if wanting to touch me but restrained by her surroundings. 'Of course. I'm not criticising you at all. Anyway, why wouldn't I come over? It's such a lovely city,' she says, tilting her head in the direction of the fluorescent commuters milling by the window.

'I'm glad you came, whatever the reason.'

'Any time. Today was fab. I think I know my way around Copenhagen like a native now. And I'm sorry for what happened at Tivoli.'

'It's okay. Thanks.'

'Is it okay? Does it happen to you a lot?'

'Not a lot. I don't attract much attention. I'm not that tall by Scandinavian standards, and I suppose three years has made some difference. The voice is sometimes a giveaway, but I've worked on it.'

She nods, though I don't know if she's acknowledging my struggle or my success so I don't react.

'But the other thing was that the guy thought we were a couple,' I continue, 'and probably just assumed because of that. He meant no harm – just a snap judgement gone wrong. I know the difference between people being cruel and people being oblivious.'

Grace's face seems to open like a dilated pupil, like she's straining to accept what I'm saying as it's given. 'Does it hurt when people are oblivious?'

'That depends. Do you want the polite answer or the impolite answer?'

She laughs. 'Impolite, definitely.'

'Well . . . I go home and cuddle the dog and then it hurts a bit less.'

Grace holds my wrist and rubs it with her thumb.

18:32 There's a man behind the bar, stubbly, salt-and-pepper, probably pushing fifty. Sweating copiously, like he's partaken in a little too much of the restaurant's warmth and has had to open the collar of his shirt to ventilate it. A manager of some description – possibly the owner of the place. From time to time he waves at departing customers, but for the most part he studies a book in front of him. Figures of some sort, probably.

It's not just Friday evening – it's the last Friday of the month. A time for examination, and a kind of commercial penance.

Grace stares through the window, lost in imperceptible calculation. We're quiet for about a minute, and then she turns and looks at me. 'Can I be a total bitch here?'

'What?'

'Just . . . like, you're probably not going to go to my thirtieth, so can I tell you why I invited you? I just . . . I just really wanted there to be another single person there.'

'Oh,' I say, though I'm quite flattered to be objectified in this way. To be referred to as a single person implies its opposite: that I might not be at some point in the future. I try to recall when I last thought of myself as a single person, and then look to Grace's tired eyes. 'That doesn't make you a total bitch.'

'I feel like one, though. These days the only thing I do with my weekends is go to weddings. Gay weddings, straight weddings, churches, art galleries, old country houses – I once went to a wedding in a barn, and instead of chairs there were bales of hay. Fucking bales of hay, that we had to sit on in our glad rags. And lesbians write their own vows, none of this lawfully wedded wife stuff. They're always beautiful and they make me cry and I hate them. It's kind of a novelty at first, when you're twenty-three and a friend gets married. It all seems really mature, like we're playing dress-up. And then it gets boring. And then it gets embarrassing.' She sighs. 'And I feel so . . . old-fashioned for caring. It's only marriage, like.'

'Does wine depress you?' I ask, and she laughs, though I know she doesn't find it funny.

18:44 Resisting my attempts to steer the conversation elsewhere, Grace is talking about her job. 'On paper,' she says, 'I'm like: yeah, mental health, I'm going to help people who are suffering. But then the money comes in, and it's not great, but it also makes me think that I'm, kind of, profiting off people being unwell. Then I'm as depressed as the customers.'

She keeps telling me how broke she is, and I keep waiting for her card to be declined. Every time it isn't, I take it as proof her situation can't be as bleak as she says. It becomes easier to deal with people if you assume they are constantly exaggerating, that the sums of their life don't really add up. It's easy to commiserate with a lie – all you have to do is reciprocate.

'You're reminding me of my parents,' I say.

'Fuck off.'

'Hear me out. I always wonder how they're so happy after forty years doing the same thing, and I think the answer is, they never thought they were doing good. It was always just a job to them. They weren't always holding themselves up to an impossible standard.'

'People aren't designed for jobs,' Grace says. 'Our brains aren't able for them. We were built for drinking mead and hitting things with sticks.'

At that moment a female waiter knocks over a glass at another table. It's only water, nothing too dramatic, but then a man sitting at the table lunges to stop the rolling glass and, crash, it ends up in pieces on the floor. If this was Ireland, the customers would cheer, but here everyone just speaks louder as if to drown out the incompetence.

'Ay, ay, ay,' the waiter says, and I realise she is foreign.

A man says something in Danish to her – it sounds so menacing it might actually be a joke. 'Fyrværkeri,' he says. Fireworks. It's not the time of year for fireworks, he says.

18:53 Grace makes a comment about how nice it must be to live alone, to be able to bring people to the apartment. 'Your friends from Lund, or hook-ups and stuff,' she says, and I don't know how to respond.

I don't know how to tell her I have only shown my body in its present form to people in their own apartments, and, by people, I mean men, and, by men, I mean a particular sort who camp out on certain dating apps looking for the likes of me. Men who don't have a problem with it, in the same way that a rabbit might profess not to have a problem with lettuce. Men with a surplus of hands but a deficit of ideas. Men who tell me they want to experience me; men for whom I have made myself an experience. When I return to the flat, I wash away the taste of them with pulpy orange juice, and shower alone.

In the end, I say I don't like to bring men to the apartment. 'Dolly doesn't like the smell of them,' I joke. 'They smell like other dogs.'

Grace hesitates, in thought. 'Now there's a side of you I didn't know about,' she says. 'You know, you being gay, as in, you know, you being into men wouldn't have shocked me before. But now it kind of does.'

'You saying you thought I was gay?'

'My friends did. Some of them were kind of adamant. But, like, good for you. I hear European men are huge sluts. I'm glad you're swinging out of them.'

'I'm still attracted to women, though.' I look downwards. 'God, this is a bit personal, isn't it?'

Grace smiles. 'Yeah, you're right, sorry.'

I don't know if it's the depredations of the game or the knowledge I'm being beaten but her smirk convinces me to keep talking. 'It's complicated. I've tried using apps but I keep getting banned from them.'

'Oh . . . ' She hesitates. 'Why?'

'Because. Because people report you because they don't want to see you there. And it hurts. Like, rejection is one thing. It happens. If I went on an app and everyone swiped left on me, I could live with that. But when you get thrown off altogether, it's like people are saying I don't like you and have decided that no one can ever like you.'

Grace looks at her glass, now empty, as if manifesting a refill.

'I can't go to bars,' I continue, 'and talk to people like norm— like other people can, you know?'

There is a long pause. Grace continues to avert her gaze, and then she speaks, 'You deserve to be loved, and to be happy.'

There is another pause. 'Thanks. You too.'

'But,' she says, 'your little dog at home is probably wondering where her mammy has gone.'

I look at my phone. 'Jesus, yeah, it's nearly seven.' And then there is another gap, another space of hesitation masquerading as something deeper, until my words mist into the air, surrounded by the foreign words of the restaurant, droplets carrying measures of unseen history. 'Here, like, would you like to come to mine this evening? I could put something on.'

'Put something on?' she says.

'Dinner, I mean. It's no trouble, I love to cook, it keeps me sane, and if you don't eat it I'm sure the dog will.'

All I can think about is the tattoo on her left thigh. It descends into my mind like a spider down a window pane. A tattoo of a woman's face – I can't remember who she is but I want to see her again. To find something in her features that I can't find in Grace's.

'Okay,' she says. 'I can be taste tester for Dolly if you want. On one condition . . . '

'Yeah?'

Grace tilts her head and hesitates. 'You have to kiss me when I get to your apartment.' She shakes her head gently as she speaks, as if making a particular effort to force the words out of her head, like they've been wedged between her teeth all day.

I look at her and she smiles at me, and suddenly we are back at Magasin du Nord first thing this morning, she so small and I only slightly bigger.

'We could do it here but I don't know how friendly this bar is,' she says, laughing. She begins to stand up, the first flinches of retreat.

'Deal, yeah, yeah,' I say. 'Let's hug on it at least.'

We go outside and hug on Rådhuspladsen and Grace puts her hand on me as we do, in a playful and uncanny way. It turns seven o'clock, and the bells of the city hall play foreign, melancholy music. We agree to meet at my apartment at nine.

She asks me to promise I'll open the door for her when she buzzes, and I say: yes, of course, I promise.

20:17 The street on which I live is greyed by lamplight and sharp with spring chill, quiet but for the swash of unseen traffic. It is a dead end, an empty pocket encircled by the arteries of the city, the aspic still of it intensified by the absence of leaves on the trees lining both sides of the road. I might be moving through a painting.

Dolly strides in front of me past lanky apartment buildings, her backside waving like a line of pendulums as she goes. She pulls against the dog lead to sniff bicycle wheels and desiccating puddles with a sureness suggesting a taxi driver's knowledge of the streetscape.

But she's a poser. At home, she barks when she hears bigger dogs howling outside. On the street she pretends she doesn't see them. What I witness this evening is the familiar coward's sashay. Dolly and I exchange courage like women swapping clothes; a friendly pursuit of comfort better worn.

Faces waver past me through unreliable light. A bald man with a prosperous-looking beard, who smiles at Dolly but doesn't look at me. A short woman with slicked-back grey hair who seems to walk without moving, like an altar boy.

I tie the dog up next to a family of plastic shopping trolleys nested inside of one another. I duct around the aisles with a little red basket in hand.

Grocery shopping serves as a reminder that all life in Copenhagen is leisure. The place sweats like nowhere else: in New York steam rises from the ground, but here it flues out of the people. The locals are always possessed of their time, no matter what they're doing – even their office jobs, all pastries and rolled-up sleeves, amount to a kind of respite.

The supermarkets here are small and stocked like hard-mode Sudoku grids, so you only ever get a fraction of what you're looking for. I suspect they train the TV detectives in Copenhagen shops, *Nordic noir* coming only after a lengthy search for petits pois. No wonder the locals are so fit: they spend their off-hours pulling on the supply chain.

Higgledy-piggledy, my father called it when he was here. Never in all his years of retail stewardship had he seen higgledy so piggledy.

As I move, I can still feel Grace's hand on me like that of a phantom groper, impelling me to curl my head back periodically so that an onlooker would see me startled by wheat pillows and double-A batteries. I fondle a selection of vegetables to ground myself, each paperish bulb of garlic or pocky cauliflower a talisman of reality, the same reality in which I have presumably always more or less dwelt. Then I stand and giggle at the iceberg lettuce and wonder why it's taken me this long to appreciate the gentle thrill of traversing a supermarket after a glass or two of wine. The twin buzzes of intoxication and energy-efficient light bulbs, married in a sickly but handsome way – like a Coke float, or a menthol cigarette.

I'm putting a salad together. Grace was a vegetarian – she'd show me morose videos about battery chickens and grumble and harrumph at the appropriate moments. I once accused her of only avoiding meat because she was too cheap for it, and she didn't talk to me for days. She didn't appreciate having her motives impugned – I'm not sure she cared for my suggesting she had motives at all.

A salad with lentils, beetroot, chickpeas and halloumi: a tiding-over meal. Best to keep her wanting more.

At the checkout it's the usual form language, straight from the beak of the bird in the mobile app. *Hej* is met with *hej*. There is no expectation of chit-chat, and the contrast between here/now and there/then only sharpens my awareness that there's far too much face and mouth to Dublin, and I am not yet at ease with mine.

If I ever start to think and dream in Danish, then, perhaps, I'll start to understand the place. As it is, perception is forever a garrulous conversation, a call and response with my vocabulary bank. Life is slower in a half-learned language, more deeply lived and more easily outrun.

Kvittering?

As I leave, the cashier asks if I want a receipt, and I do, because these minutes promise to be a source of nostalgia to come.

Ja, ja, tak skal du have.

As we make our way back, I mutter all delerious at Dolly, pleading and incantation, asking her to be on her best behaviour, to keep the volume down, to spare Grace's shoes. Then my phone buzzes, and I wince in the street, as though hooked up to an electrical charge, or a sex toy.

A message. Not from Grace. A picture of my grandfather in his nursing home, wearing a top hat on his bald head. I don't know the occasion. His face is the colour of a Gala apple.

He met Grace once, when he had more of his faculties. He called her pass-remarkable, and I took it as a compliment. Any sort of remarkable was good enough for me.

He wouldn't remember her now. He knows neither of my incarnations. As I slip under the metro station overpass at Lindevang, watching commuters babble onto the street, past the ticket machines and the *BT* newspaper stand, I consider what a privilege it is to still move with my memory, however imperfectly. Sometimes the future only begins once its alternatives have been tested to destruction. I tell myself I am lucky, and for once I believe it.

20:56 I sit and wait in my good silver blouse. Salad made, hair-removal appliances out of sight, apartment cleaned, bed tested – my own bed, like I don't know what it feels like – and the dog drenched in Camilla's canine cologne so she smells nappy-fresh.

Eight o'clock comes and goes, and I'm still on my perch, nothing to do but congratulate myself for making a salad and not ending up privy to food going cold.

There is a metallic peal at twenty-five past, and I buzz Grace in without saying a word. The dog starts mewling, I make an unsuccessful plea for calm, and there is a knock at the door, which only further rattles her.

And Grace has changed into another outfit: under her jacket she's wearing a blue polka-dot thing that sets her hair off. There is a plastic bag filled with clothes.

And I envy her hotel mirrors, though I say nothing.

And then everything is happening, locked within quiet moments heralding little in the grand scheme. How I've missed them: the small, empty seconds.

And Grace.

Grace.

Grace.

She tastes of spearmint chewing gum.

'Sorry I'm late,' she says.

'It was worth the wait.'

She laughs. 'Only seven years.'

I smile, though it doesn't feel like seven years to me: it feels like longer, and shorter, and like something completely new, like my life is constantly shifting orbits around a distant but essential axis. I nod towards the wall to my right. 'Come and have a seat, dinner is ready.'

'Your apartment is so lovely.'

'Yeah, you said yesterday.'

'I'm not allowed to hang anything on the walls of my place,' she says, with a gaze suggesting the wrong side of a conjugal visit.

'Don't get too jealous, most of this stuff isn't even mine.'

'I think I can tell what's yours and what's Camilla's.'

'Because you know me so well?'

She nods. 'This yoke here,' she says, pointing a finger at a snapshot of a craggy butte next to the bathroom door, 'is hers. And this lady's album cover is yours.' She gestures towards a pair of sepia-toned female legs, tastefully shot, made into a canvas and hung on the wall next to my bedroom. Grace's nails are painted black, so as she flicks a finger it looks like there is a deciduous bud at the end of it, the promise of something greater than itself.

'Well remembered,' I say.

'Mylène Farmer,' she notes, reading from the picture. 'She was the French one you used to listen to who was a bit slutty, but in a good way. See, I do know you.'

'I sort of rediscovered her over the last couple of years. There was a lot of that – finding my way back to things I used to like but was a bit ashamed of.'

She smirks. 'Like me.'

I laugh. 'Yeah, in the form of Grace Keaney, my sordid past reasserts itself.'

She smiles and looks at the floor. 'I'm asserting myself all over you.' In her voice I can hear pride and relief and hopeful wickedness, the thrill of jumping on a plane and finding the least exotic spot in a foreign city, of knowing that home is a four-letter word that abides stubbornly in the unlikeliest places.

I have no response to it so I kiss her again.

21:33 I have decorated a table, candles and all, the meagre yield of an academic salary and a Jysk loyalty card. I pull out a chair for Grace, but that gives me pause to doubt myself. Like a rookie waitress summer-jobbing in a doughty tourist trap, I try to keep my soles on the ground and my plates in the air as I go. Training without a mentor, touristing in courtesy: new grammar and syntax pervade but I'm far from fluent, so I immerse myself and hope to get by.

I offer her wine. It seems a failsafe.

'Don't mind if I do,' she says. 'Is it the same as yesterday?'

'No, it's red, it goes better with the food,' I say, walking towards the kitchen. I bring out the bottle and pour it into her glass.

Then I go back to the kitchen, and, as I carry over the halloumi salad, I make a rehearsed preamble: 'There comes a time in every little girl's life when she flies the nest and realises that her mammy was wrong – that vegetables are always nicer raw.'

And it looks fine on the table: a tiding-over meal, like I wanted, sitting dutifully on its plate in a stance of poised insouciance – a vagrant chickpea, a wodge of squeaky cheese. But it's bereft of heat and steam. It owes more to a canteen than a restaurant. It wants for romance, and so it betrays me, but as I quietly berate myself Grace interrupts my thought.

'Wow, Phoebe, this looks amazing,' she says.

I can't tell if she really means it, so I grin in appreciation as I sit down opposite her. 'I wasn't sure if you were still a vegetarian so I went with something without meat. I hope that's okay.'

'Shut up, this is more than okay. This is fabola.'

'So *are* you still a vegetarian?'

'Nah,' she says, curling up her shoulders. 'I gave up on it years ago.'

'At least you don't seem to smoke anymore. Very health-conscious.'

'At thirteen euro a pack, I can't afford not to be. Robbing bastards.' Grace takes a fork to her salad and shifts a mouthful. 'Oh, this . . . great,' she muffles, nodding, her mouth still half-full.

'Cheers,' I say, giving her a window of swallowing time.

'No, seriously,' she says, 'how did this happen? I don't remember you being good in the kitchen.'

'Well, I guess cooking is a bit like chemistry. You just put the different elements together and come up with something new. A stove is just a big Bunsen burner,' I say, making a flame gesture with my fingers. 'And I've had to get better with, you know, substances over the last few years, trying things out and seeing what works, experimenting, and I suppose I took that with me to the kitchen.'

'Your eating used to be terrible,' she says. 'I remember. You'd have snacks instead of meals, we'd go for lunch and you'd just have coffee. Like you were anorexic or something. Your body was probably crying out for vitamins.'

'My body was crying out for lots of things.'

She pauses for a moment and smiles. 'You know what this is? All this?' she says, gesturing towards the spread between us like it's a rickle of tombola prizes. 'It's growth.' She gives a shit-eating nod and swigs from her glass.

I raise a toast. 'To growth.'

We repeat in unison, clink, and drink.

21:58 Minutes pass, and out of a welter of words and damp chewing noises comes a story about a laser pointer and a quiet road in south-west Dublin. Grace tells me that some kids, and she's sure it's some kids, have been aiming one at the house next door to her.

'That sounds annoying,' I say, distracted, deep in halloumi country.

'It gets worse. They've put on one of those filters – you know the filters they used to have on laser pointers? They've got one with Santa Claus on it. So there's a big green Santa on the front of the house. In March. People probably think it's a drug den.'

'God.'

'The woman who lives there is a barrister. Collette or Clodagh or something. One of those girls who's come up from the country and thinks she's the dog's bollocks. I think she's in Opus Dei. She's all teeth. Half her face is teeth. She called the guards on them once.'

'Your street sounds interesting.'

Grace's shoulders drop. 'Jesus, I'm so boring. I'm sitting here talking about my curtain-twitching. Fucking hell.' She has a look, downward and inward, like she has left the funhouse and seen her own life in a real mirror, seen it flawed to the brink of failure, and finds herself without time or wherewithal to gussy it up.

'You're not boring,' I say.

'How do you know?'

'If you were, I'd know, believe me. There's a difference between being boring and being sad or shy. Boring people flaunt it. The most boring person in an office is the person whose life everyone knows about in intimate detail. You know they're going to the recycling centre on Saturday and you know which faulty electrical appliances they're bringing and why. You know they're going on a first date tonight and you know they seldom have seconds. In Ireland, I used to work with someone who gave her budgie an anthropomorphic voice. An awful, squeaky thing. "Betty thought it was very cold this morning. Betty is happy that excise duty has gone up in the Budget because she doesn't like cigarettes." See, now, that's boring,' I say, jabbing my finger on the table. 'Zealous, militant, in-your-face boringness. Conversational terrorism.'

'You have strong opinions on this.'

'I've read enough trans memoirs to know what boring is. Anyway, it's nice to be an observer.'

She looks sceptical. 'What do you observe? What's the goss around here? Any rapists?'

I pause. 'Do you remember when you heard "Funkytown" here last night?'

She nods.

'That was Tommy and Lise. They live next door. Mid-fifties, not married, though that's not unusual here, and they live in a kind of suspended reality where it's always 1980. You get used to hearing Diana Ross and Olivia Newton-John through the walls after a while.'

She raises a half-smile. 'That sounds class.'

'I'm glad people like them exist. They remind me there's still happiness in the world. Reject modernity, embrace tradition, celebrate good times, come on. But there is one thing.'

'Are they sex people?' she asks.

'Yeah. How did you know?'

'Just . . . logic.' She takes another mouthful, and in the process a piece of beetroot falls and lands on the table but she quickly rescues it.

'They're car-keys-in-a-bowl people,' I say. 'I turn up my music on those evenings. Not for my sake, but, you know, for Dolly's.'

'Ah, yeah, of course,' Grace says, and we both look at the dog, akimbo on the floor next to the sitting-room door.

'Dolly stays with Tommy and Lise when I'm away. She's seen things you wouldn't believe.'

The dog snores and extends her limbs, ambling in her sleep.

Grace looks at me. 'You have a nice life here.'

I smile. 'A nice boring life.'

I realise at this moment that we are the same thing, and imagine her coming with quiet satisfaction to the same conclusion. Two people whose existences have lived down to and past the depths of their own cynicism. Two people cursed to be what they were always going to be.

We tenant in each other's aftermath. It is a kind of furious freedom, attempting romance with someone you have already failed it with. The question of ever-after has been answered, so we are offered new and distinct ambitions, hope of making do at making-do. It is life's wage for learning: a second chance.

In the absence of an example to follow, a template or a rule book, we decide what happiness is, moment by moment, sweetness by sweetness, and its joy is heavier, because it belongs only to us.

22:15 Grace asks for the Wi-Fi password. I interpret it as a gesture of intimacy: now we are Wi-Fi official. I open the Notes app on my phone and show her a morass of numbers and capital letters.

About a minute later, as she sits on the sofa looking at the screen, she howls laughing to herself. 'Phoebe! What *is* this?'

'What?' I ask, coming out from the kitchen, towelling my hand.

'Here.' She hands me back the phone, open on another note. It says: *I beg your hardon.*

I can feel my face, like an outdoor heater humming into life. 'Oh.'

She smiles at me in a giddy, childish way. 'Who was *that* for?'

'It wasn't for anyone. Sometimes . . . I don't know, sometimes I just write down funny lines I think of.'

'That *is* a funny line. Nice one.'

'The Notes app is kind of like a cutlery drawer, you know? There's useful stuff in there and then there are bits of string, a gammy corkscrew you haven't used in years, you know.'

'I know, yeah, yeah.' She nods slowly and then snorts laughing again.

22:53 Dinner gives way to rooibos gives way to the night gives way to intent. On the couch, mollified by the residual taste of each other's lips. Grace shifts towards me and runs her fingers through my hair like a clutch of curling ribbons.

'Y'know what really makes me sad, Phoebe?' she asks, the slender vowels of my name revealing her teeth, discoloured by Primitivo. 'You didn't inherit your mam's boobs. That makes me sad. Very sad.' She curls her mouth in a mock frown.

'You saying you were attracted to my mother?'

'I'm saying she had great boobs.' A thin smile appears on her face as if in a developing photograph. 'That's all I'm saying.'

'I don't think they're genetic. Every day she brings a box of Jaffa Cakes to work because she knows her co-workers don't like them, and every day she eats them all herself.'

Grace looks at the balcony door. 'Nora Forde. What a hero,' she says, tripping over a laugh.

'*Nooora Fooorde*,' I say, lugging the words so they seem to creak.

Grace plays with her hair, less gently than with mine, like it is a well-drilled choreography. 'Coming back here has been kind of like coming back to a fruit that wasn't ripe first time around. Does that make sense?' And she kisses me, furtively, like a teenager. The dog peers at us, awake for now.

'Yeah, it does,' I say, tired of waiting for a ministration of sense and happy to cinch myself to hers. 'I've missed you,' I say, and it is a ghost of a sentiment, which catches me by surprise. 'I think I'm homesick for something, but I don't really know what.'

'Here,' she says, standing up in front of me. 'Do you have a speaker?'

Before I have the time to say anything she is a tension of limbs, coolly impelling the coffee table to the side of the room, and I am wishing myself into the position of being inched across the floor by Grace Keaney.

I could be anything, really. The furniture she ruts herself into. I could be a footstool, an armrest, an orthopaedic pillow. The grated mozzarella she sprinkles into her face when she can't sleep at night. I could make myself whatever shape and size is necessary. It's no trouble. I have done it before.

The creeping seconds ignite, and we heave propulsively around the apartment, from wall to sliding door and back again, not jigging but flaunting and wobbling about the place, to the tune of the Saw Doctors' 'I Useta Lover' – while Dolly looks on, a paw half-covering her eyes, curled into something resembling the foetal position.

We sing about an apocryphal, glorious arse as though members of an exhalatory choir of invisible revellers. Our hips touch, and she skates her hand through my hair, and she twirls me, and we are finding our way through the collaterals of our history under the tent cover of early nineties folk rock, cast by a moment into the beauty we never found.

'D'you play the spoons?' Grace asks, with a raised voice.

'I haven't the spoons to play the spoons.'

Grace draws me out of myself, the spirit at my own séance, in my own home, my presence once and finally felt in the world of the living. Our bodies, time-and-trusted, garble among the bric-a-brac of the apartment: the obstinate sofa and its curious dog, the empty wine bottles on the table on the other side of the room, the potentiating lights of the city behind them.

It is not merely a melding of old and new, but a kind of perverse nostalgia. The fallout shelter existence back home returns to me, the comfortable banality of a life lived for its own sake, and maybe, maybe, I miss it.

The worst thing you can do in Ireland is lose the run of yourself. But now we are a thousand miles away, casting off the run of ourselves like snakes shedding skin. That might be why there are no snakes in Ireland – they have all departed to lose the run of themselves.

I grab Grace's phone from the couch. I stab at buttons, the small text on the screen lurching across my eyes from side to side. And then it begins to play: the prickling synthetic strings of the intro to Des'ree's 'Life'.

Grace sings the chorus about forty seconds too early.

'Stall the ball. We haven't had the ghost or the toast yet.'

We blab over the music, like leotarded fitness fanatics gasping for words.

'Whatever happened to Des'ree?' Grace hollers.

'Dot-com bust. Selling rabbits' tails over the internet. Didn't work out. Very sad.'

'Come on.'

'I don't know. Maybe she didn't like being a singer.'

'Maybe she wanted to be a one-hit wonder. More airplay with one hit than two, you know?'

'That must be it,' I say, smiling. 'You're so clever.'

She gives me the finger. 'You always danced like a watery shite. Remember the time you knocked over that woman's drink at the silent disco at Tripod? She was screaming at you and you thought she wanted to shift you.'

I raise my hands, laughing. 'In my defence, once "Dragostea Din Tei" comes on I can't be held responsible for my actions.'

We haven't merely demonstrated survival – we have mastered what it means to be alive. In the twenty-first century, the mediocre people are writing essays with words like *heterodox*, *evidentiary* and *illiberalism* in them, while the really brilliant types are in their apartments, slopping red wine everywhere and throwing shapes like the luminous, fluorescent clapper-switch clowns they are. Intelligence aspires to genius, but genius aspires to flimflam.

Saturday, 00:04 Grace identifies herself as a 'versatile top' in the manner one might say 'good with figures' or 'allergic to pine cones'. She is spread out over the edge of the couch, her head gogging off the side like a loose slice of bread.

She asks me what I am into. I examine and re-examine the question. I lack a satisfactory lie by way of response. I had once taken myself for granted. I strode the world as a smiling reflex. It said, *How are you?* and I said, *Not too bad*. How good is not too bad? Now my desires are a half-written sentence: I know the first few words, but after a swivelling comma, things could go anywhere. It seems the trick to always knowing what you want is to never ask.

Grace nabs my wrist and pulls me towards her, so I am staring down at her face as it drapes horizontally at waist height. 'I hope this isn't a shock,' she says, 'but I've never been with someone like you before.'

'You've been with me before.'

She grunts with laughter and smiles at me upside-down, and it becomes apparent through her brio that she doesn't know she is the only woman I've ever fucked.

'I have a vibrator in the wardrobe,' I say, like I'm telling a thief where the better jewellery is.

'Now we're cooking with diesel. And, like, what would you normally do with the vibrator?' she asks.

'Do all your sexual encounters start with this much dissection?'

She presents a hand and it lands on the side of my knee. In a miscreant voice she says, 'You'll thank me for this later, babes.'

I decide to stop asking questions.

00:11 Grace is in control, firmly and by default – the one left wearing the jeans as I lie on the bed and feel her removing my leggings, running her finger over a hole in the fabric. It seems there is something to be longed for.

We are listening to Mylène Farmer. 'C'est une belle journée'. The singer was her choice – she called her *that French one* – but the song was mine; the intent to drown out a skittish dog scratching on the dark side of the door.

I recline at anaesthetic convenience to her, near-naked but not near enough. For she is there, beneath a layer of fabric: Lady Protuberance, not quite present, but a presence, like dread at the scene of a pileup, or unease in a drift that has yet to become one.

I look at Grace and smirk, creasing my face in a way that broadcasts a certain turmoil. 'Are you going to do this fully clothed?'

'What do you mean? I've taken my shoes off.'

She mocks me, but who wouldn't? It is a horrible thing to love, the power Grace has over me, to be simultaneously virginal and barbarous, bride and corpse.

She comes back from the closet furthest from the door with the bulbous yellow contraption in hand. Looking at the black mushroom head of it with squirish pride, she tells me it's not a vibrator at all. 'It's a wand. You can do more with it. You obviously knew what you were doing when you bought this,' she says, politely.

Grace kisses my nipples so that there is lipstick on me, a weltish smack across my chest, and she says something about how I've changed, and I pass a remark about it being down to the hormones, which she ignores.

Haven't we all changed? Isn't that the point? I am not a spectator anymore. I have been plucked from the audience of life like a gameshow contestant, arms fluttering, breasts bouncing.

There's even a buzzer. Emergent from the electrical socket like a hand outstretching a grave, the wand spasms into life and emits its own questioning hum.

Her arm hair is so beautiful. Seductive. Freshly cut grass. Grass so fresh it needs no cutting. It sits etched across her, each copper-brown line representing an atom of her worldliness. She is delightfully self-containing, and I am smeared all over her.

The effort she puts in, looking at her, all tension lines, while I do not twinge at all. Her hair falling over her face and its look of deep seriousness, like she is staring through me. All I can think of is how amusing it would be if she stuck her tongue out the way people do when they're concentrating.

Good sex is supposed to be funny, but I am trying not to laugh.

The ticklish but empty rumble of the appliance against my body, a current that runs through me, out of my body, through the bed and beneath the room on its way to the ground. I might be made of damp wood: all I do is crumble and smoulder, all wand and no magic.

Every so often she runs her free hand over me, her thumb grazing me, over my nipple, down to sweep the glom of fat that has accumulated on my middle, hormonal padding intended to protect a foetus during pregnancy, and she stops before she goes too low. I tell her it feels good.

I know how it usually goes. The way it feels like falling, sinking deliciously into waves, not the way it did before, like ketchup bursting from a dissociative squeezy bottle. The leached, gooey aftermath of an out-of-body experience – or, rather, two out-of-body experiences.

I seem to have changed my internal map, to reflect a newfound position in the hierarchy: the upward-and-outward of ejaculation, the graffiti-tag of it, replaced with the downward-and-inward, the hypothetical downward-and-inward. And the way I always need to go to the toilet afterwards, the bulk of my expulsions now hygienic in nature, less a reflection of physiology than moral judgement.

I know it so well. Would she know if I faked it?

I put my hand on her upper arm, the synthetic fabric of her top, through which I can feel the tone of her body. 'It's okay, Grace. I'm not going to get there. It's okay.'

She presses a button and the device judders to a stop. 'Pourvu qu'elles soient douces' is playing. 'Are you sure?' Grace says.

'Yeah, yeah. I'm just not in the right frame of mind. Antidepressants, you know?'

Grace pulls her legs out from under her and sits guru-style on the bed. 'Phoebe . . . are you attracted to me? I don't know. Maybe I pressured you into something you didn't want.' She speaks like she is trying to justify her actions to herself, trying to clarify them in her own mind.

I give her a look of self-pity veiled in outward concern. 'It's not your fault. It might have been just . . . too much at once.'

The dog is breathing heavily on the other side of the door.

There is an outbreak of apologies, which Grace interrupts by saying, 'It's not good when sex ends with everyone saying sorry. That usually means an ambulance has been called.'

She says we don't have to try this again, but I say I want to. We decide to take things slowly. To try some things. Some implements. Utensils. Different ones. To go shopping. Isn't that what you do on a city break?

Grace has monitored my performance and in lieu of a sabbatical, she recommends a bespoke programme of retraining and redeployment.

We lie together, the lights off, early hours, beginning after end, and I stare ceilingwards, hoping she is still awake. 'You came a thousand miles for this,' I say, feigning a phlegmatic detachment.

'It's pretty common,' she says. 'Queer women travelling thousands of miles to have sex with their exes. It's a stereotype, kind of.'

Queer women. That's us now. Here we are. Make way for the queer women.

Minutes pass and Grace's breath deepens and becomes throatier, and the hours stretch out, and I remain wide awake, neurons firing faster and faster, suddenly on all cylinders, to remind me of the day that's gone and the mistakes I've made and how important and defining it all is. The room carousels around me, even when I close my eyes.

Tomorrow, tomorrow, fucking hell, tomorrow.

At three in the morning, I move to the couch.

Ten thousand nine hundred and ninety-four

Saturday

08:58 I can smell the portents of breakfast from the kitchen behind me: flimsy, savoury and discernibly meatless. Grace kisses me on the cheek once I sit up on the sofa.

'Hello, sleepy head. I thought I'd make something nice for us,' she says, before straying back to her in-progress.

'Cool, great,' I say, sensing the crawl of a flat smile across my face. 'You're amazing.' A more decent me would start helping out, but between the couch and the aftereffects of yesterday's walking I am scarcely able to move.

But she doesn't mind. She never seems to mind. The membrane between me and other people, between dreams and reality, has never been slenderer. I am a limbo pole. She is in constant coil around me, avoiding any false moves – and to be seen by her as someone capable of hurt or even inconvenience comes readily to me as a kind of affection.

She's making pancakes. A set of ingredients has been marshalled and bled into the pan in the Irish style, resulting not in decadent Yankee slabs but thin crêpes with minor-hurler freckles.

Morning light hazards around us as we sit at the table. Scattered like chess pieces are a coffee pot, a bottle of honey and a bowl of sugar with a teaspoon in it. To all intents and purposes, we are unsupervised children in the little flat – Grace, a friend who has stayed the night, now having us dive into the sweetest and unwholesomest breakfast possible.

It's a slightly hackneyed source of liberation for women to live together without men, but it's harder to do when you've spent twenty-seven years sharing vital organs with one. As we sit there, though, I might for once be convinced that he is actually dead. We could be slavering cannibals, feasting upon him.

Grace flings a morsel of greasy dough at Dolly. It hits the side of her snout and falls to the floor. She picks it up and takes it to the kitchen.

Grace smiles at me. 'We're all eating unhealthy today.'

'Actually,' I say, 'if you want unhealthy food there's a place at Nyhavn that does a great breakfast buffet. Danish bacon and those little red sausages. The right side of continental. Not too much cheese and cucumber. Maybe we could go there tomorrow, before we go to Lund.'

'I'm game for that. What are we doing today, madam tour guide?' She seems to uncork a thought, and then smirks. 'Apart from buying a strap-on.'

'I was thinking art again, unless you want to go to the Carlsberg factory.'

'Have you been? Do they give out samples?'

'They give out samples of the beer that's not good enough to sell. I started seeing the face of Peig Sayers in the paving stones after. Two stars. Not recommended.'

I take out my phone, and scroll with one hand while tapping a fork against the table with another. 'We have two options. The Glyptotek in the city centre, and Louisiana, which is about an hour out of the city. The Glyptotek has classical art and sculpture. Louisiana is modern.'

'Modern. Modern, modern, modern.' She bounces on the chair as she speaks.

'The Glyptotek has the wall of noses, though.'

'Is that what it sounds like?'

'Yep. They take all the noses that have fallen off the statues and put them there.' I gulp some coffee. 'But maybe this isn't the weekend for removed appendages.'

'No, we'll save that for when you get to the top of your waiting list, won't we?'

I smile. A swing and a hit. 'Maybe one day I'll get my nose done and they'll put it there.'

'Maybe,' she says. 'I'd visit your nose.'

10:51 A bump in the journey, from platform to platform. We go up three storeys but we're still underground, on the main line, the hard-swallowing oesophagus of the station.

We sit on a metal bench, waiting for our connection. A moribund tunnel breeze shears the air, while people in heavy jackets come and go.

A group of young women, early twenties probably, pass us in identical black duffel coats, chatting loudly among themselves. The blondes of their hair vary from white to straw to strawberry, so they look like pallbearers carrying the earthlies of an unusually sleek dog.

'I don't know how you live here,' Grace says, into my ear. 'Everyone is stupidly good-looking.'

'The beautiful people dress in black and beige turtlenecks and granny glasses. Like they're toning themselves down. If you want to be attractive in Scandinavia, you can't show off.'

'Sickening,' Grace says, and I hum in agreement.

She moves her hand, then hesitates and puts a claw of fingers on my leg. 'Still,' she says, 'I love Copenhagen.'

'You barely know Copenhagen.' An announcement, a

delayed train from Sweden, an unlawful incursion on the Øresund bridge, forces a pause, then I speak again. 'Sorry about last night. And thanks.'

'For what?'

'For not leaving. You didn't come over here expecting things to be this weird.'

Grace gives me a face like a high heel snapping. 'You don't know that. Weird is all right. Weird is interesting. Maybe I want to help you get more comfortable with yourself. Help you tag off the struggle bus.' Then her eyes lunge and she laughs abruptly. 'Ah, would you look at that,' she says, labouring over the last two words.

'What?'

'Look.' She points at a long metal sign that says *Nørreport* in blue letters.

'I don't follow.'

'Nora Forde Station.'

I let out a sigh, which folds into a smile. 'How long did it take you to come up with that?'

'Fifteen seconds. Here's another one. What do the conductors say when the train is leaving the station?'

I say nothing and shake my head.

'Nora Forde!' she yells. One of the blonde girls turns and looks. 'You know,' Grace says, 'like *all aboard*.'

'Very good.' And it is good. It's what I need, really: ironic detachment from my own history – to be haunted by it as a ludicrous phantasm, so many tanned messiahs in so many pieces of toast.

Eventually a grey train pulls in, and Grace and I end up opposite one another with a small table between us. There is a whistle-peep from outside and we rattle away.

I gesture towards the window, on my left as I'm hauled backwards. 'It's a nice journey, this. Once you get out of the city. There's lovely scenery along the coast.'

We slice past walls covered in graffiti – gibberish, mostly, though I spot *all cops are baseballs* on an electricity box – then the new buildings around the port at Nordhavn, brown and white towers, like weathered teeth in the mouth of the city. Glassy boxes, expensive apartments, gritty sea air, something out of the fever dream of a money-grubbing window cleaner.

This might be London, if the train was busier. It might be Dublin, if it was slower. Urban renewal hews the corners of the world. For those of us with a bent towards regeneration, it's a little underwhelming – life's new lease offered by the rattiest of landlords.

Humanity has tripped face first into the future. Now buildings look like anaemic refrigerators, telephones look like small anaemic refrigerators, and refrigerators, anaemic or not, also function as telephones, for reasons no one can explain.

But there is a certain glimmer of logic in the apex of the morning. Distantly, beyond the pane of water in the harbour basin, wind turbines stand in staggered succession, as if stitching the sky to the sound.

11:24 The train slows, and the quiet platform at Klampenborg eases into view. A man in a trucker cap walks past us towards the exit. On his way, he paws the corner of each row of seats.

'Hamlet is Danish, right?' Grace says, sitting with her head resting on the window.

I nod. 'His castle is near where we're going. Kronborg.'

She narrows her eyes. 'Which one is Hamlet?'

'To be or not to be.'

She raises her thumb, rested on the table between us, like I have aced a test: that was the question.

The train begins to pull away.

'Tycho Brahe is my favourite Danish person,' I say. 'Historical, I mean. He was an astronomer. He proved that the stars in the sky were moving. Before him, everyone thought stars were fixed objects, and supernovas were just comets in the atmosphere. That was what Aristotle had said.'

'That's quite a cute legacy. Being famous for watching the stars.'

'That's not why I like him, though. I like him because of how he died.'

She smirks and flares her nostrils. 'Of course you do.'

'He was at a banquet in Prague. He refused to go to the toilet because it was against etiquette to leave when there were royals in the room. The urinary leash got him. I relate.'

She smiles. The train wobbles and we pass a set of clay tennis courts.

'He developed an infection and died a week later,' I continue. 'That's what happens if you care too much about not offending people. If you worry too much about not making a fuss. When you think about it, most people die of politeness.'

We flutter by the back gardens of amiable commuter houses – vacant furniture and trampolines and the odd greenhouse making a spark of the cold sun.

11:45 Humlebæk is riven by the railway and humble in a way only money can buy. Around the station sit an assembly of pretty little shops, selling understatements: jewellery, French bobs, pointless wicker chairs. Estate agents display a curation of second and third houses for the attention of the upwardly upscale, a floor-length grid of them, cards for a bingo game in which the only dabbers belong to those who have already won.

A long wide road leads to the museum. Ahead of us walk two women dipped in navy polyester. Tourists, obviously, on the receiving end of a mobile phone app. 'Follow Ham-Le-Back Strand-vigh for five hundred metres,' commands a voice demonic and secretarial in Estuary English.

The street is only half a kilometre but it has the endlessness of status, of earned permanence, of iron and granite and Teslas charging in driveways.

The houses on either side are large, detached and luxuriantly distanced. Gardens fluoresce with cherry blossoms and tidy rows of new daffodils. Satellite dishes protrude from sloped rooves. Family names are painted in gothic script beside each postbox: Morgard, Randrup, Fisker.

Grace continually peeks over the hedges as we walk. This goes on for perhaps a hundred and fifty or even two hundred of our metres – her helicoptering past the dwellings and their surrounding vegetation like a child pining conspicuously for a coveted toy.

And then she says it: 'This is such a wonderful place to live. I'm so jealous of you.'

I don't know how to respond, so I just mutter 'God,' and I don't know what I mean by it. I can't quite explain to Grace that I don't live here, that I barely know this street lined with houses I've never entered, populated by people I've never met. I am not a Randrup or a Fisker or a Ludvigsen or even a Schmidt.

But I suppose what makes her jealous is that I live a life that isn't hers. She is escaping from something, even if it's just a routine. The more she moves, the less she is.

She probably walks like this around Dublin, circumnavigating the place like an auburn canal, past the big windows, the sale-agreed signs, the superheat of the latest boom. I develop a mental picture of her there, in the drizzle, out of luck, but the thought of it is simply too much – her, in that country, thumbed down by the low expectations of a people whose finest hour was a scoreless draw with Romania.

At once I find myself so protective of her, wishing to keep my body between her and that emerald tormentor – but my body, that's another problem.

As we walk, our hands keep touching – which might be romantic, but it would be fairer to say that Grace's hand is hitting my wrist while mine rests underneath. There might be five inches between us. I have come to the conclusion that I prefer talking to her sitting down. It draws less attention to our differences. It creates a pretence of equality. We don't fit together – at least, not the way I want us to.

Comparison always leaves you on your back, looking up, afflicting the floor to spite the ceiling. It's not just material things, but the knowledge that others have fewer worries and more of their own time. To look to the future is to stare at the sky at the end of a long, straight road, to see it blinding and luminous, escalating to a great nothing, full of carbon dioxide and space junk and people who will always contrive to stay above you.

Grace stops in her tracks next to a collection of evergreens and weeping birch trees. 'Look, Phoebe, look,' she says, with childish excitement.

'What?'

'The sea.' She points at a scrap of ocean, little more than a worry in the blue of the sky, visible beyond the end of the road. 'Don't you love it when the sea sneaks up on you?'

'I suppose.'

'Ah, come on. Like when you were a kid and you ran past the sand dunes, along the wooden planks, and then it was there, this fucking huge thing. Life is the Brittas Bay car park and you're always looking for the sea. I love it. It's such a great feeling.' As she speaks, she looks like she is resisting the urge to run towards it, and I could watch her for ever, splattering words and chugging dopamine.

'Something huge and unexpected and wonderful,' I say. 'Yeah, yeah, that is a good feeling.'

12:16 It is the sort of place that makes me wish I had the constitution for psychedelics.

I'm stood here in darkness, draped in coloured light, in neon and pastels hanging from a ceiling whose existence is implied but unprovable. Purples fading to reds and blues, crystals emitting light to christen me with minute waves. The space is antenatal. In it, the inadequacies of the human body are remedied by their own irrelevance. I may as well have gills to breathe.

It is like sitting in the centre of my own brain and watching it locomote, observing the sparks and confusion, the great groaning into life. A feat of engineering and re-engineering, programming and de-programming.

I have been to the core of my consciousness, and it is a shimmering void, as I might have expected.

I keep thinking about drugs. Grace has probably done them all – all the good ones. She comes over as addled by experience. She was probably all see-through tops and cocaine, all cistern lids and social welfare cards, a shimmering void of her own, before she slipped into her rut.

There is a door, and the outside blinks in through the cracks. Beside it, there is a plaque. It says the installation is called *Digital Detention*: a meditation on the way technology disorients us, and separates us from ourselves.

And I imagine that the disorienting effect of technology is a particular issue for drug dealers, who might have four or five mobile phones. They must be forever in a two-front battle, fighting spiritual alienation and the rozzers. A defence they may later rely on in court: your honour, I want not for incarceration – I have already been imprisoned by the apps.

Welcome to the age of estrangement, the write-up says. And how bizarre and twisted it is – a sick and boring life, indeed! – to regard estrangement as a curse. Birth is our first exile, and it is only after the second or third that life is lived.

The attendees, Grace included, seem to have taken it for granted that the purpose of these meditations is to give pretentious tourists an opportunity to upload a snapshot of themselves standing in the midst of some natty lights.

The whole thing has a winking quality. 'Look at me: I'm art,' the gathered gawkers seem to say, but the joke is that, really, these people are forever doomed to be the Tallulah-from-Missouris they've always been. They will resume their stolid personas the moment they leave this room, lacking the determination for anything else.

They resemble nothing more than attendees at a hanging or a lynching – smiling proof that human beings may overcome the threat of technology, of their own looming, expectorating future. Old humanity vanquishes new for its own entertainment.

When we leave the room, Grace asks me what the display was about.

'I'm not sure,' I say.

12:42 Grace and I drift into a display of etchings. A local artist, with two dates under her name. The studio lights are harsh, illuminating couples and posh children and men in sheepskin jackets clicking over a wooden floor.

We stand and gaze, and gaze, until we've spent ten minutes staring down the barrel of a monochromatic blue drawing of a newborn baby in swaddling clothes. We laugh to each other because it looks like the child has his fingers crossed, like he's telling a lie.

'It's funny we're looking at babies,' Grace says, and I ask why, but she responds with a question. 'How can you tell it's a boy?' she says, and she's right. The background colour hardly amounts to evidence of anything.

This child is keeping all sorts of secrets.

'I never told you,' Grace says, a little quieter than before, aware of her surroundings, 'Caoimhe, my sister, is an animator now. She studied it at NCAD, she was on RTÉ News about it last year.'

I lower my voice. 'NCAD, very swish. The last I remember of her she was this quiet thing in a school uniform.'

'She was, oh, sixteen when we were together.'

'And now she's a professional animator.'

Grace gives a leavened sigh. 'She works in a bakery most of the time.' Now she is quieter again.

'What does she animate there?' I say, louder than her.

'She waitresses,' Grace whispers, and a hardness saturates her face. 'Not everyone gets what they want, you know?'

'What does that mean?'

'It doesn't matter,' she says, almost not saying, and hurriedly shakes her head. She is completely quiet after that, and I fear I have embarrassed myself in the presence of this infant who stares hungrily into me, hardly nourished by my expression. But we stay there for another five minutes, as if looking to him, or her, or whatever, for an explanation.

Babies are not people, not really, though they pretend to be. They are flesh and blood and little else, a vehicle for a million futures, none of them yet seized. I suppose that is what I see in the picture. I don't know what Grace sees, and now sense it would be an imposition to ask.

Sometimes it is like we are in the middle of a drill, as in fire, but with no fire – just the knowledge we are not each other's escape route.

13:39 It starts with a flurry of offhand remarks that spiral into a story. A trickle of sentences that turns into sliding mud.

We sit on scuddy grass at the back of the museum. There is a collection of sculptures here, around which visitors thread, eyes wide, hands held, cameras out. We drink frothy coffee from café paper cups.

We dither from inanity to inanity. Grace speculates on the backgrounds of the museumgoers: which of the men engage in boudoir photography and call it art, how many fractions of a polycule are in our midst, which of the couples are secretly brother and sister.

'Straight couples who look like they're related give me the ick,' she says, propping herself up on the grass with her palms downturned. 'Paging Doctor Freud.'

I tell her Scandinavia is full of them – part of Jante's Law, probably, formally mandated equality leading to a kind of incestuous eugenics.

Our home country doesn't have this problem, we agree, because Irish men are spud-headed stunt singles with porn-bush beards they all grew within six months of each other in 2014.

'What's the opposite of hostile architecture?' Grace asks. 'That's what beards are on Irish men.' Then she sits up on the grass. 'God. You used to have a beard.'

'I know. Her name was Grace Keaney.'

She laughs and flings her head back so I can see the workings of her throat. And it might be a mystery that she's not offended, but now she's got me where she wants me. With my back to history, sitting beneath its shadow, predated on both sides.

On a day like today, Sweden can be seen quite distinctly. The port of Helsingborg looks like art itself, a drab confusion of factories, chimneys and warehouses – a commentary on the one-time promise of industry. The Øresund, a smooth fillet of water, forms a velvet rope of sorts, behind which we watch from the dewy serenity of the Danish side.

There is a ferry that goes back and forth, itself a permanent fixture. It is a half-hour journey, repeated dozens of times each day like a nautical dumbwaiter.

And there must be something to this act of zipping across the interstice, because the ferry is popular, not just as a way of getting over, but as something people sit on for hours. Bottled beer, hot dogs and chit-chat à la whipsaw, all journey and no destination.

'Anyway,' I say to Grace, 'it's nearly two o'clock, we should make tracks.'

But we go nowhere.

Before I know it, I am setting to the lace trimmings of the story. 'I got here on a plane four years ago. The flight was on time so they did the little fanfare at the end.'

'Oh, come on,' she says. 'You know what I'm *really* asking about. You. *You*. Spill.'

'We're supposed to be going shopping this afternoon.'

'Forget about that. I'll get presents at the airport.'

'All right. You know those Danish butter cookie tins they keep sewing equipment in?' I say, raising a finger. 'Here they put biscuits in them.'

'*Do they.* Danish culture is so strange,' she says, monotonically, lilting her head from side to side.

'I don't know where they store their dressmaking stuff here. They must have crisper drawers full of buttons and thimbles.'

'Stop stalling.'

It is only history. A series of events with no great meaning or significance. Morals are for fairy tales. In the real world, the arc of the universe bends, and it keeps bending.

I look up at Grace and exhale. 'Remember what I said to you the other night, about the girl in school called Phoebe?'

Grace looks askance. 'Oh. Yeah. I didn't think we'd be going back that far.'

'Not quite that far, I guess. But a couple of months after I moved away, I noticed that my whole inner secret life had disappeared. For a while, I thought I was okay. I thought emigrating had cured whatever had been going on in my head all those years. I thought I was finally going to be normal.'

. . .

Mellanakt: första delen

You have to come up with an allegory.

I am a mermaid. I am a butterfly. I am bread stiffening in an oven. I am Jesus with tits. I am Keanu Reeves in the 1999 blockbuster *The Matrix*.

I am a sneeze without any snot. I am walking with a pebble in my oh-no-size-nine but the pebble is a diamond, maybe. I am a fish with no friends. I am three friendless fish in a trench coat, altercating, and now the trench coat is damp.

It's hard to explain. It's not a specific problem. It's not two specific problems. It's not a broken leg, a crack, a shatter, an ache, or a bleed.

It's turning the colour knob on an old television. Greens become yellows and yellows become reds and reds become purples and it's an alien landscape and it's hilarious but it's not because it's the entire world and you know no better. All your love, your accumulated knowledge, your being incorporate is contained in it.

It is you, but you will never be it. You reside in a gap, in the maddening crescent between two circles that refuse to overlap in any sense-making sense.

And the thing about old televisions is they couldn't be recorded from, so what was seen wrongly or not at all could never be recovered. Biblical epics, bloody-bandage rugby, Benny Hill, Vinegar Hill, inflatable swimming pools, the archbishop on his throne, the living and the dead, all of it, gone. Life was ephemeral – all you had of anything was grazed memory.

And I know this isn't how these stories are supposed to start. Jan Morris's memoir, published fifteen years before I was born, opens with her talking of being three years old, or maybe four. People want a three-or-maybe-four tale, and like most stories, the effect of it is not in its grasp of truth.

People empathise more with a child in their head than the adult in front of their face. Invent an infant, make her beautiful and frightened, brutalise her – only then may they respect you.

Still, still, I always felt different. I probably felt different when I was three or maybe four.

The film is damaged but I roll it anyway: I played with tea sets and wore my mother's high heels. I remember how my feet were too small for the shoes, how comically minute I was. Was that out of the ordinary? It raised no particular eyebrows then.

The images flicker and fade.

The earliest films – not the movies, I mean, but the rolls of film themselves – were made from nitrocellulose, an explosive that came to prominence in the American Civil War. An explosive made in large part from oxygen itself, so it could burn without air, even while submerged in water.

In the beginning, film reels would go up with devastating regularity, taking picture houses and people with them, the first victims of the recorded image, of mass-dispensed recollection. In 1926, a tenth of the population of a village in County Cork perished during a screening of *The Ten Commandments*.

You have to come up with an allegory.

Andra delen

2016 started, as they all do, in January. I came to live in boxy student halls in Norra Fäladen, on the curling outskirts of the city of Lund – science labs on one side, fields of rapeseed on the other. The halls were built in the nineties and the common area was a time capsule, encrusted with posters of Jim Carrey as *The Mask* and Bart Simpson's impertinent speech bubbles.

Those who lived there were usual by usual standards – badminton hobbyists and bawdy limerick enthusiasts, people with places to go and Tupperware to fill.

When I moved in, amid the first real snow I had encountered in Sweden, my room was empty but for a desk, a dusty swivel chair and a stripped bed. The midwinter sun was amplified by the disaffected white outside. The place was full of echoes.

I never bothered to decorate, because it seemed frivolous to spend money on what was clearly a holding area. Still lacking a concept of home, I knew any definition developed too soon would quickly outgrow itself. I appreciated the underwhelm of life in white space.

I longed to be an explosion of light and colour, finely tuned. I would decorate the walls with myself. Or maybe I just wanted to blow up, and had convinced myself through careful self-delusion that beams and splashes would follow.

What I really needed was to take a risk. To get out there, and meet people, out there.

A few dates occurred. With women. Halting conversations that lurched from the app into real life. They were fine. They were nice. They swayed to and fro like efficient doctor's appointments, the sort where no one has to take any clothes off. The women were usually expats, because the locals intimidated me. They and I were so much alike – shy and self-conscious, unsure of ourselves.

They asked me about my family and I asked them how much the caramel slices were.

Slowly, I realised I wasn't attracted to any of them. I would go on nutritious lunchtime nibble-offs and emerge in a state of self-loathing clarity that was post-orgasmic and essentially masturbatory.

And so the vodka drank me in the spring of 2016. I had a need for something, and every interaction I had with the fresh faces around me only served to remind me that I could not find what I was so fervently looking for. Freedom from, freedom to. Half-thoughts with no pay-off. Clear liquid on white space, which in time fades back to nothing; a litmus test in want of a procedure.

Sitting on the bed, I talked to the furniture. I concluded straight off that the chair was unfit for human habitation, its doddering cushion covered as it was in a splodge of dried mud. It looked like it had been recovered from a landfill, a loot-me-down proffered by the housing agency.

For one reason or another, or a combination of reasons, the patch of dirt seemed to have a shape. For a time, I looked on it as a tree, tilting towards the ground as if investigating its origins, like an American in a small Irish town. But then I saw a stately nose in it, delicate, coming to a prolific rhinoplasty point, and accepted rapidly and with almost no hawing that what I was gazing at and not sitting upon was the authoritative head of a man.

Mad, yes, maybe, but it seemed entirely logical that, in a world in which I was subject to all manner of manipulation and salesmanship, I could put my faith more securely in the wisdom of this unoptimised stain. He was good because he was ghastly; he was decent; he was beautiful.

He became an advisor to me, as the days lengthened. I would ask him why I wasn't in control. Why it was that, having moved away and struck out and fled the nest and all the other clichés, I still felt completely trapped.

He told me that I was not trying hard enough. He told me that my failings were my own. He told me I needed to come to terms with myself. He was cruel and brutal to me in my hour of need. I might say he was like a parent, but in truth he was much sterner than that. It was like I had conjured up my own worst enemy.

I would boil over alone in conversation with him, while others in the house came and went, doors slamming, feet bouncing, cutlery smacking, caps and sandals, *tjena tjena mittbena*.

I became indescribably angry. I went out and fetched a scouring sponge from the communal supply closet, at three in the afternoon on an exam day, the house quiet and bathed in fetid heat, and scrubbed and scrubbed away at him, until he faded, until he became increasingly unrecognisable as himself, *eat that you bastard*, reduced to a discolouration, a podge of grey and plastic-mesh green.

It was like I had smothered him in chemical gas, like an act of righteous war. I had murdered the man, and in so doing had killed the sense within me that gave or took pause. I came to see myself, to record myself, as a scientific experiment. Such thoughts are both vainglorious and a little suicidal – but then, but then.

I am the brain to my own body and I decided (that I would decide, that I would decide, that I would decide) what my body is for. It was layered execution of the executive, a slow unpacking of will.

But was I a woman?

~~Of course not, you stupid cunt (nb unladylike language)~~

~~Why not though?~~

~~Do you have a death wish?~~

~~I have yet to be granted one~~

I ran headlong into ambiguity.

Books were ordered, ones with titles like *Womanhood is a Muddy Step on the Stairway of Destiny*, essay collections in which writers in roomy Brooklyn apartments would survey their labia majora in a hand mirror and spend fifty pages elucidating their spiritual properties – but all they told me was that womanhood involved spending more money on amphetamines and bad psychoanalysis than I could reasonably afford.

The terminology, it turned out, was cheap; the costs of claiming it entirely self-imposed.

I concluded I did not need to *be* anything. I would study my body, without regard to context or the record or the colour or the burning rolls of film. I would have a life of pure experience, like an animal, nameless.

I had no more questions to answer.

Tredje delen

The pills were sent by a woman living in a small town in Spain. Santa Something de la Something. I never looked it up but assumed it had a busy beach, a gigantic Franco-era church and a football team who played in stripes. From email to email, she would change her name – Doris to Irene, Irene to Helen, Helen to Stephanie – but I was happy to go along. The sex-change grey market requires a supply of new names and faces to meet its demand for same.

In June, I told my mother what I wanted. She asked me if I thought I'd been born in the wrong body. I said I had been born in my own body, and that was the point.

A doctor on the internet gave advice on dosages. From his base in a coastal city in America, he helped us find the sweet spot between pointlessly ineffective and dangerously ineffective. He had gained a certain personal mythos, the way professionals who spend their days burnishing themselves on social media frequently do. He obtained an instinctive deference from the rest of us: in the world of the blind, the man with the sight-pill prescriptions is king.

There was crowdsourced medical advice. We told each other things the doctors wouldn't tell us. Swallow nothing – everything must go the other way. Nourishment must be arse-about-mouth from now on. Buy some sex toys, and avoid grapefruit juice at all costs. You won't get boobs if you're too thin – but for heaven's sake don't be fat!

The whole effort was terrifying, yet to turn away seemed even more so. There was something energising about the casual way we discussed the process, like we were valiant explorers and not merely victims of chronic medical neglect. Perhaps the very reluctance of doctors to prescribe to us had heightened the appeal. Moralism always backfires. Stigma is its own allure. We were like teenage mothers. We weren't to blame – the rest of you had made us this way.

Eventually it was just me and the city. The student town becomes a scar of itself during the summer months, exactly the seclusion required for my little enterprise. The heat, in the twenties and occasionally beyond, constituted a revolutionary potential, like I was sweat and steam rising from myself, emergent. I was under the red-hot element, getting closer and closer, all commas and ellipses, nearly, nearly.

One Friday mid-morning, I went to the postal kiosk at the supermarket to pick up the package. Wordlessly, I handed my slip of paper to a dry toothbrush of a woman behind the counter. What I was doing was not criminal, not really, but the Swedish combination post-desk, library stack, tobacco shop and hot-dog stand carried with it an air of illicit hybrid.

She wore a yellow T-shirt with insistent bubble writing: *GLAD SOMMAR*. A greeting intuitive yet oddly untranslatable: *happy summer*, yes, but who has ever said, 'Happy summer'?

It was thrilling, the way my bank transfers, the incognito pill traders, this woman standing in front of me, the entire mangled airmail system became part of the working of my body. Europe was now my jagged archipelago of organs. I did not have ovaries, but instead I had Åsa once-overing my ID and giving me a jiffy bag full of who-knows-what.

There was logic to it. Human beings are social creatures, and I had made myself more social, and thereby more human. I had secretly joined society.

And then I reached ten thousand.

Ten thousand days.

It seemed a good jumping-off point. A hundred times a hundred: a figure both round and square. The tenth of July 2016 was exactly ten thousand days after the twenty-second of February 1989. Having tried one life for ten thousand days, I couldn't be said to have quit prematurely.

Several times in life, existence collapses to a point. There is before and there is after, and between there is an heirloom of a moment, like the crackable spine of a book, with no value but sentimental. I thought it prudent to leave such an occasion where it could readily be found, to put history away for safekeeping.

Blue and white pills, like a summer sky, prostate medication and birth control repurposed for my use. A blister packet and a wheel that went click-click-click. Tablets for old men, tablets for young women, a gradient I traversed. I sat on my chair – yes, the swivel chair! – and, having cut the blue one with a dinner knife, I waited eucharistically for it to melt on my tongue. Its taste was weak and bitter, and my disgust was a kind of verification.

My body became an experimental and experiential diary.

Ten thousand. Still alive. Lethargic. I dreamt that night – I can't remember what, but to dream was itself a breakthrough. My subconscious had returned like a hero from war. Great spaces existed within me. The lights had been raised. It was wasteland mutating into forest, the way everything comes to live if it is only left alone.

Ten thousand and two. Alive, still. Urine smell: rancid popcorn butter. I went for a walk to expel some nervous energy, up to the mound at Klosterängshöjden from which the whole city can be seen, from which it glimmers like found treasure, but I had to return home because the feeling of the T-shirt rubbing against my chest was excruciating, like insects were living under my skin.

And I was, yes, alive, go, still, alive, yes, go.

Back in my room, I began feeling an odd pain in my arms, an aching twinge in the muscle around my elbow. I decided immediately, with a shiver of excitement, that I was now going to die. I lay in bed, in wait, for the remainder of the day for fear that I would corpse myself in some exposed public location. I fell asleep, and when I awoke it was Wednesday, and the pain was gone, and I was still alive.

Ten thousand and eleven. I had a vivid dream in which I was being fucked. By what or whom I could not say. It shocked me enough to wake me up.

At what point does a person become someone else? Ten thousand was a convenient figure, but change is a moveable feast. The process does not have a clear beginning or end. I cannot, after all, pinpoint the day when I began to want. It came over me like a season. Perhaps the truth is that I have remained all along the same person, differently interpreted.

Ten thousand and thirty-seven. I looked at myself in the mirror, and I saw everything that had come before me.

There is a narrative of transition that says it is a rejection of the self. We are always accused of running away from something – cutting something off, one way or another. But what was I rejecting? Half my ancestors were women. Half my DNA is female. That is a biological fact. I am doing nothing but accentuating a heritage that is all my own. I have appropriated nothing.

I looked in the mirror and the flickering film had become full, marvellous colour in front of me. The futures ground out, reclaimed and reconstructed. I saw the women who looted fur coats on the rubbled streets of Dublin. I saw the women who worked in garment factories in the north-west of England, and grotty telephone exchanges in London, nicked hands and hoarse voices.

I looked in the mirror and saw those from whom I had been made, and to whom, by a certain alchemy of the person, I had now been returned.

. . .

14:52 Our tickets are left in waste-paper baskets and we make our way back to the train station – back to the city, the way we came. Grace's questions are an encore to my story. The afternoon is a fulcrum around which we move, coming only for the gift of going back, different now. *How did the name change happen? When did you get your passport sorted? Were the college okay with everything?* It is like she is trying to prevent me from running away from what I have just said.

I am leaving a trail, dropping aspects behind me, but she picks them up, ensuring that they will follow, whether I want them or not.

So much of the weekend might simply be chalked down to fate, deemed a sign of cosmic alignment, something in the stars Grace looked to before boarding her plane. And yet, now we are here, the story I tell is of the power of choice: that rules, even extra-terrestrial ones, are made to be broken. We have seen fate and rejected it. We draw our own stars. We understand how distant they are.

I ran away from Ireland in pursuit of a truth and now I have run away from the city to dispose of it.

Grace is still asking questions. It is a procedural drama, I tell her, full of stamped addressed envelopes and *personnummers*, and I don't have the time to explain what all of it means. It transpired mostly in the form of queues and waiting, and, in that sense, it was similar enough to the rest of life.

I feel more vulnerable here than I did in my bed last night. Like I have revealed something below the surface level of my own body, something no one has ever seen before, something unfamiliar even to me, and now I am in a kind of exhausted ecstasy.

I talk to Grace about my name change. 'My mam helped a lot with things,' I say. 'The morning I got it all done, at the Four Courts, we went to Smithfield afterwards and had coffee. I was so relieved and glad to have someone to talk to.'

'That's so nice. One more thing,' Grace says, as we walk into the underpass to get to the southbound platform.

'Go on.'

'Did you tell your ma about the sex dreams?'

I smile. 'No,' I say. 'You heard it first.'

I am free, now, of a shame I once carried, and a responsibility too. It is as if all the days of my life have been leading to the moment when I would sit on grass overlooking the sea, unburdening myself to the woman I sort-of loved so many years ago, the woman who loved a version of me long-ago discarded, like a ticket to somewhere better.

And there it is again: fate.

15:14 A rapport is carried on an engine's impersonation of power, all noise, thwacks of progress and assertion, as if in rebellion against its confinement to the rails. Its life is an incline to a brief performance of self-sufficiency, which comes and goes like indiscretion – then childhood returns, and it is delivered unto the commune of the scrapheap.

For the moment, though, it gives us a sense of direction.

Grace sits back in her train seat, one hand wrapped around a paper cup, as copious conifer shadows slew across her face. 'Gender,' she says, free-standingly, in the manner of a Mad Lib, and I begin to tense, a survivor of prior homilies on the subject. 'It's interesting, isn't it?' she continues. 'I was a tomboy growing up, kind of. I mean, what is a tomboy nowadays? But I never thought I was a boy, you know? I related to girls. To women. Sorry, I'm rambling.'

'No, that's fine,' I say, and a set of juddering gears seem to crunch in my head, now-you-see-it, now-you-see-it, now-you-see-it. The way men get to define their own perfection, while women are presented with a premade unattainable, a teetering, toddling in-tray of handwork and heartwork and etceterawork. That is Grace's problem.

Perhaps she has come to prove my womanhood by exhausting me completely. That's the one thing all women seem to have in common: they are tired.

Then I realise she's talking about her dad – the influence of her dad, maybe?

'I feel like I know nothing about him,' I say. 'What age were you when he died?'

'Ten. Stomach cancer,' she says, with the as-it-were tone of a fact acutely known but now only sporadically felt. 'It was incurable by the time they caught it. He was thirty-nine. He'll be twenty years gone in October.'

Neither of us speaks for a few seconds. The train passes under a bridge, a fleck of darkness darting down the carriage, and out of view.

Grace continues, 'Sometimes I think about how, by the time he and my ma were my age, they already had me. I don't know how they managed it. They were superheroes.'

'My mam was twenty-six when she had me. When she was thirty, she had two and a third on the way. All I have is a dog that doesn't like me.'

The mark of matrimony puts women on the rails – that's why wedding dresses are followed by trains. There is a certain pride to be taken in us, sitting here, a sisterhood of squeaky wheels.

'I'm sure things will work out for us,' I continue, thought-terminating, but mid-sentence my hand knocks over the empty paper cup in front of me. It lands on the floor of the carriage and rolls away before we can get it. Grace mugs at me like an overinflated beach ball.

Slowly the trees give way, and the city resumes.

15:39 The concourse of the central station is so vast that the sounds in it combine to a hollow, ringing echo, an octave higher than the sum of its parts: the turbine-hum of luggage wheeling to and fro, passengers-to-be pacing with anticipation in black berets and super-skinny jeans, and pigeons, of course, fighting on the ground beneath our feet, caught in a tangle of feathers and deformed city-bird limbs. A guitared man sings 'Nothing Else Matters' into a cheap microphone – amid the hubbub, he is distinct, if not distinguished.

Every time I walk through this place, I think it looks like a church: sweeping wooden arches, stained-glass windows and careful light. Then I berate myself for the notion, evidence of a peasant mentality – taking a monument to public enterprise and reducing it to the status of a mere smell-and-bell dispensary – until the next time, until I emerge once more from the top of an escalator and think: this *does* look like a church, full as it is of those waiting to be transported.

Outside the station entrance, back in the sour cold, we walk as Grace hatches a plan. 'We should celebrate,' she says. 'What do you think? A party for our mutual thirtieth?'

'Mutual?'

'Like, it basically is. Why don't we go somewhere later? Saturday night, it's party time, *priddy baybay*.'

'Where do you want to go?'

'There's got to be a queer club here somewhere.'

'Oh.' I look downwards. 'Okay.'

'You not up for that?'

'I don't know. I'm not really a club person these days. I haven't gone in years.'

Grace puts her hand on my shoulder and squeezes it like a joint of meat. 'Listen to me: you're a thirty-year-old woman. I'm probably the last person who'll ever ask you to do this. Let's do the business tonight and then you can sit at home watching Jessica Fletcher solve murders for the rest of your life.'

'You have such an accurate read of what my life is like.'

She laughs, and her breath is visible in the cold. 'Now's your chance to prove me wrong.'

Now we are back on Rådhuspladsen, the central square, the spot from which the entire kingdom of Denmark seems to radiate. White vans flit acircle, cleaning firms and security companies, with *We work for Denmark* written on their sides. Yellow buses move cautiously, red and white flags quivering out of driver's-side windows. And, in the cycle lanes, the future of the nation, blond and bouncing, is carried in the spacious trailers of bicycles that coast-overlap-coast at varying speeds.

The city is music and we a pair of gulping marimbas.

I could get caught up in this – in being part of a real country. The comparison cannot help itself. Ireland is a state that smirks at the fact of its own sovereignty, deadbeat, looking to offload its responsibilities. A nation with an asterisk to the north-east.

Then Grace smiles at me in front of the city hall, and I love it, its public nature. A smile I can show off. Her cheeks are flush with the cold of the late afternoon, the redness standing out against the blonde of her hair, and the sight of it makes me wonder if I look the same to her.

She moves closer and speaks to me, her plans further loosened.

16:02 A lumbered dredge of Saturday-afternoonites remains on Strøget, even now, as the sun dips and the light begins to wane.

The street is narrow and masterly, mediaeval, as if business is intimidating its way to custom. Shapeless dresses and cigarette pants adorn wide windows, boutiques keen to sell summer clothes, but shoppers not yet sure enough to buy them. The masses move with a stuttered anxiety, snarling breath into the air like a crowd of racehorses waiting for a signal. A man walks, lecturing a child in the pushchair in front of him, speaking an indecipherable language with preacherly confidence. The street is a meeting of routine and peccadillo, a calibrated madness of people.

For about fifteen minutes, Grace pulls me around a Lego shop like a child hauling a helium balloon. I am a human italic next to her and her boldness. She doesn't hold my hand, but she doesn't need to.

She buys a model of the Berlin Fernsehturm for three hundred kroner, a figure meaningless to her and one I opt not to translate. I suggest it looks like an air traffic control tower, and she tells me I lack imagination. 'The world is full of amazing things,' she says, imploring me to view it through her eyes. I decide to take up the offer.

She swings me again through streets, past quiet restaurants where waitresses adjust outdoor heaters, past moody, green-tinted adverts for streaming TV thrillers, past tourist shops selling plastic Viking swords and magnets shaped like the head of Queen Margrethe, with no cigarette.

We land at a department store depurated with the smell of expense: perfume, treated wood, unread books and bath salts – a compound of empty affluence, the sort of air they will one day charge us rent to breathe.

Grace is drawn to a blown-glass ornament in the shape of an owl. It is a brownish-green colour, looking like an oversized thimble with googly eyes. She jokes about buying it for me as a present, 'You can look at it when you're doing your magic in the kitchen,' but, in truth, this weekend is making up for all the unmade gestures, the unwritten history. A gap is being filled, hour by hour.

They say if a product is free, the consumer is the product, and, as we flitter through the unbought and ungiven trinkets, I think to conclude that we exist now as gifts to one another – so much so that the owl, the perturbed wooden elk and the multiracial plush dolls are redundant.

And then another unexpected visitor. 'Phoebe, hello!'

Sofia Bäckström, deputy head of the Department of Global Development and International Studies, DOGDIS, at Lund University. Fifty-five, or so, brown hair fading into grey, wearing a deep-green jacket lined with white fur, which is undoubtedly fake. We are about the same height, and she stands before me like an empty vase, sturdy yet aspiring of more.

She speaks with a clipped English accent, also a put-on, so disliking her requires almost no effort at all. The academy is an odd setting for a woman who seems to have devoted herself to a lifelong Katharine Hepburn impression, but the opulence of her personality has done nothing to impede an escalator-like rise through the faculty.

'Gosh, Sofia, how are you?' First-name terms, always first-name terms with local academics. 'This is my friend Laura, from Ireland. She's come to visit,' I say, gesturing towards Grace, who, from her expression, might as well be listening to a conversation about imputed multilateral aid flows.

'Hello, Laura, nice to meet you,' Sofia says, extending a diplomatic hand.

'We've just come to look for presents for Laura's little son at home, isn't that right?' I say, giving my eyebrows a lift.

'Yes,' Grace says. 'This is a gorgeous shop.'

We natter about Lego and Laura's imaginary son, who lives for it, as evinced by our bag. Grace says his name is Bruno, a choice so deranged that no tactful Scandinavian would dare question it.

We're Irish, so we say 'yeah' in the form of a gasp, a minced assent. Sofia is Swedish, so she says 'okay' like it's a ski slope she's pulling us down.

The prof and I end up in a conversational metronome: we drift towards work, then recognise the gaucheness of discussing it; we hurtle towards our personal lives, and remember we have nothing in common. The fictitious babby becomes a load-bearing talking point.

'It looks like you're having a very excite-ning time,' Sofia says, nodding towards nothing in particular. 'I won't get in your way. Have a nice trip, Laura. See you on Monday, Phoebe.'

'Absolutely, Monday, see you then,' I say.

Sofia drifts away and starts inspecting price tags. Grace looks at me quizzically. 'What was all that about?'

'I don't know. I don't know where Laura came from.'

Grace straitens her gaze. 'I don't look like a Laura.'

'What about Bruno? Who inspired that, Mars or Tonioli?'

'You started it. You didn't have to change my name. Are you ashamed of me?'

'More ashamed of walking around the toy section of a fancy department store with no intention of buying anything. Did you hear her, though?'

'Hear what?'

'Excite-ning. Swedish people speak fluent English, and sometimes they have great English or American accents, and, every so often, they come out with excite-ning, or they pronounce chair as cher. It's like a robot glitching.'

'I bet they say the same thing about your Swedish.'

'If I'm lucky. I'm sure they have lots to say about me behind my back. There are so many adjectives I could use to describe that faculty.' I inhale sharply. 'But I usually go with "thundering".'

'Why are you doing this PhD?'

'I don't know. Inertia. Is inertia a good enough reason? I have nothing better to do.' I restrain myself from explaining that a PhD isn't proof of intelligence, merely that you can mash your head into an angle grinder for four years and still have enough of it left over to fit into a mortarboard.

Sofia was one of my referees when I applied for the doctoral programme. She was a champion of mine – though I was easy enough to champion, having got straight As during the final year of my master's, when I was on hormones but still half-closeted. I was welcomed into the cloister of a Swedish PhD: decent pay, trade union membership, practically unsackable, as long as I kept showing up. Yet I applied under an old name, and I can never quite shake the sense that they would have laughed me out of the room if they had known who I really was. I am now reduced to working at it out of a kind of psychodramatic spite, fighting a battalion of uncorroborated thoughts in my head.

And maybe I simply don't want to see my day-to-day through Grace's valuable eyes. I am comfortable here and now, in this space between know-not vacationer and bone-tired émigré, in the way she sees the place as supple and negotiable, still believes the stories it tells. I hold out hope of repatriating her illusions. I don't want to lose them.

'Here's something better to do,' Grace says, making her way towards a troupe of cow-eyed toy sloths.

16:46 The city is a garden; it beckons us off the beaten path. The shop is on a side street, between a small kebab place and an outlet selling vacuum cleaner parts. Grace and I move towards it, out of public view, like a pair of Jane Austen characters. There is an unspoken consensus that this visit to *Michaels Kondombutik* carries with it a dramaturgical thrill.

Behind a heavy wooden door, the place is orderly and surprisingly well lit. There is a man behind the counter, slight in build, with a good head of hair for his age and a neat moustache in the shape of Mount Kilimanjaro. He looks like a maths teacher, a shop steward or both – a man whose vista speaks to the likelihood of a sizeable collection of old magazines in his name.

He greets us in Danish and watches our pottering with a canny librarian eye, and I feel like an errant schoolchild, being dragged into trouble by my more adventurous classmate.

It is a woodland of the abject and I suppose we are squirrels. Feathers, eggs, leather, all organic, all budding, blossoming, pouchy, earthy, damp, deeply rooted and various other filthy nature words.

'You'll need this after your surgery,' Grace says, more than once, and I appreciate the advice, the consideration of where I will be when I shake off the shakeoffable.

The man at the counter asks us in English if we need any help, proof he has been listening, which serves to shut me up, but has no effect at all on Grace. She states baldly that we are on the lookout for a strap-on, and by the time those words are out it is too late to pretend I'm not with her, so I smile as if to associate myself with the remark.

His eyes brighten and he skips towards a shelf just in front of where we are standing. 'Here you are,' he says. 'We have a good selection.'

It is the most expensive thing we've bought today, but it is an investment, a matter of sowing and reaping.

I pay for it, and a generous bottle of lube – water-based, all-natural ingredients – on condition that we figure out a way to split the bill later. After all, we are both deriving some use from it.

As Grace makes chit-chat with the shopkeeper – where she's from, how long she's been in town; he went to Wexford once apparently, Wexford of all places – he keeps his gaze lasered on me, and smiles. A joke about inviting him for a threesome surfaces in my mind, but I shoo it away, lest he find a way to overhear it.

The man places our goods in a paper bag, discreet and biodegradable. 'Enjoy your evening,' he says, as we leave.

'Take it handy,' Grace replies, and I am a rustle of knife-cut tension, trying not to laugh.

As the door thuds behind us, she calls him a creep from central casting.

17:56 'I keep meaning to ask,' Grace says, 'do you cycle?'

We are back in Frederiksberg, the day reduced now to a thinning film of light, passing yet another island of parked bicycles, another puddle of aluminium.

'No, no,' I say. 'I tried it and it wasn't for me. I'm too anxious.'

'But the bike lanes are so big!' Grace says, loudly. 'It's not like in Dublin where you're taking your life into your hands, you could be squashed by Eddie Stobart in two seconds flat.'

'Yeah, I know. I'm not afraid of being run over.'

'What is it then? Were you beaten up by a bicycle?'

'It's just, you know, I'd watch women cycling down the street without a care in the world, wearing jackets ruffling in the wind, looking like something out of *Amélie*, and I'd immediately think of Isadora Duncan getting decapitated by her car wheel.'

I like to think there's something poetic about this explanation, that I have developed a motherly protective instinct over the body I have subscribed to, though the truth is that subscription has done nothing for my co-ordination, a famine of zigs spoiling a feast of zags.

Grace laughs with acid pity. 'You're like Domestos for craic, Phoebe. You kill ninety-nine per cent of it dead.'

We pass some young men playing Kendrick Lamar on the loudspeaker of a phone. Grace shushes them theatrically and they yell something back in Danish, and then they are gone. I am silent and forward-facing throughout.

Sometimes, it seems like Grace wants bad things to happen, that she is engaged in a lost-cause confrontation with life. But her flightiness has some merit: a more risk-averse her would not have ended up here in the first place, and a more risk-averse me would have waved goodbye on Thursday and made an endeavour of forgetting.

All I can be is an obedient self to myself, to decide where I wish to go and slither and wobble until I get there – a skill that would be unforgettable had I not overlooked the need to learn it.

We walk down the street where I live. There are tables and chairs perched on balconies, the odd person sat on high, reading or knitting, too far away to tell which.

The city is an experience repeated over time, in short rhythms and long. It folds back onto itself over and over, cyclically, bodily, perceived slightly differently with each repetition, revealed in a process of persistent but gradual disclosure.

18:08 'She couldn't hold it in,' I say. 'There but for the grace of God go any of us. Camilla tried to toilet train her, but all it did was make her feel guilty about shitting all over the place.'

When we got back to the flat, Dolly drifted towards us silently, in hiding from herself as much as Grace's throaty effort to sing Louis Armstrong at her. A familiar sight: the irregular waddle of a woman who knows she is of a species that won't land on its feet.

And in the vicinity of the balcony door, the cause of her anguish: a lumpy little raisin whirl, curled next to the sofa.

'Do dogs feel guilt?' Grace asks, taking her coat off.

'Absolutely. Dolly contains multitudes.'

'It's good you have something to look after,' she says, as I carry the houseguest to the bathroom wrapped in toilet paper.

I don't know if she's joking or not. 'Definitely, it keeps you sane,' is all I can say, as the flush begins to rumble.

Quickly the dog rallies, blessed by impunity, liberated from the consequences of her movements.

18:19 Last night's red-wine glasses, washed this morning, become this evening's white-wine glasses. It is an achievement of sorts that we've made it to this stage of the day without a drink. It raises questions, second thoughts of what was juddering through us yesterday that warranted our polite sips and the occasional glugs they obscured.

There is a point at which two people no longer need a filter between them: that of alcohol, effusive but empty text messages, or factitious dating bios. When there is no more pretence. If we reached that milestone, it is for the first time.

We speak in eulogy to our late romance. In other words, we are silent.

Grace empties the paper bag onto the bed. For a few minutes, we battle cardboard and fiddly stickers, until the intervention of a pair of scissors. There is a map-sized instruction leaflet in twelve languages. Grace doesn't need it, she knows where the clips are, but starts reading Italian for me anyway. '*Strapponi*,' she says, theatrically, '*il strapponi*.'

I crease my mouth. 'I think *strapponi* is a type of pasta.'

'Yeah,' she says. 'It's the type they eat at hen parties.'

The moment I see the jet-black strap-on in its fullness, thick with silicone veins and tributaries, I laugh through my nose. There is something about the phallus separated from the body, just a schlong floating discourteously through time and space, that makes it inherently disarming – like seeing someone with a distinctive facial feature, a big nose or no chin or pencilled-on eyebrows, and feeling instinctively at ease with them and their imperfections. The manless penis is more conversation piece than tool of oppression – like an ice sculpture that may or may not be about to melt.

We undress, and I see the tattoo of the woman on Grace's thigh, and all I can see in her face is serenity. We are shorn of the inhibitions that kept us beneath layers last night. Now we hide in each other.

My old friend makes a stranger of me.

19:24 We're chirping with giggles as we finish.

Once the thing, glistening, is put away, we lie there, my head on her shoulder, in a blend of kissing and laughter. We are now mature enough to be properly adolescent – leave-taken of our senses, sense made of ourselves.

My hair is covering the side of her face, draped over her like a vulgar tarpaulin. She moves it over and looks down at me. 'Do Danish people having sex speak Danish while they're doing it?'

'I suppose so. In my experience, they don't say much.' I start chuckling to myself. 'Swedish guys would be like: "*Nu kommer jag, herrrrrrrregud!*" They'd have to roll their Rs and come at the same time,' I say, dissolving into laughter, which is only partially shared, and gradually peters out.

'Can I let you in on a secret?' she says, smiling, mindless, filling a moment's quiet. 'No one knows I'm here.'

It scarcely registers as a sentence, so I just giggle with well-now bonhomie. She stares at me, still open-eyed, expectant of a response. Eventually I muster a what.

'No one knows I'm here,' she says.

I lift my head slightly. 'Yeah, no, I heard you, but, like, no one knows that you're in bed with me right now? Is that what you mean?'

'No one knows I'm in Copenhagen.'

'Right,' I say, in a voice clammy with self-pity. For all that I thought I wanted to know Grace, for all that she appeared like something, someone to explore, I already seem to know too much. Is it selfish to say I don't really care who we are when we are not each other?

'I didn't tell anyone I was coming here,' she says. 'I didn't want people to ask questions.' She is talking for the sake of talking now, saying things she doesn't want to say, things I don't want to hear, reflexively, a discharge of words.

'Why did you come here?' I reply.

She says nothing.

I look into Grace's eyes. To look at her is like staring at an ancient text. It implies profundity, it might even be beautiful, but I'm without a key and its meaning is a door slammed to me. 'What if something had happened?' I say.

She tilts her head back. 'I could have called someone. I'm not stupid.'

'So what did you say to people? Was it like "I'm off for a few days, I'll see you when I see you"?'

'I have a friend, Mags, who lives in Eindhoven. She says she's quirky, but she's not, really. She's a video game producer. It's really interesting.'

'I'm sure it is.'

'Anyway, I told everyone I was visiting her.'

Each new detail of this scheme adds both to its intricacy and its sheer pointlessness. I've been spitting around Copenhagen putting the rube in Rube Goldberg these last forty-eight hours.

'So Mags knows I'm here,' Grace continues, 'but she doesn't know you, so she doesn't know why I'm here.'

'Grace, I don't get this at all. Why are you telling me this now? What are you playing at?'

'I just didn't want people getting the wrong impression.'

'The problem with that,' I say, 'is I don't know what the right impression is.' Maybe my problem is that I seem much of the time to be more impression than anything else.

'I just thought people would think it was strange that I was visiting my ex,' she says.

'I get that.' I put my hand above her collar-bone and sigh. 'All your behaviour makes more sense now.'

'Like what?'

'Like not buying presents for anyone.' I pause. 'I don't know. Is there something weird going on here?'

'Weird, sure.' Her voice takes off like a small chorister bird. 'Everything I do is weird. I'm sorry for telling you this. I think it was the wine. Or the endorphins. Sorry, sorry, sorry.'

I shift myself up on the bed, so that I'm kneeling next to Grace's body, her right hand resting on my upper thigh. 'Listen, you didn't lie to me. I actually seem to be the only person you didn't lie to, apart from Mags, whoever she is. So I suppose I'm not the one you need to apologise to.'

There is danger in seeing too much. A single mirror has some use, but with each addition, another buff of confusion is inflicted, until you have a perplexity of them, and what you see is indistinguishable from the face of madness itself. Grace sits in front of me, a gathering of scattered glimpses, naked, mirrored and muddled, but I cleave to the idea that, beneath it all, if seen through a lens I am not yet privy to, she exists coherently.

We end up showering together. The apartment bathroom is windowless, stale and sticky, possessing no consideration for the erotic, but I do my best to fit around her.

20:21 Grace is two and a half quaffs into her glass of wine when she tells me she's going to quit her job. We're on the sofa together, side by side, waiting for a pizza delivery, something light and chickeny with peppers – a bland, consensus choice. The television is on, a dour programme about art deco clocks, but we have it muted.

I ask her what brought this on, through a glaze of bemusement.

'Do you ever think about running away?' she asks, skidding a hand over Dolly, who rests on her lap.

'Think about it?' I say. 'I thought I already did it. I changed my name and everything.'

'I mean, like, *really* running away. And never being found. I do sometimes.'

'You can't really run away these days,' I say. 'Not with technology. There are bungee cords attached to us, and if you run too far you get snapped back to where you came from. Kept in your place. So – and sorry, I'm just backtracking here – do you want to leave your job and run away?'

'I might quit my job right now,' she says, taking out her phone, as if to prove my point about tech and its risks. Hintlessly, I'm being winched into Grace's life in Dublin, a mediator without an antagonist, without context or any detail at all to go on.

I start brandishing traffic-warden arms. 'Hang on, *hang* on, can we calm down a bit? Let's not do things we can't undo.'

'You're very cautious all of a sudden,' she says, and there is diode-emitted light on her vagaries, so she is illuminated but I am clueless. 'Forget it, I can't think straight,' she says, and puts the phone down.

'What's wrong with your job?' I ask. 'Maybe instead of quitting you could talk to me about it.'

'I'm in a quarter-life crisis.'

I contort my face in an approximation of sympathy. At this point, this more-like-three-eighths mark, 'quarter-life crisis' is a word combination that inspires a pinprick chill, like 'listening session' or 'sibling entrepreneurs'.

'I might as well be a touchscreen,' she continues. 'That's what I feel like at work. A robot with a face like a slapped arse. If I was a robot, people could just go into the clinic and press a few buttons. Beep, beep, beep. The touchscreen would be nicer to them, as well. It wouldn't complain.'

'Well, you know, a lot of jobs are like that. Isn't that what they say: work to live, don't live for work?'

She leans back and looks to the ceiling. 'Fuck *off*. You sound like one of them.'

'One of who?'

'A therapist,' she says, spitting consonants.

'Is this about you turning thirty?'

She gently shakes her head, which I take as a yes. 'Did you ever hear about the woman in America who ran away from home and pretended to be a high-school girl?' she asks. 'She went from town to town saying she was a teenage orphan. I think it was in the eighties. By the time she was caught she was, like, thirty-five and still going to school every day. They sent her to prison.'

'And . . . do *you* want to do that? Pretend to be a teenager?'

'I just want to start over again. To get things right for once. One last go on the rollercoaster.' Then she sighs, and her breath seems to contain years of suppressed feeling.

'Society looks down on people who act younger than their age,' I say. 'Mutton dressed as lamb. I've always thought it's because the world doesn't want to be reminded of its failures. Sometimes people get left in suspended animation. They don't come of age. They just become older and older children and have to find ways to hide it.'

'I was so strong when I was younger. Now look at me. I'm stale bread.'

'Better than being brown bread. You're only twenty-nine.'

'I've missed out,' she says, and looks to the window, to the darkness outside. Grace has a flair for drama, which would be useful if the roles she acted out were not always ones of twitchy reproach. A hard-boiled bisexual she may be, one who was inside me barely an hour ago, but a bent towards damsel-in-distressism remains, a vestigial tail of heteropassivity.

And I know I could ask her what she thinks she's missed out on, but it's not that kind of talk. This woman is caught between acute grief and the faint suspicion that what she is mourning was all along unalive. Like falling in love with a fictional character – cringey, but real.

She is learning how not to want while I am doing the opposite, but I can't tell which of us is the leading indicator. It might be easiest to conclude that life is supposed to be a great spiral, as our tyres continue to squeal and our surroundings churn about us.

'We all end up making choices before we know who we really are,' I say. 'But knowing who you are is a burden too.'

'Yeah, it is.' She pauses. 'How?'

I tell her a story I read, one of my second-hand brutalities, about a fifteen-year-old trans girl, a Black girl living in Kentucky before I was born, who wrote to her gender clinic doctor – 'John Money, a real arsehole,' I explain – saying she saw herself in the Fleetwood Mac song, 'Rhiannon'. 'You can find your future anywhere, if you look around,' I say.

I start singing winefully, my voice monochrome and quivering. 'Sometimes I lose myself thinking about what must have happened to that girl.' I take a drink. 'She'd be the same age as my mam, but I'm certain she didn't make it. And I hate that I always jump to that conclusion, but I do.'

Grace says nothing in response, and we're one-apiece in stories lost in transmission, a banquet of pressure-cooked squib, damp.

'I suppose what I'm trying to say,' I continue, 'is that sometimes the decisions you make when you're young are made to protect yourself, and they're not bad choices if they do that.'

Grace immediately offloads the dog. Dolly casts an instinctive paw to avoid the floor, and is left hanging precariat off the weave of the throw.

'Here, look, this'll cheer us up,' Grace says, as she skips towards the door and out of view. And as the apartment fluctuates around me, I am ready for upcheer. A bird is not tamed by a cage, merely imbued with a cannier form of wildness. The surest sign that pain has been fully felt is when nothing is taken seriously at all.

Grace returns. The strap-on is with her and mischief greased onto her face. 'When the pizza comes,' she says, 'go down to the front door and collect it with this in your hand. It'll be funny.'

Dolly stares at it with the captivation reserved for unidentified food-sized objects. She approaches the air in its direction forensically.

I look at it as the home remedy it is. 'Is this part of running away and becoming a teenager?' I ask. 'Making me do silly pranks? Anyway, I don't think I'll be able to carry that and the pizza boxes all by myself.'

'I'll go down and help. But you have to answer, and you *have* to be holding it.'

I smirk and sarcast. 'You like bossing me around, don't you?'

She smiles and throws the toy at me. It embarks on an unforeseeable turn, a golfer's backspin, and hits me glans-first on the wrist.

20:42 By the time the buzzer goes we're on our second bottle of wine, pacing ourselves less in the way of a marathon than a children's sports day, shiny spoons and long-gone eggs.

We stagger a little as we make our way down the stairs – keep left, turn left, keep left. I walk with the strap-on in one hand and Grace in the other, hoping my footsteps obscure the door-hinge creak of my knees. If our old friend Hans Christian Andersen could see us now, he might build for us a fairy tale in which a pair of ugly ducklings are transformed by the magic of pubescence into juvenile, revanchist ducks.

The delivery guy speaks Danish with an accent – we are met with an eye-sparkle of delight when he realises he can speak English with an accent to us instead. He has a gold tooth and responds to everything Grace says with *excellent*. 'Ha ha ha, excellent,' he says. His bicycle saddle has a hole in it, not yet an inconvenience but obviously on the grow.

Grace is still making small talk with him – I'm not listening too intently, but at one point she asks him where he bought his North Face jacket – when he spots the thing. He covers his face as though protective of a sneeze that never comes.

Grace smiles and says, 'Oh, sorry, we meant to leave that in with a neighbour.' Then we give him his two hundred and fifty kroner and he's still rattling like an old teapot as he makes his way.

20:51 'Over here the politicians complain about pizza-*dansk*,' I say to Grace from the kitchen, as I try to cut slices with a dinner knife. 'The way immigrants don't speak Danish properly and sprinkle it with foreign words like they're bits of pineapple. Course, I avoid that problem by hardly speaking the language at all.'

I make smaller pieces for Dolly and put them in her bowl, a stew of carbs and topping, but she's more interested in the scavenge.

I give Grace a plate and sit down with her. I try to get her to talk about her situation, even as gossip, something external to us, but she is reticent now.

Then out of the broil she starts talking about supermarkets. 'Imagine you're, like, walking around buying toothpaste,' she says, 'and everything seems normal. Then you hear a song playing.'

I nod along, mostly relieved that unlike our previous attempts to explain ourselves to each other, this one has no intention of making sense.

'Let's say the song is "California King Bed". And you're like, "Oh, that's a good tune, haven't heard that in a few years."'

'It is a good tune.'

'Yeah. And then you listen closely and you realise that the voice on the song doesn't sound like you remember it. And you're like, "Is that Rihanna? Does Rihanna sound like that? Have I gone doolally?" And it's probably some cheapo session singer they've got because they can't afford Rihanna. But you can't really remember so you start to wonder if maybe Rihanna's voice wasn't what you remembered it to be.'

'Yeah,' I say, absently, increasingly aware that I am talking to a Billy bookcase. Not literally – not this time – what I mean is that the trouble with other people is you have to assemble them yourself. But telling a story is a way of saying yes: permission to see what is and need not be there.

Grace gestures with her right arm and starts ranting, her words sharp and thirsty as a guillotine. 'You know what I'm getting at? The whole word is just . . . fake all the time. Fake jobs, fake music, fake news, fake everything. I got an email from a takeaway app earlier. The subject line was: *Are you feeling lucky?* Like, what the fuck is that? Actual people don't care about me, but the Ginger House Thai Restaurant is trying it on. I wouldn't drop my drawers for their pad prik.' She sips a glass of Diet Coke, placed strategically in front of her. 'All that's going on in my life at the moment,' she says, 'is work on Tuesday, a set of fucking maths puzzles for a job application I'm definitely going to fail, and tickets for Richard Ashcroft at the Olympia that I don't even want. This isn't real life at all.'

'I think "uncanny" is the word you're looking for,' I say, because 'uncanny' is the word I'm looking for.

It is strange, strange beyond interpretation, to hear a mouth from my past damn the problems of the present. Hers is not a face that should know of AirPods, or undercuts, or the US president's tan suit, or the US president's tanned successor, or the eleven years left to prevent irreversible warming – yet it is grounding and soothing to hear her, like a comforting voicemail from beyond the grave, like watching a thrusty performance by a hologram of Elvis Presley. Grace doesn't belong to the world of Fake Rihanna; she belongs to the world of Real Rihanna, and, briefly, I return to that world too.

Grace raises her eyes. 'I'm not looking for a word.'

No, but I'm looking for a word. Atomised, maybe. A scientific word for a curtly unscientific process, as though there is something natural, chemical about loneliness, like it simply happens: people dissolving into mist just like water.

I am looking for a word for an overload of context, a feedback loop of context: the sense that things are bad but someone else has it worse but things are bad but someone else has it worse; the labour of endlessly tweezering your stupid, intractable concerns into and out of an imaginary world-hierarchy of discontent; of going nowhere fast while envying others their fractional speed advantage; the feeling of clinging, hanging on to the teeth-grinding, eye-blinking, watch-watching, cutting *and indeed spewing* edge of a century ostensibly young but plainly unburgeoning, gasping, coughing, reaching impotently for dirty air. How does one thrive in this thickness of things?

I am looking for a word. A beautiful, hold-the-front-page, kick-up-the-arse term, for the way I have to swim through her, the way I am fish-mouthing for clues as a child might bob for fruit, the way people fill out like liquid and take up more space than could possibly contain them.

I am looking for a word for a world – bruised, browning, nourishing still, but visibly in decay, not getting any better, not coming back.

He looked like an apple and I said nothing. 'Gala apple,' I say.

'What?' Grace responds, interrupted.

'My grandfather,' I mutter, unaware I had spoken aloud. 'My mam sent me a picture of my grandad last night.' I feel like I am winded by my own thoughts.

'Oh,' she says. 'How is he?'

'He's fine, he's fine. He's great for ninety-one. That's not the point. I didn't reply. I've been pushing people away. I can't believe I sat in this flat for so long, just me and the dog.'

I negotiate silently with myself, come to see the obvious, and nod, satisfied. 'I will go to your thirtieth. I promise. I owe it to you. I'm going to make amends. I think we should have more weekends like this.'

She agrees, and I kiss her, and our escape is accompliced. A cacophony fades as we hurtle-clatter-faster-faster on the truth that happiness is our just desert, because we have made it so, made it ours to seize, made it.

It is like sleep. It is just so easy to fall into.

21:46 'Here, tell me what you think of this,' she shouts, from behind a door, ajar.

I'm in front of my bedroom mirror hair-brushing myself when Grace flits in and starts stabbing at the screen of her phone, like we're old-marrieds on a road trip seeking detours or antidotes to prior ones.

She tells me she's found a nice lesbian bar in Vesterbro, the trendiest part of the city – then clarifies it had better be nice, because it's the only place for queer women in a ten-mile radius. It's inclusive, she says, without feeling the need to unpack the word.

22:19 A full bus, steaming cologne and burped cider, a journey thick with the wafted exuberance of a Saturday night, a metal cage of raucous talk progressing over the suburbs.

Grace and I put our heads together in development of a plan, a manner of trying ourselves out for something. We will pretend to be an old couple – correction: an established couple – on a weekend break. But in its way, the relationship counteracts the lie. All romances are an accumulation of references, memories and language indistinguishable from the outside from a work of fiction. Observers will expect us to be peculiar and impenetrable, elusive, even evasive. We won't be surprising anyone.

Indeed, as the trip proceeds along the streets and their corners, as marinara and fermented grape backwash inside us like the contents of a milk carton, the lie makes so much sense that it becomes its own diamantine truth. It is increasingly obvious that if we told the bargoers we were anything other than a loving couple they would simply never believe us.

I drain a bottle of white on the bus and dispose of it in a metal road-side litter bin overspilled with beer bottles and the odd nitrous-oxide canister.

We move as triple agents, triple-airhorn-blasting through the city, high in pitch and spirit, copen-honking.

22:41 The bar is on a narrow and sonorous side street, tucked within the tucked-within. Its only indicator is an unlit sign over the door, a permanent fixture impersonating a temporary one, which reads, simply, *Machi*, as if to say: if you don't know what this is, you don't need to be here.

The place is small on the inside, fit for no more than forty people, lit in a faltering fashion by small lamps on the tables and along the far wall, so everything is smeared with a dusky glow. The windows are covered with pride flags and posters of geisha girls, invisible from outside but eye-catching from the position of patronage.

We're only there half a minute when a couple offers to buy us a drink. 'We're always happy to see new people,' one of them says, as she approaches with an eager smile.

Grace demurs. 'You're grand, thanks,' she says, and the grand woman looks confused.

Instead, Grace buys me something expensive with berries, which goes down as easy as Calpol: a triumphant red concoction with crushed ice on top, and an intact strawberry and mint leaf to garnish.

There are no free seats, so we bring our teetering cocktail glasses back to the couple. They scoot over to make room for us on their bench, which backs into the wall facing the windows so we're all sitting in a row, like a Broadway troupe, stars in the centre, hangers-on at the sides. I am at the end closest the door.

Emma and Danielle are their names – they're both stout and blonde and probably about forty, but distinguishable by Emma's boxy glasses and Danielle's sweater, which says: *Anything You Can Do, I Can Do Bleeding.*

Emma asks us where we're from, over the sound of chatter and Tori Amos.

Grace detaches from her straw. 'Ireland. We're here to visit,' she says, as if talking to a passport inspector.

'Oh, Ireland,' Emma says, the wall preventing her from slipping fully backwards as she flops into memory. 'We've been to Ireland. Galway is wonderful. And the *countryside!* Where in Ireland are you from?'

'We're from Dublin.'

'Oh, yes. Dublin is very nice.'

'Dublin's a kip,' Grace says, in the grip of her cocktail.

'A what?'

'It's not nice. It's ugly and expensive and everyone is homeless.'

I assume people think the Irish are being bashful when we come out with these complaints, a this-old-thing response to our pretty little country. But the truth – well, people like us, the oppressed, don't get to define the truth, do we? So maybe it's youthful disillusionment, or post-colonial landschmertz, or maybe we're like James Baldwin's white gays, bemoaning our thwarted entitlement to the wages of our race, to riches and power and dominance.

I take a drink. You would too.

Danielle tilts her head forward, emerging as if from nowhere. 'Yes, it was expensive when we were there.' Grace and I nod sagely.

Eventually, we allow them to invest in us, and over second cocktails Emma imparts the history of the bar. It's a hundred years old and was once reputed as a meeting spot for sex workers, who came from Asia to serve and service a local clientele – hence the cultural appropriation on the walls. The reason the bar is so small is that no one ever stayed for long: the girls would perch themselves against the counter and the men would strut in and take them away.

Emma tells us that the place was known as a *luderbar,* and explains that *luder* is the Danish for 'a prostitute, as in whore', a definition charmingly jurisprudential. It's enjoyable too that a place that was once an escape for a certain kind of man now falls under the feet of a certain kind of woman – there is a satisfying symmetry to it, like the reclamation of a slur once grunted under breath.

My phone buzzes. A text from Grace, saying:

wanna take ya to a whorebar whorebar x

23:35 When Emma and Danielle's friends arrive, we begin to feel like the fifth and sixth wheels of their Saturday night. Off we drift, assuming the role of outsiders at someone else's party, stalking on the outskirts of relevance, looking for a way in.

We end up with a group of Americans, three of them, who leave words with us like belongings. Remarks, compliments, impersonations – I feel inhabited by them like a rental car. The man in the group mentions having dated a girl from Celbridge. Grace says Celbridge girls have a reputation back home, and he takes the bait without question.

I suppose it reminds me why I once enjoyed socialising as an Irish person: because abroad I am Irish, but in Ireland I was no one. Talking to foreigners, I can see in their eyes their desire to imagine I am of the rainy little rock, the insufferable man with the beard, the pompous man with the sunglasses, the lady in the castle who sings about boats, of them all.

In Scandinavia, Irishness became another mothy cloak to be dwelt under – then my life changed, and now that kind of perfidy doesn't work anymore. My nationality is no longer the first thing people notice about me.

One of the women is thrilled to hear of our craggy psychogeography. 'A gorgeous, gorgeous city,' she says of Dublin, surely two gorgeouses too many, and her tidy mousey fringe swishes as she talks.

After a time we curl ourselves around another set of names. Aubrey is the one with the fringe and the other woman is Mamie – 'not Amy, I'll hit you if you call me Amy' – who wears avocado earrings that merit an admiring remark from Grace. (Twenty-five dollars on Etsy. Mamie doesn't know what that is in euros.)

The man's name is Mark. ('Aubrey, Mamie and Mark,' Grace says. 'You guys should be a band!') He has a Tom-from-MySpace grin and declares he is straight but will be on his best behaviour for the night, to which I smile and nod politely, platonically, pews-at-a-funerally. As part of his cultural exchange he's brought with him a quantity of dandruff, which decorates his shoulders like stars on a flag.

The group went to college together in Ohio and are now travelling through Europe for the spring, with a view to spending the summer in Berlin. (Grace and I trade a smirk at this.)

The three of them were in Lapland a month ago, and show us toothy pictures of themselves being pulled by huskies, then a picture of a perturbed reindeer. '*Vaadin*, that's what the reindeer are called,' Mark says. '*Vaaaaadin*,' he says again, stretching out the first syllable so his mouth is ellipsoid and just as worldly as the rest of him. 'Not Rudolph.' He laughs, and I do too, even though I want to strangle him.

I imagine asking them about the Sámi and them telling me they've never heard of her. The whole thing reminds me of nothing more than being in my early twenties and hearing stories of the Camino and the Inca Trail and Northern California, the adventures other people got to go on by dint of being other people.

While I'm on my way back from the toilet, one of the women, once again nameless, comes over and tells me she's very proud of me, then puts her hand on my arm and mutters something about 'that motherfucker Trump' so I can smell a snap of gin on her breath.

I say thank you, bereft of a more inspiring reply, then mention that the bathroom is nice, to which the woman doubles with deep-chewed laughter. 'Very good,' she says, in by-the-way acknowledgement of a secret code I'm not sure I have used.

Sunday, 00:08 When she first sees me, I want to run away.

Caught in the teeth of the stalwart sound, the portentous chatter heavy with false promise, the bubble-pop sound of wet glass on wood, I look for an escape from this woman, cut more delicately from the same pattern as me.

I have floated on the crowd like a lotus, but now I sink beneath her as she smiles, and walks, still smiling.

Grace carries on talking to the Americans, but I have gone mad. I am silently calculating the distance between this woman's nose and mouth, to prove a point, to sign a warrant by which I may hang myself.

She has black hair, chrome-black, so black I take it for granted it is dyed. Green eyes. A mid-Atlantic accent. Next to me, I see she is half a foot taller. I am a flattened-out piece of cardboard. Her name is Leyla.

'Nice to meet you,' she says, and I feel like a duck being hand-given bits of bread.

I introduce myself, and by the farts of my brain a pronoun declaration breaks out. I am given a choice, but the last thing I want now is responsibility for anything.

They go to shake my hand, but I end up manoeuvring it into a hug, because I get it into my head that that's the Scandinavian way, but of course it's not the way with strangers. We embrace unfully, like an old fridge door bulging shut.

'I've never said hello to someone at a bar and given them my pronouns before,' they say.

I shake my head. 'I'm a huge dope.'

'Are you Irish?'

'Yeah. Maybe that's why I did it.'

We find some space against the countertop, between beermats and wiped droplets. 'Are you based in the city?' I ask.

They live in Herlev, a nothing-much suburb pocked with outlet stores and spired by a twenty-five-storey hospital. Leyla is originally from a town near the German border, but doesn't bother telling me which one. 'Herlev is better,' they say.

'I live in Frederiksberg,' I say.

'Holy shit, are you rich?'

'No. I don't think so. I have a dog.' I take out my phone and start moving through the photo gallery, through selfies and colour-chart scenery until I find a decent one of Dolly, sat in front of me on the bed with her right front paw raised.

'Oh, she's amazing! She looks like a baby cloud. You live in Frederiksberg with a little dog? What a cute lifestyle. Like a film.'

'Yeah, it is.' I look at the shining image in front of me with satisfaction. Perhaps it's the lifestyle, or maybe it's the compliments – either way, I have found water to tread where once there was only useless air.

Leyla possesses an unearned ease with the world. There is so much home in them, a half-light sufficiency, as they tell me of their room in someone else's house, their bar job, a cartoon – *Bertie* something – I've never seen before, the life of human yieldings under which they have fallen like a crab beneath a second-hand shell.

The less of ourselves we surrender, the more we get to keep. A misshape life has its small acts of revelation, in domesticity, in care, in family found and stumbled upon. It is highly charged. It is a distillation of everything. We paint nails instead of walls, standing no less solid for that.

I ask them how they stay sane, and they point to a group of friends sitting at a table.

'How did you meet them?' I ask, quivering adolescently on the borderline between small talk and a plea for guidance.

'I met them a few years ago, when I was in college.'

'What did you do in college?' I respond, unable to hide my expectations of this free spirit, this self-clamping umbilicus.

They close their eyes. 'Lots of stuff. Dropped out, mainly. It's no big deal.'

'Oh. I'm sorry to hear that. And it is no big deal.'

'But I make prints and stuff.'

'Prints?'

'Art. Let me show you.' They present to me on their phone a dreamy picture of a setting sun – on our planet or another, it hardly matters – the image a war of colour, all blues and conflicted oranges. It is both rage and serenity. It balances them.

'Did you draw this?' I ask, and they nod.

The screen is too small for the image, so to see it properly I have to manipulate it, to manipulate myself, my tequila fingers and nothing-a.m. eyes, zooming in and out, over and back. Instead of a picture, it's more like a picture book: a thread of glimpses summing to meaning, a satiating piecemeal. It is probably the way life should be read. So much is obscured by the absolute.

I stand and stare and ponder Leyla's silence, how frequently they find it, and what it would be like to encounter.

There are black figures on a plain, walking, a pack of them. 'Are these wolves?' I ask.

'They're just creatures,' Leyla says. 'They're not really anything.'

'I was thinking if they were wolves we could say we had exchanged dog pics.'

They smile at me, one wasted on this or any bar. 'Please buy a copy,' they say. 'I could use the money. If you liked it.'

I say yes, and in my head it already decorates my borrowed rooms.

If you spend a weekend walking anywhere, you might never meet your exact likeness, but, in the aggregate, you'll find that no part of you is without precedent, or without hope. The city has its ways. It yawns and I awake.

Grace spots us and comes over, carrying a drink I don't remember her buying. Realising I have not yet mentioned her to Leyla, I am left with the task of crafting another falsity, tailored to the ear of the recipient.

01:41 Dirty shoes, washing machine heart, usual lipstick.

The same song, for the second time in an hour. Grace and I slow-dance, somehow, awkwardly, in drain-circles.

She smells of Leyla's cigarettes. She grazes me on the cheek, once and again and again.

The women from before are here, the ones who bought us drinks, and one of them is wearing star-shaped glasses. She smiles at me. I can't remember her name.

Leyla's coming to visit us. We agreed before they left. We're going to show them everything. We will demonstrate the country like an airplane seatbelt. We will pull on it tightly. The pissy pubs. The small-person museum. The coastal route from suburb A to suburb B. They will hate it.

I don't know where I live anymore. It is hallucination upon hallucination. Phoebe, Phoebe, figment, something into which I have thrown myself so forcefully that I am free of reality's cut.

It could be, it might be, it is, it is a wedding, not mine, one I have picked up off the ground, and it is dreadful. It is a three-star hotel. My belly is full of mashed carrot and biscuit cake.

Why not me? Why not me?

The music is quieter, rhythms, concentric. Lines of light, lines of sound, lines on her palms on which I am traced, time lines, dual.

Excuses to go back, there have been so many, so many too-perfect excuses to go back, to go back to where I left my adulthood, to be excused back there.

Grace whispers noiselessly, wordlessly, blurredly into my ear. A passion without language thrills along my lobe and up the side of my head.

The world now seen through curious hands.

There is a cumulation. The music stops and someone swears in a woman's voice.

Grace whispers that she loves me, and we are long gone, raw air in our lungs, and the city we share with a heaving infantry of busy faces presents itself to us. Its darknesses, its promising absences, its sparse, fecund corners are now spots in which we may at last live and grow, like mould on wholesome bread, like some exquisite disease.

We are the secrets of the city and we are infectious.

Grace is drunk. To the twenty-four-hour metro we walk as if to fly. Down Vesterbrogade, past glassy financial buildings and dormant roadworks, until she sees a poster for Dua Lipa and sings and sings, cries of sultry freedom, desolate bodies given voice. The maleness of untrammelled femininity.

The red bricks and copper rooves give way to a greenish light in which we seem to swim.

'That's it,' I say. 'I'm officially never going to a bar again. I'm old now.'

'You're not old,' Grace says.

'I want to be old. I want to live in a big house and drink wine out of a cardboard box while suitors come and go. And,' I say, wielding a sanguine index, 'I want to have Dolly by my side, in an urn on the mantelpiece.'

There is fizzing laughter, in the form of applause, in the form of congratulation. We chant, 'No-ra Forde, No-ra Forde.'

I lip-kiss her on the scuffed outlie of a shuttered Vietnamese restaurant. It is five past three in the morning.

03:32 Grace wants another cigarette, so we enter a 7-Eleven whose frontage hums like Christmas artifice.

Inside, an immediate thump of fluorescence and sterility, and something unwelcoming in night-time eyes, eyes knowing and given to mete out.

I tell Grace I'll wait on the street as she joins a queue

of about half a dozen, purse and phone in hand. She says nothing, deferring with a nod.

Out I stand, nestled by the shop window, humoured by the deranged caffeine-light of my phone.

It is now the last day of March. In a matter of weeks, the people here will rent boats and sunbathe on canals – ostentatious heaty displays, the turning season not merely an experience but a gesture.

As I stand in blackness, body in retreat against the fabric of my coat, I stitch myself into thoughts of summer.

Life trickles by in near-silence. Like swimming birds surrounded by surface tension, the fine detail of the people is indiscernible. Shadows move over the skin of the street: couples stewarding themselves, solitary traipsing strangers, the occasional sour policeman. An ambulance strings itself through the narrowness.

Shapes with hoarse football-chant voices inch towards me from my right, stereophonic.

One of them shouts, melody in menace, and instinct warns that I am the target, but I don't move. He continues. Maybe it's shouting, or maybe I am so unused to the casual talk of men that I mistake it for rage.

I could close my eyes, pick a fight with object permanence, but nothing lives as short as I want it to. I have been socialised an object, not acting but acted upon.

Another man comes over and tries to drag the loud man away. They speak quickly and with force, breathing complicated air at each another.

I say nothing.

I don't know why they are here, what they want from me. There is no explanation I could offer that would not make things worse. I have no voice but the wrong one.

Grace hears them and leaves the shop. She starts talking at the men in English. She makes armour of herself, baring teeth, a scar-tissue disposition. She says, 'Leave her alone,' again and again like a running motor. Then there is a sudden movement, unseen, and the loud man is restrained, and we

go
left
right
left
right

stereophonic. beep test. conditions: baltic. difficulty: medium(??)

I rush through the personal space of a middle-aged woman in a fur coat. She has red double-barrel hair, a turret of it, and scowls in chastisement, motherly.

I am spat out by the street as by my own biography. It was all eyes and I couldn't bear the looking.

left
right
left
right

The body has a sound – strike it and there is a tone. The way he used to grind in his uniform, the worried threads of his school crest, the way he made suitable use of me, all those years ago. The sensation of him against me. The way I wanted to be there. The way he was proving a point that rang with truth like the bell on the church beside the school grounds. The way half the world sniffs out freshness and selfhood and difference and thrashes it about like so many cats and so many mice. The way girls are treated in boys' schools. The way everyone knew before I did. Who am I to question it? Who am I at all?

I make myself an echo in an act of protection.

left
right
left

right

There is nothing behind me, but still I run, until the delusion of my limbs becomes its own exhilaration. The pressure of the ground against my feet as I move over it becomes an embrace, so I could go on for ever.

I sink into the street, into a pureness. It is a thrill to live life in endless battle. The problem is, I have mistaken my skirmishes for life itself. I see life without struggle as a kind of death, so I run and run, until I fall again, and then everything is familiar, and I am under my mother's roof. Pain has become a heartbeat more real than the one within me.

I am
left
left
left

on the ground outside Michael Kors.

A small piece of broken glass has pierced the palm of my right hand, and my body gasps into life, hasty throbs of blood trickling over my skin. I lie there, subject to a flash from a phone camera, to a shape that moves away.

Grace stops and turns around. She helps me up and we walk the final two hundred metres to the station slowly, holding one another, muttering startled apologies to the sides of one another's heads.

The weekend collapses on itself, re-experienced as bristles of white and grey, colour drained, bled onto cold streets, three hearts, two hearts, one heart, stop.

04:02 The light is harsh and the sound of the electric engine resembles a Hammond organ.

There are only a few people on the train, silent save for a group of girls behind us who speak periodically over the sound of music from a phone speaker. The singing, like the light, is jagged: daring intruders, pushing them away. It is a border that polices itself.

I realise after a minute or two that Grace is crying, spilling from untidily made-up eyes onto the back of her hand as it covers her mouth, nail polish eroded.

'Here, here,' she says.

'Where?'

'Here.'

04:27 Grace holds my hand as the cold tap runs over it, and there is an ache down to the child-bones in my palm. She asks me where Camilla puts the plasters, and I can't remember, so I sit on the couch while she courses through the flat, until she finds them in a drawer beneath the cutlery.

'Now,' she says, as she places the rectangle carefully on my hand and wraps a bandage around it. The only noise is the sound of the dog snoring next to us.

I start talking to her about hospitals. I tell her that I broke my arm once when I was a child, on holiday in Lancashire. I was six years old, standing on a wall, and as I jumped off my legs moved awkwardly and I landed on my side, and the weight of me, slight as it was, landed entirely on my forearm. I spent a night in the infirmary. I was a little soldier – that's what they called me. The nurse offered me butties and I laughed because I didn't know what a butty was. And the hospital at night, the wonder of it: the darkened institution, to a child's eye reminiscent of being in an empty school after hours, awesome and terrifying.

I loved hospitals then. I wanted to be solved like a jigsaw puzzle over a bank-holiday weekend, to have the collected parts of me assembled in their proper place. I needed to believe that someone would know what to do with me.

Now, I no longer see myself as something to be cured.

Now, I will hobble around on a mass of broken bones and take pride in them, because if what lies within me is sick then I no longer care to be well.

'I remember,' I say to her. I am full of rememberings.

Somewhere in the midst of my chatter I manage to fall asleep, and I dream of the sea, and what Grace said earlier in the day proves itself: its vastness is humbling. I dream of the hidden beach on Howth Head, with its back to the city of Dublin and the harbour in the village, facing away, contemplating escape. A stamp of stones and sand on an envelope of jagged sky-scraping rock. The arduous stairway-to-heaven walk to it, over crags and through stinging nettles. The way the vast monster of the sea is bound, channelled by this fluke of nature, so that it becomes a private tapestry for the select few willing and capable of the journey.

How nothing is ever as terrifying as it looks from the common vantage point.

08:10 I am awoken by Dolly licking my face. By a contrivance, we've both ended up on the bed, in our traditional positions, though I have no memory of how. I hear the scrambled roar of rain outside the window, a noise that seems to claw at the back of my eyes. I kiss the top of the dog's head and she licks my wrist, careful to avoid the bandage.

The place is empty. I look to the kitchen and sitting room. I grab my phone from the coffee table, running at six per cent battery, and there is a single text message on it. It says, simply, again:

Sorry

Ten thousand nine hundred and ninety-five

Sunday

10:05 To start with, a raggy white T-shirt and a pair of pea-green pyjama bottoms chequered with hundreds of iterations of the word *wonderful*.

I am dry heaving into a toilet bowl, sting of stomach acid cresting behind my face, awakened again into the dregs of the night before. My retching is unproductive. All that comes out is a stream of transparent gloop forming an island of bubbles on the surface of the water. Though it looks like nothing, I flush it anyway.

The plaster on my hand has congealed into a mass of the rubbery and sticky and my mouth tastes of the same. I wash my hands and replace the bandage.

The dining table: I go to it, but do not eat. Its four legs and flat surface are lacking in anything and all but empty of me. Breakfast is for beginnings. Nothing here is broken. Nothing new has been revealed. Grace can look after herself – it's the one thing she has always been good at. She suits herself and the rest of us have to wear her.

I'm vaguely aware of where she's staying – or rather, where she was supposed to be before she took to me. A flat-pack hotel near the airport, more vending machine than minibar, twenty minutes on a train. But ambush comes less naturally to me. I am setting a good example by leaving her alone.

The same white wooden chair on which Grace ate dinner on Friday evening, where she told me how boring she thought she was, and I reassured her parentally. And maybe I was lying then, maybe, but she has proven me right. Now she is gone and knuckle-crack quiet is all I have for accompaniment.

Dolly is absent with leave, still dozing at the end of my bed. There's nothing strange about the scene at all: a slice of life, albeit one thin as paper. Today I have yawned and shambled into the same existence I have stepped into every Sunday morning for a burrow of years.

The morning has the consistency of a swallowed belch. Through the window in front of me, misted with patches of condensation like diced onion, the apartment block across the courtyard is visible, its brickwork darkened so it is the colour of blood. An Irish downpour is in progress outside, rain like sin, sticking to everything. The weary daylight scatters on the blinds so they come to resemble bars, a mechanism of control.

Amid everything, the clocks have gone forward, so what little light there is has itself a new name. In a different universe, I will have made sure to change them shortly before bed last night, sometime between half past ten and eleven. I will have adjusted the small alarm clock beside my bed that I do not need and do not look at. I will have manipulated the clock beside the plate cupboard in the kitchen, whose small plastic hands I will have turned manually, for fear that, if I take it down, I will never be able to hang it up again. Like clockwork, I will have worked the clocks. Yet now, days and hours prevail to blindside me.

Grace has taken my routine and, for the moment, I opt to let her keep it.

I am so secure here that I could be persuaded these walls have been built around me – that I am a quiet part of the masonry, a nick waiting to expand into a crack waiting to expand into the awful open. Existence teases with the repellence of routine. But isn't that how it always goes? Choice becomes habit, habit becomes necessity, necessity becomes restraint. People are impaled on the pointed and painted front gates of their own lives.

Dolly strides in quietly, sweating across the floor, stretching her legs with each step. I put some food in a bowl for her, into which she eagerly presses her face, the combination producing a wet scarfing noise. I also give her a dog treat shaped like a length of rope, which looks like liquorice and smells disgraceful.

I go to the kitchen and make coffee, watching the granules surprise back and forth behind the glass of the cafetière. The livid randomness of small things. The stochastic nature of everything. Knowing how something is made doesn't stop each iteration being slightly different from the last – so much can go thrillingly awry between the hard lines of A and B. What I'm in it for mostly, though, is the smell. In lieu of sitting with myself, I sit with this.

A mug steadying from hot to merely warm. After fifteen minutes staring at the words *You Are Loved* on its side, trying to remember if the thing was a gift or if I bought it for myself, I pour the liquid down the sink, rinsing it away like it's wine I have tasted and dutifully spat out.

On the sofa, crying and I don't know why. Dolly is at my feet. I am not sad – all I feel is the oppressive heat against the back of my eyes. It is an honour to cry. It didn't always come so easily. It is permission. It is a foundation. Every time I do it, I make a fortress of myself, great stones and cannons and drawbridges, something strong and distinct. People are born in blood but baptised by the saltwater of subjectivity, which tells us we are free and separate – spiritedly and hauntedly separate.

I take out my phone and write a message to Grace.

I love you. Let me know if you need anything.

I hope you're safe x

And away it goes.

11:23 Ana is there, always. A thought, disguised as a person, against which other thoughts may be bounced.

Instead of texting her for advice, I simply unfurl the conversation in my head. She'd see Grace and me as characters in a romance novel. 'The one-bed trope,' she'd say, and I'd have to explain that we haven't yet made it a whole night in the same bed. She'd want us to be together. She'd want to meet Grace, to bake cherry strudel for us to eat at her flat as we tell her how we permanently and irrevocably fell in love over an ice-slip of a weekend.

More than anything, though, she'd see that moments like the one surrounding me are the staff of life. The trouble is that Ana's dreams always exceed her. I've had these conversations in reverse. I get texts about guys she knows at work, a dude she saw tonguing a vanilla pastry at Espresso House, another of life's great loves stood behind the cash desk at Åhléns. A procession of bullion-haired six-foot-twos whom I hear of once and never again. Ana has a dramatist's body, with the defined neck muscles of someone constantly scoping for chance encounters.

I'm not sure she ever even talks to these men. Her stories have the quality of a monologue, events unrequited. She makes sure to tell me them anyway, as if to remind me that love is all around as long as you reach out for it – it's just that she never does.

Ana would tell me to go to Grace's hotel, and that would be a disaster.

I am surrounded by makers of bad decisions, limpeted

to those who have planted mistakes and let them grow to shadowy heights.

When I am alone and there is no one around to laugh at me, I like to think I have in my being an honourable ascetic quality. But, really, I'm just looking for the same validation as everyone else. People get caught between peculiar and its opposite, they pick the one closest to them and then spend the rest of their lives reassuring themselves they have made the right choice, a war with an imagined enemy fought on the terrain of their own regret.

11:45 The search for distractions becomes a pastime in its own right. All I stumble upon are cartoons, canned-laughter sitcoms and tedious Danish talk shows hosted by mannequin-people far more attractive than they have any business being at this time of day. As I comb through programmes, I mutter comments to Dolly – 'She's had work done on that jawline, hasn't she, my baby?', 'They used to show that on TG4 back in the day, my beautiful darling' – but she just lies next to me twisted like a pastry, taking no notice.

I decide to check. And there they are: two blue ticks. She has seen the message. She is alive.

In a search bar, I write *leyla herlev*. A floor-plan of words appears and it takes a few seconds to make sense of it. Herlev has a hospital – they mentioned a hospital, didn't they – so all that appears on the screen are doctors called Leyla. It's a relief, I tell myself – isn't it? The only meaningful thing that could possibly emerge from this search is a record of criminal behaviour. I wasn't looking for that. I don't know what I was looking for. The prosecutorial nature of a deep creep is such that it's best not to examine motives too closely.

Last night, while Grace and Leyla were smoking outside, we all talked about breast milk – which men in history would have had the tastiest breast milk. We must have been discussing transition, and then Grace did what Grace so frequently does, latching onto the topic, so to speak. We agreed it would vary from man to man, without a stereotypical flavour. Leyla said Marlon Brando's breast milk would be like cheese. Grace said ricotta, and we all laughed.

I said Michael Collins's milk would be salty and weak. West Cork: seafood diet.

Leyla said if men, cis men, could make breast milk, it would be like cryptocurrency. People would invest in it – thousands of dollars in every squirt. It would be prestige milk.

There was a song. We wrote our own lyrics. Not about Brando or Collins, about Napoleon. We all agreed Napoleon would've had hearty breast milk, sufficient to feed the population of Elba. He'd have an army of loyalists boiling water to keep it fresh. And the song – ABBA, of course. *Waterloo, something something.* I can't remember it now.

I stop trying to reminisce and start playing music through the Bluetooth speaker. It is lo-fi and ambient – deluxe, premium silence, really; ad-free if you pay for it. I pick up Dolly and start swinging her around the room. She panics and claw-grasps my arm. Then I put her on the sofa and she immediately lies flat as a meatloaf, as if to prevent me lifting her.

I turn the music off and look again at my phone, at the one-word text Grace sent to me and the longer one I sent in response. I stare at it for over a minute, as if by the power of mind something might happen. I close the app and tell my phone to fuck off as I put it down again.

And then I remember: *Waterloo, Bonaparte's jugs are for me and you.*

12:23 There is only one person I can talk to about this: someone with whom I share DNA and little else. Michelle, her husband and their one-year-old son live in a newbuild near Malahide which they'll still be paying for by the heat death of the universe. They have rail and road connections to Dublin city centre, a kitchen island, and an artisanal coffee grinder they never use because they never drink coffee that isn't made professionally and served in a compostable paper cup.

Michelle has pushed a small person out of herself – largely, I suspect, in an effort to keep up with her friend group, and, perhaps, to exploit the various parental perks offered by the government department where she is employed.

Her name is Michelle McCabe on my phone. I changed it when she got married.

I listen to an Irish dial tone as I wait for her to pick up.

'Hello?'

'Hi, Shell.'

'Hmmm, howdy stranger! How are you?'

'I'm okay. Weather's miserable here. How are you? How's Sam?'

'Sam's grand, his teeth are annoying him. I'm about to give him a feed. Is everything okay?'

'Yeah, why wouldn't it be?'

'Because I don't think I've ever got a phone call from you on a Sunday morning before.'

'It's just . . . it's Grace.'

'Grace?'

'Keaney.'

'Oh! Grace Keaney. Blast from the past. Actually, I heard from her a few weeks ago.'

'Yeah, I know. She's here. Not right here. But she's in Copenhagen. You gave her my address and now she's here.'

'Wow. God, she was always a bit, you know, a bit mad

like that, wasn't she? Impulsive. Sorry for turning you in. She didn't tell me she was going to visit.'

'It's fine, listen, that's not why I'm ringing. There was an incident last night and now Grace is gone.'

'An incident?'

'It's a long story. I injured my hand.'

'Are you all right? Did you go to hospital?'

'No . . . it's not like that. It's been disinfected and all. It's fine.'

'Is Grace okay?'

'I don't know . . . I think so.'

'Do you want me to tell Mam?'

'Jesus, no, she'll be on the first plane over. I'm just . . . I suppose I wanted to vent. It doesn't matter.'

'Did you hear about the drama at home?'

'Drama?'

'Mam was on to me about it at seven yesterday evening, while I was in the middle of putting Sam down. She's had three kids herself and still no consideration. Anyway, breaking news. The shower's broken. It kept cutting out when Mam was using it. She thought she was going to get electrocuted. They've had it since we were kids, now she says it's clapped out.'

'Right.'

'Dad said he was going to fix it himself. Dad, who couldn't fix a drink! Mam said she didn't trust him not to kill her. She said if it was a choice between divorce and being six feet under Glasnevin, she'd choose divorce.'

'Christ.'

'I think she was joking. She also said the only thing she has to live for is Idris Elba's next film. Course, Liam's going spare. He's having to shower at the girlfriend's house.'

'Fleur?'

'Is that her name? I haven't a breeze.'

'I think that's her name, yeah.'

'Right. Are . . . are you sure you're okay?'

'No, I'm fine. What do you think I should do, though?'

'I don't know. I . . . don't . . . know. Grow up, maybe? You and Grace are a bit old for this craic. You're doing a PhD, not the Leaving Cert.'

'Yeah. True. Sorry for bothering you.'

'Ah no, it's grand. Sorry if I'm being harsh, I've been up since quarter to five. Sometimes I wish I was globetrotting like you. Seeing the world. Sowing your . . . well, you know, seeing the world. You can call and bother me whenever you want. I wish you'd do it more. We all do. We're always thinking of you. Give my regards to the bitch.'

'What?'

'Dolly, isn't that what she's called?'

'Oh, right. Thanks, Shell.'

12:37 Michelle and I were close enough in age that we might have been friends, but distinct enough in personality that we never fully took to it. She's never called me her sister, not to my face – but it was never in my nature to make demands of my family. They are freshwater people. It took the imposition of so much saltwater between us to make our differences clear.

Michelle saved my life once – though we never called it that, either. It was just one of the many mishaps that afflicts a young child. It'll probably happen to Sam soon enough, and then Michelle will have the opportunity to rescue another small boy.

My hair was blond then. I had a shock of fair curls, like a spaghetti-twirl of yellow wool on a ragdoll, which grew darker and straighter over time.

We were at a holiday camp in the Cork countryside. It was the summer of 1993, I think, shortly before I started school.

My parents could always afford foreign holidays, but went without – perhaps they wanted us to appreciate the beauty of our own country. How much beauty there was to imbibe in faux chalets, miniature golf and smoky canteens is another thing altogether.

The park had an indoor swimming pool, vast by a child's standards, which was encircled by a snaky yellow water slide. In those days, visiting a swimming pool was a once-a-year event for Irish children, and getting to one with a slide was a Kodak moment on a par with having your school visited by aging basketball players or President Mary Robinson.

I dawdled in the toddlers' pool. My father was sitting on a lounger reading the *Sunday Independent*, probably poring over Terry Keane's gossip column and muttering to himself about the behaviour of C-listers he could scarcely have identified in a police line-up. (These events took place before the Moriarty Tribunal robbed him of his faith in the rich and famous.) My mother was elsewhere – her idea of a holiday didn't involve looking after children.

The warm, chlorinated water gave me the kind of hug no human being could ever provide. It was a being which held the potential of righting wrongs.

I didn't so much get into difficulty as create it for myself. I threw my head under the surface, allowing the recirculated liquid to pillow me. But then I lost control, I tried to breathe, and felt the sting of the water against the back of my nose and knew I had erred again. Michelle was there to grab me and haul me out of the water, all buck-teeth, 'What do you think you're doing?'

A lifeguard came over with a whistle and a sing-song accent, but by the time his hairy wet legs carried him to us the mission was complete.

I was never more comfortable with Michelle than I was when she was saving me. She was every inch the older sibling:

bigger, and practical, and protective. She knew how the world worked, and, at some point, I assumed she'd take the time to teach me. Hers was a shadow in which I was content to grow quietly, slowly.

At some age, some early teens age, I realised I had become taller than her. I ended up outstanding her by about eight inches. That was why I needed to run away: because I outgrew her. She tells me to grow up, but growing up is all I have ever done. That was the problem.

Michelle's life went through phases. She played hockey, for a time. She was into some sort of rock music, for a time. She socialised exclusively with gay men, for a time. My life was conspicuously without this ebb and flow. Invisibility was my antidote to size. I became dutiful and predictable. I chose not to live. I made myself vast and forgettable, like a great plain on which anonymous grains are grown to be processed into nothing foods, big and unimportant.

I cannot explain to my sister how she broke my heart. I cannot explain it to myself. Perhaps it is best to think of it as a sickness: amoral, defying rational thought.

Ten minutes after the call ends, my phone buzzes with a set of pictures from Michelle. Sam is sitting with his plush toys: Elmo caught in his right arm, smile on his face. He is also blond.

13:02 The post, on the sixteenth of November 2016. I remember what I said: *I'll still be the same person you've always known.* That was a lie, these people didn't know me, but, more than that, it was a hostage to fortune – how could I know who I'd end up being?

Three days later, I woke up in my flat in Lund and discovered the announcement had gained two more likes in the early hours of that morning. Numbers 112 and 113. They were two women I had gone to college with. I knew the two of them knew each other. I imagined them, out for a Friday night, in the smoking area of some club in Dublin, talking about what had become of that sheepish lad from Intro to Sociology.

Grace is here because of that post, and her own reaction to it, whatever it was.

The past is parented: it is something that may be crawled back into, like a mother. The past belongs to everyone, while the present aches with solitude. That is why people fear the present and the future – because they are a confrontation with the unknown forces of others, to say nothing of themselves. Better instead to be a constant and unwilling diarist, innocent of all but the committing of words to paper, because, if there is no future, there is nothing left to do but endlessly scrutinise the past, to inspect it for proof we've got what we deserve.

Grace has left so much here. Literally. She has two days' worth of clothes in my bedroom. A tranche of personal history. She has taken nothing but keys, her phone and money. Everything is still here. She has done this deliberately. She has run away because she wants to be found, because she wants to be looked for.

Now I have a wild goose to chase.

In the kitchen, with my phone in my hand, I mentally draft and redraft a message for her – but, by the time my brain connects to my fingers, what emerges is simple:

Hi. I'd like to talk to you in person. Please let me know if that's okay and where you are x

Forty-five seconds later there is a response.

Room 142

I listen to the fizzing rain outside, exhale deeply, and go to get my heaviest coat.

13:51 'Smooth Operator' is playing at a low volume. I sweep across the hotel lobby, drying the soles of my boots on purple carpet as I go, every third step a covert slide, so that equal attention is given to left and right. There is a pomo chandelier teetering over the foyer, an assortment of plastic balls thinly coated with gold paint – impressive from a distance, but, the closer I get, the more it resembles a molecular model from a science lab owned by Liberace.

A group of young women on my right are sitting on what looks like a large ottoman, surrounded by cabin-size suitcases, obviously too early for check-in. All are wearing earphones and one is hiding behind a pair of large round sunglasses. A pile of coats steams on the floor beside them.

I smile at the receptionist as I squeak past. She says nothing, just watches – a helpful non-response, given I have no coherent explanation for my presence. Perhaps I have learned to fake a kind of confident self-assurance, or maybe she recognises that stopping me will only exacerbate the puddle of rain drippings in front of her desk.

Presently I am a shark: surrounded by water, in need of constant movement. That is the palliative effect of a downpour; it is therapy for Irish people.

I drift between a series of indistinguishable hospital-red doors, around several corners, following the signs for Rooms 130 to 149. The purposeless propulsion of it puts me in mind of going to the departure gate at an airport – the way the walk at Kastrup seems to take you further than the plane does. The world is cheap but you pay with your knees.

Behind the door of Room 142, I hear the muffled sound of staccato talk from a television, and then, after four knocks, some movement.

Grace opens up. She has been crying, as have I, but the rain serves to disguise me. Our red eyes are ambiguous, born equally of despair and last night's cocktails.

She speaks first. 'Hi. Come in. How's your hand?'

'I'll survive. How are you?'

'I'm good. Sorry, the room is a total mess.'

Taking off my coat, I look around and see a strewn white duvet, an unzipped Adidas holdall and an empty share-bag of paprika crisps. As messes go, it is far from total.

'Do you need a towel?' she asks.

'No, you're grand.' I pause and see damp brown strings coming down over my face, so wet my infant curls look to be returning. 'Actually, yeah, no, a towel would be good.'

Grace fetches a large white towel from the bathroom and hands it to me.

I look at her as I dry my hair. 'What's going on?'

She sits down on the end of the bed and sighs, and for a moment it looks like she's going to cry again. 'I got a taxi back here. First thing this morning. Sorry for not telling you. I just wasn't able for things. It was too much.'

'You're not to blame for what happened last night.'

'I am. I shouldn't have come over here. It was a stupid thing to do.'

'That's not true. None of this is your fault. I'm glad you were here. Other people suck. I thought we agreed that other people were the problem.'

'Sit down,' Grace says. Even in despondency, she retains a flair for the frogmarch. I prop myself next to her and my additional weight perches us insecurely on the bed, so we have to heave ourselves back onto it. Grace picks up the remote control and switches off BBC World News. Behind her, through the window, I see a damp church steeple, camouflaged by a flurry of wafting trees.

We sit in silence for about thirty seconds. It is as if the truth needs to build up a head of steam within her.

Then she speaks. 'I'm sorry. For everything.'

'You have nothing to be sorry for.'

'I fuck up everything.'

'You don't. That's not true. Stop being so hard on yourself,' I say, like I am taking offence on her behalf.

'I quit my job. I did it this morning. I sent an email and then I sat here staring at the telly. And I had crisps. And then you came.'

My stomach deflates, and I sigh. 'Okay. If that's what you want, okay. You're right to move on from it if it's getting you down. Put yourself first. You'll get another job, I'm sure. You'll be fine.' I put my hand on her knee, but she shifts away immediately.

'Do you want to see my resignation email?' she asks.

'Not really, no.'

'Here.' She takes out her phone and fumbles with it for a few seconds, then hands it to me. 'Here you go.'

I look at the screen. The subject line is *I Quit*. Title case, all terrifically *J'accuse . . . !* in its righteous indignation. For a moment, I admire it. The email starts *Hiya Craig*, with no comma.

The body of the message is long, and I decide not to read it. The specifics aren't important. Work is all the same. I could say that to her, could tell her how every job, every nixer, every academic posting, increasingly every hobby, is simply a means by which interchangeable people compress themselves into the fixed identities of elsewhere profit, becoming a hideous no one in the service of a presumably beautiful someone. I could tell her that, as an inevitable consequence, all of life now seems a contoured fraudulence, every success unearned and unsustainable, every failure a scathing proof positive. But even that would sound like criticism – after all, if every option is identical, what is there to quit?

Grace probably wants to be on a permanent holiday, an entirely rational aspiration. We've been conjoined this weekend, more intimate than ever, but what she really wants is freedom, of the sort lacking in the torrid privacy of my everyday. There has been a pattern to the weekend: over and over we have ventured out only to find ourselves slug-salted by people. Perhaps we should have gone on a road trip, taken ourselves apart in every sense, made a wet fish of the world around us – but where would we go, and how would we get there? To chase horizons, you have to believe in horizons, to know they are not empty and sheer, and we've both been too hopesick for that.

'On Monday evening, at the reception desk,' Grace says, 'I had to charge someone fifty euro for a therapy session. Discount rate. He must have been unemployed or a student or something. And when I asked for the money, he just looked at me and said, "You're right, I'd be better off killing myself." And I said nothing, I just laughed and said, "Yeah," and took the fifty euro. Put it in the little cash folder. That man's dead now. I'm such a fucking bitch to people.'

'I'm sure he didn't mean it. He was probably just upset. They shouldn't make you deal with people who are suicidal.'

'They shouldn't make me deal with lots of things. Like Darren.'

I say nothing. In Grace's present voice, a man's name is story enough.

'Darren Meehan,' she says. 'Gold-standard clinical psychologist and fucking gold-standard groper. He tried to kiss me on Wednesday, the night before I arrived here. Not his first time. Nine o'clock, just as I was about to clock off for the night. Big weekend ahead of me, you know? Cunt's married with kids. I wonder what *he's* doing this weekend. Fucker's probably bringing his kids to Gaelic training, being Mister Perfect Dad. Anywhere's better than being back there,' she says, faltering. 'I can't go back.'

I stare at the wall, at the small black reading light above a desk she surely hasn't had the time to sit at. 'I'm sorry to hear that. And sorry for his wife and kids too.' I'm about to ask her if she's complained about him – indeed, if she's told anyone at all – but the rage and release in her side-profile keeps me quiet.

'He knows all the tricks,' she says. 'He knows exactly what to say to make me sound crazy. It's literally his job.'

'Gaslighting.'

'Shut up,' she grumbles. 'I didn't ask for a dictionary.' A pause. 'Sorry. It's just . . . the world is full of guys like that. People who know exactly what buttons to press to get what they want. There's diddly-shite I can do about him.'

'Yeah,' I say, punctuated by a laboured exhale. 'That's very true.' Maybe we should have spent more of this weekend bonding over a shared disdain for mental health professionals – but, in a sense, we've already spent seventy-two hours disrespecting them.

'I'm just so fucking worthless,' she says. 'It's not like depression, where you feel bad but it's irrational. You know it's just a chemical imbalance in the brain. Right now, everyone keeps showing me how worthless I am. I thought I'd get older and life would get easier. I'd figure things out. I thought – and fuck me dead, here's me being crazy – I thought people would start to respect me.'

'You'll get there,' I say. I don't know what role to play. A mothering ear, a friendly insult. Perhaps I should be the woman behind the glass screen at the dole office, asking what she wants to do next. 'Do you need a tissue?' I ask.

Grace nods.

On my way to the bathroom, I look at the top of her bed, the red headboard that covers most of the far wall, and see the faint outline of a pair of feet on it, a film of sweaty discolouration. She might have been lying like that when she sent the email. It would explain the rush of blood.

The ensuite bathroom is smaller than I expect. I get her a bundle of toilet paper, the worst possible remedy but the only one available. As before – as always, perhaps – we are children fashioning adulthood out of nothing.

I sit back down and ask her if there's anything that makes her happy. She hesitates before saying no, which is as close to a promising sign as can be expected, but, if there are any dreams in her, she draws a veil around them before I can see.

'I wish I had a neat and tidy life like you,' she says.

I bunch up my face. 'I don't think my life is neat and tidy.'

'Your life is ridiculously neat and tidy. You don't have any problems. You have an easy, boring job that pays well enough for you to live alone. Your family support you but you ignore them.'

I quickly catch and release a breath. 'It's not as straightforward as that.'

'You know what I think?' she says, and then she laughs to herself. 'I think you feel guilty that things have worked out so well for you.'

There is a long pause.

'You're entitled to your opinion,' I say.

She falls back onto the bed, onto bedsheets congealed like half-scrambled egg, and laughs to herself again. 'Here's some news from home. Here's what the gang are up to at home. I woke up this morning and there was a message on my phone from Naz. My flatmate Naz. She was on a date last night.'

'Okay,' I say, craning my neck.

'I was looking at it in the taxi on the way here. Lovely looking lad. Beautiful eyes. A marketing executive. Executive – that's at least fifty grand a year. His dick's probably phenomenal and all. Picture perfect. One thing's going to lead to another, and soon I'll be alone and homeless.' Grace's trowelled-on sincerity is indistinguishable from cynicism. She carries around a set of suppositions she can smother over others like a sheet of acetate – and perhaps it's bittersweet delusion, and maybe it's a learned reflex. I simply don't know her well enough to tell.

There is the growing sense that this weekend was the encore performance of a person who no longer truly exists – that we've been sleeping in a derelict house the night before it is to be imploded. In our own way, all either of us wants is one more day. What is catching up to Grace is not merely age, but the knowledge she is running out of new people to whom she may orient herself, like stars. It makes me wonder what damage we could have done to each other, given the chance, given more time.

I turn around and put my hand on her shoulder. 'It's not so bad. I mean, it could be worse. It's not like you have a mortgage or kids to worry about.'

She lifts her head and glares at me. 'Yeah. Lucky me. I don't have kids or a mortgage. I don't have anyone.'

'You have me.'

She quickly sits up again, and swallows. 'No. No, I don't. But I used to have someone. Someone else. Do you want to hear about her?'

'No.'

'Her name was Valerie. She was five years older than me. Her mother was French, I think that was where the name came from. A grandmother or a great-grandmother. She lived in Shoreditch. I wanted to live in Shoreditch but I had to live in Brent because I was poorer than her.'

'All right. Okay. You lived in Brent. Why are you telling me this?'

'Why not? She was wonderful. Such a beautiful soul, inside and out.'

'Where is this going?'

'I don't know. It's going somewhere.'

'Is she dead?'

'You wish,' she says, flashing her front teeth.

'Are you still with her?'

'Would you shut up and let me finish,' she growls, stamping her right foot against the floor. 'I was in love with her. I don't know if you've ever been in love with someone, what it's like.'

'Why are you talking to me like this?'

'Valerie was an English student,' she says. 'Doing a PhD on modernist something-or-other. I don't know. She really cared about her subject. She was so passionate about it, unlike some. I was at home with her. She carried my hopes and dreams around London Fields in her little brown bag. I was always looking for something, but with her I wasn't looking for anything. I had everything I needed. But then . . . ' Grace pauses.

'Then what?'

'You really want to know what happened, don't you?'

'Not really. Just . . . go ahead.'

She smiles. 'No, it's not important. I don't want to upset you.'

Grace revels in the control of knowing the end. It's funny, how secrets that can only really hurt develop an addictive quality. You can be driven mad by a half-told story. That's what happens at the end of your twenties. You began it with an infantile sense of life as a many-ended thing, but by the time you turn thirty you begin to see the lines and curvature of a personality. You begin to see the unbreakable narrative of yourself. You know life only ends one way. Hopes wither on the vine of a half-finished story, and the truth becomes a thing to be fought against. I think that's why people have children – the hope of another dice throw.

'It didn't work out,' Grace says, in a smug, podcasterly voice. 'Valerie had an accident. A car accident. A van went into the back of her near Chalk Farm tube station.' She gives me her best rictus. 'Just as well you and me can't drive, eh?'

I say nothing.

'She was in hospital for a couple of days after,' Grace continues. 'Some neck injuries but nothing too serious. She was okay. It was a lucky escape. Very, very lucky. She was wearing a seatbelt. She was always sensible. She drove like a pensioner.'

'Can't imagine you'd get much speed driving around London anyway.'

She glares at me. 'The whole thing really affected her,' she says. 'Near-death experience. It gave her perspective. It was, as Oprah says, an a-ha moment. It made her rethink her priorities. And it turned out, would you believe it, I wasn't one of them. She didn't see a future with me.'

'When did this happen?'

'She dumped me five months ago.'

'That's . . . recent.'

She shrugs, giving the look of someone for whom time has lately meant very little. 'I don't know how to be the kind of person people can love,' she says. 'We're getting old now, Phoebe, you know that. It all fades away until there's nothing left. I'm not clever or interesting. I'm not likeable. I'm just a body, and not much of a body at that. Soon I'll be invisible.' She looks at me. 'Welcome to being a woman.'

Our time together, then and now, has only ever had an attritive effect. We are ruining one another. Her, by her envy for my silent life; me, by my envy for her righteous heartache. Drowning is so often a dual endeavour, perpetrator and victim constantly swapping roles, both equally murderous and equally innocent. We could never be enough to keep each other going.

'I'm sorry you went through all this,' I say, still unsure if I believe Grace at all.

'It gets worse,' she says. 'I stopped going to work after Valerie ended it. I worked for a company that made labels. Yeah, labels. Putting my communication degree to good use. You know what happens to people who stop turning up for work? And that's how I ended up back in Ireland.' Then she says, 'Do you want to see a picture?'

'Of what?'

'Of Valerie.'

'No, of course I don't.'

Grace leans back on the bed and rifles through a small leather bag. She hands me a Polaroid. She doesn't tell me what it is – I am expected to know. It is a window into world I do not wish to see. There is a woman sitting on a blanket in a park somewhere. A picnic. There are other picknickers in the background, but they are irrelevant. Only this woman I am looking at matters.

Valerie looks shorter than me. She has long, brown hair tied in plaits, and is wearing black circular prescription glasses. She is chubby and not especially attractive. She looks business-like and warm, like a schoolteacher or an experienced au pair. She is feminine, naturally so.

'You should have told me about this earlier,' I say.

'Maybe I should,' she says, turning away from me slightly.

'You should have told me this was all a rebound.'

'That's not what this was,' she says, sighing. 'I don't know what this was. It's just a mess. Sorry.'

I stand up. 'Of course you're sorry. Everyone's sorry. But still you manage to find a way to remind me that I'm just here for other people's enjoyment. I'm an object to you just like I am to everyone else. Just another disposable tranny. An emotional support tranny. The next best thing to an actual woman, isn't that it?'

The more I speak, the more obvious it becomes that I no longer have the ability to anger myself properly. Everything simply devolves into a self-directed rage. I glare at the world and say, 'Look at the state of me! Look what has become of me! Look what a mess I am!' By accident or by design, the finger of accusation is always curling inwards.

'Jesus Christ,' Grace says. 'That talk says more about you than it does about me.'

'I'm just so sick of people and their ulterior motives. Pretending to get it. Pretending to care. You have no fucking idea what it's like.'

She sniffs, restraining tears. 'Yeah. You're right. I do have no idea. Can I talk now?'

'Go ahead.'

'Can you sit down? I want us to talk like adults.'

It rankles that she's suddenly so reasonable. I resume sitting on the bed. 'Why couldn't you just leave me alone?' I ask. 'I didn't need this.'

'No one else understood, Phoebe, and I thought you would. I thought I would learn to grow from it.' As she talks she moves her hand, extending it into an open palm as though she is presenting me with the truth unpolluted, but all it does is give the impression of a lecture. Even the way she says my name, like she is congratulating herself for remembering it and getting it right every time, only bothers me more.

I look up at Grace. 'Why do you always end up hurting me?'

'I don't think that's fair either.'

'I'm never going to be good enough for you. You don't give a shit about me. You're all about yourself, you always were.'

'You're being ridiculous.'

I'm on my feet again. 'You used me for a few months in your early twenties and now you're using me again, ready to walk away the minute something better comes along.'

She raises her hands. 'Okay. Right. Okay, Phoebe. Do you want to know why I broke up with you back then, if you're still so fucking sore about it?'

'Here we go, I can't wait to hear this.'

She breathes sharply. 'I broke up with you because you got me pregnant and I had to have an abortion, all right? I had to break the law. I had to get pills off the internet. I couldn't tell you because I'd no idea how you'd react. It made me realise that I didn't know you and I didn't trust you the way I needed to and now I'm starting to remember why.' She pauses. 'Jesus, I thought you had changed. I thought you were a better person now. But you're the same self-absorbed, touchy prick you always were.'

There is a silence in which our whole lives seem to breathe.

'Sorry,' Grace says, 'I shouldn't have called you that.'

'No,' I say, shaking my head, 'it's fine, it's fine. I have to go.'

I throw on my jacket, half-dripping and half-scorched by the radiator.

I pull open a red door with an evacuation map of the ground floor on it, Room 142 marked with a purple dot.

Back through the unwinding hotel, a warm bath of rectangles and deep colour, as redolent of asylum as anything else. Suddenly the predictability of the place is reassuring, medicinal.

I walk expressionlessly past reception. As the revolving door creeps towards me, I imagine myself striding up to the receptionist and calmly explaining to her that having violated one of their rooms and yelled at one of their customers, I am just about ready to check out.

It is still pouring rain outside. There is a man beside the door smoking a cigarette and wearing a windbreaker and a pair of tartan pyjama bottoms.

Half an hour from home, I cannot see, and now I'm the one running away.

18:17 So there's me, now, standing in my kitchen, peeling potatoes into the sink. A bouquet of potatoes, not too many, eight or so. They expose themselves sensuously like open eyes – eyes peeled! I laugh, because I get it now, because everything makes a fraction more sense than it did five seconds ago. The spuds smell damp and metallic. They corrode my skin so that the serrations on the pads of my fingers seem to scrape one another, so I am a gear-crunch body mismatch.

So deprived of sleep and gorged on circumstance am I that my senses have heightened. I have bat radar: coo-ee, coo-ee! The potatoes talk to me as I peel them. They say *shit, shit, shit, shit, shit.* Minutes go by, and the plaster on my hand becomes so wet it hugs itself morbidly and falls into the basin, and every time coarse tuber skin touches the wound there is a sting, which too becomes part of the process but

let

me

rewind.

15:17 The train carried me back from the hotel like a cowboy in a country song, or something. The moment didn't lend itself to poetry. It was blood-draw solemn in its acuteness. Sitting by myself, I decided, attempting, maybe, to put icing on the day, that it takes a real intimacy to see that someone is, and always will be, a stranger. Sometimes the best insights available about a person are in the negative realm: the absences of which you can be sure, the known noes. My head was now stuffed to bursting with anti-facts.

I couldn't cry when she told me, so I decided to laugh about it instead, to construct a joke and place myself in on it, as I zipped beneath the city listening to an acoustic song with the word serotonin in the lyrics.

The principle was no great surprise. Grace once saw a placard for a pro-life event – it was poorly placed, far too low – on Cuffe Street, and wrote *wankers* on it so it looked like a statement coming out of the mouth of this exhortative and prophylactic baby. She wrote in biro and cursive, a southpaw scrawl emerging from a downward-pointing, claw-like hand, which I took as proof that this sort of criminal damage was new to her, that she was finding a voice, emerging as an activist of sorts. I was nurturing her. I had to be nurturing someone.

And so, present day, I was sitting on the metro, front seat, driverless train, clear view of the track in front of me, two straight lines spirit-levelled with light, laughing away to myself. If only we'd listened to the baby! If only we'd been wankers!

No, no, Grace wasn't the surprise package here. The package of surprises was me. Visceral, it was, visceral and disgusting, to imagine I had left a part of myself, a most inhuman form of humanity, inside Grace. Potent, I was, shockingly potent. My body raised questions, questions symptomatic of regret, and I had scarcely finished asking them when I decided not to answer.

15:33 A discordant set of rooms. An apartment, cold as a morgue. The spoilage of the old routine: key to door, shoes off, second door on the right, my unmade bed, the bobbled duvet cover, the big pillows, the painted white ceiling with straight-line grooves across it, tears, hands on my face, a face that had seen so little.

There I was, in the middle of a great push-and-pull of place against place, time against time. In one corner, a life that performed the illusion of being simple; in another, a simplicity that performed the illusion of being a life. It was like being an over-wanted child, watching two parents fall out and slowly go their separate ways, devolved from a unity of sanctuary into two petty, embittered people, high-handed deadbeats whose cheaply sold love never ceases to be craved.

I lay and drifted on my weeping, the dog next to me, gormless and judgemental – priestly, really, a set of features prepared to deliver a languorous Tridentine on my behalf, jutting from a head shaped like a baby shoe.

I was crying for the things absent: degrees on the wall with the right name on them, graduation photos, maybe, a proud mother and a father who has never set foot on this campus and never will again, a career that did more than career, holidays without the dynamic of reconnaissance, the smell of sex, the experience of love, such as it was, such as it might have been. The sense of a life of which stock might conceivably be taken.

It was the way I had come to live not in my life but in my reaction to it. Living in fear, you might say. People are constantly told not to live in fear, of family-annihilator types, of wet-bulb temperatures, of teenage boys spitting puddles on street corners. But fear is an awfully comfortable thing to dwell in. To live in fear is a life of pure experience, because fear itself is a skin: it cannot be seen fully from the inside.

I had left my contradictions in hard-to-reach places. I thought I would never see them again. I hadn't reckoned on the ability of time to make them slip helplessly to the floor. History is not a library, but an exhibition – not a safe-keep, but a display.

Now I felt like a real person. The last twenty-four hours were the realest thing that had ever happened to me. I was at the mercy. I was living, living around corners and beyond horizons, but I was living.

16:04 A clear memory, possessed of a quiet violence. There were only seven candles on the cake, as many as could be found at the short notice of a trivial, prime-number age.

For my birthday, my mother bought me a hardback book about self-confidence – quite possibly one of those airport books with an asterisked curse word in the title: *Sort Yourself Out, You Stupid Little B****cks*. I can't remember what Grace bought me. What do you buy a soon-to-be nobody? What is the horse's head in this scenario? But I could remember them singing 'Happy Birthday'. My whole family and Grace, stood around my parents' kitchen table, scattered around a tune.

I was twenty-three. It was February of 2012. Syria was disintegrating and Greece was being bailed out. A famous singer had died in her bathtub and a famous footballer couldn't believe it. No one was quite sure why any of this was happening – merely that it was, and, like everything, it had a significance that would only be understood by posterity.

Grace and I said nothing to each other.

He was a jolly good fellow, by popular acclamation, and so say all of us. There might even have been a round of applause. The room smelled of damp towels. My mother was emotional and my father didn't know what age I was. Michelle was in her work uniform. I can't remember if Liam was still in school, so for the sake of argument I put him in a red school jumper. I sat over a cake with icing the colour of an eye infection and through my peripheral vision the others looked like Benetton models, or a troupe of Muppets telling me to get things started. All of us were funny and kind-hearted and we'd never be this good-looking again.

There were messages on social media. College guys stretching their youth trying out words like 'deportment' and 'teleological' for size, who sang Fenian rebel songs at commuters walking by in skirts and tights and trainers, young lads affecting a posture somewhere between Stephen Dedalus and Alan Partridge. People who hardly knew who I was. *HBD, man. Have a good one, man.*

Everyone was nice to me, and I was happy.

16:29 I had fertilised this woman, like a panting stallion. I was a daddy. I was a patriarch, big and swinging. There was no way of thinking about it that didn't lapse into pornography. Did it feel like success? Suffice it to say: it didn't feel like failure. It felt like a blackout story, like someone else's limby adventure being recounted second-hand. Like someone else's violence. It had the voyeuristic quality of true crime – just another of those awful things that happen, to be avoided with a main character's abundance of caution.

When, two years ago, I looked at my own birth certificate and saw the word Female in eight-point Times New Roman, I felt nothing – just the healthy scepticism that should always meet announcements on official paper. The document was sharp-edged and smelled fresh. Maybe I was embarrassed by it. How could I live up to the word? I was so much smaller than my identity, yet it left a deal of me uncovered.

I was an impostor – but, really, so is everyone else. The syndrome is spread like infectious disease. People are constantly trying to prove the world around them is a fake, to pull back the curtain and prove the sweet lies of their childhood were true, after all. Humanity has discovered that narratives are better than real life. We are unable to live up to the glorious paper idea of ourselves, man and woman, man and beast, man the measure of all things.

The apocalypse is a world without forgiveness, without heaven in heaven or heaven on earth. I am a harbinger of it, allegedly, of society's downfall, of the collapse of something at once ancient and vulnerable, something innate and fundamental which is presently being talked into disappearing. But in a manner of speaking, I am already post-apocalyptic: I have nothing much to lose. I am endlessly accountable. The tongue is unbitten, and it spills and spills.

16:43 I once saw a statistic, in an academic paper that might have been paywalled. It said that in 1951, more than one per cent of the entire Irish population was incarcerated. Gulags at the crossroads: nearly forty thousand people, only a few hundred of whom had been convicted of a crime.

Some of these people were fallen women, bastard children, the shame-ridden flotsam of a pious society, but most of them were simply mad. The majority were in mental institutions, run not by the church, but the state – places with high ceilings and cold chessboard floors. Places where unfortunates could sleep on creaky metal and rest in oversight. Places for people with ideas, and grievances, and inopportune claims on inheritance, capital forms of madness: mad to the point of inconvenience.

Society showed them their due regard. That was what it said in the constitution: *due regard to the equal right to life of the mother* – the right to life being, by a quintessentially Hiberno-English trick of language, a right not to live, but to respire, much as a farm animal does, as a bacterial spore does.

Grace and I would both have been locked up, for different reasons, but with the same general aim: to keep society clean. They'd have beaten the shite out of us in the name of empathy and a judge's due regard, for our own good, because they felt sorry for us. That's the problem with empathy: like love, it is blind.

17:19 Grace and I went out for dinner on the evening of my birthday, at a poky restaurant surrounded by *gerroumeway* adolescents in matching tracksuits and discordant hair. We were greeted by a server, a tortoise-headed bald man in narrow glasses. 'Table for two? Yes.' Grace asked me if I wanted her to tell the staff about my birthday, but I said no.

The ceiling was made of wood and covered with fluorescent lights like razor blade scars. We spoke in short sentences and ate quesadillas, next to a large painting of Frida Kahlo and a sign for cheap margaritas. One of us used the hot sauce bottle and the other did not.

Grace was upset with me but she didn't say why – or maybe she did, and I don't recall. She and my memory amount to a double knot. She said she hoped my twenty-third year was the best of my life. I smiled and told her this was actually my twenty-fourth year. I can't remember how she responded.

She was already looking through me. We were about six weeks from breaking up, doubts surely dribbling like foam from an overboiled pot. It makes perfect sense that she got pregnant that night, in my bedroom, in my parents' house, with me floating in the air somewhere, unable to face the immediacy.

You don't learn from your mistakes. Not really. Each one begets another five. I had hurt myself, yes, but I had hurt so many others besides. I had made myself an infliction. The reward for honouring a misstep is that you see, more and more, like a fractal pattern of human error, the way the shoreline is of infinite length if you measure it closely enough.

Everything I did in my youth was done with the express intention of preventing it from becoming a source of nostalgia. That was my main fear: that I would enjoy it too much. In the end, though, it wasn't my own caution that made the difference, but Grace's. She saved me from what I might well have wanted.

I was suddenly struck by the troubling sense that I no longer had access to the thoughts that had propelled me back then. It was like I had been speaking a different language, strange impulses emerging from a past self as if from a tomb.

Everything that had happened to me, all the autonomy I had stored up like grain in a silo, all of it was the product of a decision made by someone else. Without Grace, I would have no existence worthy of the name. I was human, after all; I was made human by her. She said she wasn't the kind of person people could love, but how on earth could I not love her?

18:04 My phone buzzed. There was a text. It said:

I'll need to come over about 7 to get my stuff. We don't have to talk if you don't want to

The clock on my phone read five past six. I asked her to wait until eight o'clock, because I was getting something ready. I wanted to show her I was no longer angry.

That is why I started peeling potatoes. But now I am tired, and the idea has lost its lustre, so I will go and buy a cheesecake and a bottle of whiskey instead.

18:41 I used to watch people die, once – online, that is. I was probably doing it while I was with Grace. Car accidents, industrial accidents, drownings. I would sit and make myself an audience to their coil-shuffling and feel nothing much. Online snuff movies are like online recipes, really: just so much preamble.

I didn't do it to upset myself, but to justify the pre-existing. I could say: yes, the world is a cruel and unforgiving place, where people die constantly by random chance, but not random chance, because death is so often a punishment for living too much. Best, therefore, to stay in the comfortable rooms of my own head.

I stopped doing this, but can't remember when.

19:18 People see more of themselves in the straightforwardly dead than the complexly living. The Irish language of grief, a language existing between two languages, has evolved from a truth: that it is easier to celebrate the idea of someone than to wrestle with their reality.

I have bought a blueberry cheesecake – gory, deoxygenated purple on top.

Home is back now all right, and we are celebrating it, and

its total lack. We are dancing in wounds, throwing up blood and flesh in a kind of frenzy.

I go to the spare room, heaving with stored items in boxes. Other people's belongings, nuisances in my space. I empty Camilla's boxes onto the bed, onto the floor everywhere.

They have to be boxes. That is certain. They have to be purpose-made by me. This place, the home of sorts, is beset with the generic: round plates, chic wooden spoons, grimy plastic window frames, all of it disgustingly elegant. It is so clean – everything is so clean! In these septic rooms, the true filth of individuality must be hidden away. The more efficient the surroundings, the more effective the repression. A home belonging to me truly would be one in which I had constructed everything myself to the blueprint of my own soul. It would be unrepressed, it would be free – it would, naturally, be a complete mess, agreeably ungovernable.

I lay boxes one by one across the coffee table in the sitting room, so that they form the steady rectangular shape of a coffin. Then I draw a cross in blue highlighter, the same blue highlighter by which I was picking out sentences in journal articles about climate change adaptation only a few days ago. How its role has changed! How the fallen have mightied!

I add a star, to make it less Christian, then a beady-eyed smiling face, so it is less Abrahamic.

I am always carrying the world that bore me. The word 'intergenerational' implies heredity, so that pain and struggle are passed on much like an eye colour or a propensity towards heart trouble. But the truth is that these structures are built for each child that is born. They are distinct, and subject to their own plans.

The Irish language of grief is truly a language, albeit a half-forgotten one. In Ireland, people do not die: they get death. *Fuair sí bás.* Like it is a possession, like it is a gift. When Irish people die, they are *imithe ar shlí na fírinne*, gone in the way of the truth.

I put on music. The Fleetwood Mac song we talked about yesterday. Soon enough, it is ready. Our little wake. Our in-between space, between truth and falsehood, between life and death. I am struck by the sense within me of a set of coping mechanisms hardening into a person.

I start talking to the dog. Telling her how true redemption is found not in the cleaning of slates, but in looking at history until it becomes a thing small and familiar. I laugh at her, and the way we have swapped roles. How ordinarily, she only exists between midday and seven in the evening, when she sticks her head into the gaps between my furniture and plays call-and-response with the upstairs floorboards. Now, I am taking up space I didn't used to. Now, I am the one howling.

She looks at me, sat like a prize ham.

19:48 The first thing Grace notices when she enters is the tang of artificial lavender. 'Christ, all the candles, what the hell have you been up to? I feel like I'm in a dream. Or a candle shop. You're not going to kill me, are you?'

Then she sees the boxes.

I gesture like a mad orchestra conductor at them, to prevent Grace second-guessing their purpose. 'I had an idea for something we could do tonight. Something special to round off the weekend.' I pause. 'And I'm not going to kill you.'

'Phoebe, I'm *really* tired. I've had, like, six hours sleep since Friday. And I've just quit my job. Things are messy enough, you know? I think I just need sleep. This is all so . . . '

'Uncanny? It's uncanny, isn't it? It's like a beautiful dream.' Not only can this not be explained, but I don't even want to explain it. It is perfect in its mindless, blissful perplexity, like a delirious sunset happening within the apartment, which demands to be gazed upon and not considered too deeply.

Grace looks at me like her eyes might be about to melt out of her face. 'Yeah. That's . . . yeah. I don't know, I was going to ask you if I'd made a huge mistake today, but I don't think I want your advice now. You've lost your marbles.'

'I know, I know, it's all very weird – as you say, correctly, RIP marbles – but it'll be worth it. I promise.'

'It feels like I've walked in on an exorcism.'

'You have! You have,' I say, walking towards the coffee table. 'That's exactly what this is. We're going to exorcise our demons. And – look! I've bought cheesecake.'

'So we can be in an exorcism episode of *The Golden Girls*?'

I spread out my arms in the manner of a crucifix. 'Yes. Yes! Absolutely yes. You are so right. You have never been more right. That's exactly what this is. It's like *The Golden Girls*. Which one will you be?'

We both agree that we're Dorothy, but we both secretly want to be Sophia.

Side by side on the sofa, good neighbours, like sublime and ridiculous. Whiskey is poured into ordinary glasses. Grace looks at me and mouths the word 'Okay,' and I wonder if I should be taking notes. We are fingertips hanging off the edge of history now, ready to chase our shared existence and its sordid implications.

She asks me if I have any spells or incantations. I tell her all I have are a dozen raw potatoes in the kitchen sink. For breakfast.

. . .

Four thousand one hundred Had I not been good? They were drowned – a pair of sodden boys' pyjamas, cotton, with a red tartan pattern. You laugh at me when I tell you of being eleven years old and wetting the bed. It is amusing, in its bygone and anecdotal way: the idea of a small child, smaller than he realises, mortified by his own excretions, by the tangy smell of it, by the texture of it against him when he wakes up in the morning, six-thirty. The way it hit his skin as an unfathomable cold descending into a shame in which he also found himself steeped. He knew his body would change, he had read all the pamphlets, even the girl ones he wasn't supposed to, and so he sat there and thought: is it finally happening? Is this growing up?

Eight thousand four hundred and forty-nine I knew something was wrong, but I told myself everything was okay. My period was late: four days, a week, ten days. I went to Clarehall to buy a pregnancy test – twenty-five minutes on the bus from the city centre, the biggest supermarket in Dublin, like an aircraft hangar. I didn't want to be seen. I don't know who I was afraid of being seen by. It was the tenth of April 2012, a grey Thursday morning. There was a plastic security tag on the box, round like a combination lock. I bought two. I wasn't going again if I made a mistake. I watched the cashier remove the tags from them, the bit with the magnets. Retail work is magic if you've never done it before. The woman said, 'It's ridiculous how expensive these are. They should be free, shouldn't they?' I said yes.

Ten thousand two hundred and eight People in books say it's a sign of stress, I told her, years later, when I brought up the bedwetting. I had been under stress. Bodily stress. My mother told me she didn't remember it. There was a lot going on, she said. Your sister was a teenager; teenage girls are hard work. She questioned me about it as if I might have pilfered it from another childhood. Surely she had noticed at the time, given the evidence. Had she not seen all the effort I had made to hide it? But then: isn't the first responsibility of a child to make themselves matter? That is why we squeal after we are born. An anguished announcement. Where was I?

Eight thousand four hundred and forty-nine The test was like the inside of a copybook: straight lines. A pregnancy test is like a horoscope, or a personality quiz. You ask it about yourself and it tells you. I didn't think about how it happened. It wasn't worth obsessing over. There was no point dwelling on it, allowing it to grow. I cried and cried and thought of my ma. I knew she would understand. She used to tell me she grew up on mean streets. I didn't know if she was joking. Her people were Dublin's first people, from the oldest part of the city. They were like Adam and Eve, except instead of eating the fruit they sold it at a profit. I knew she had seen it all. The problem was you.

Ten thousand The problem was me. (Work backwards from here.)

Five thousand six hundred and thirty-two I wasn't alone. I was always a duplicate or triplicate presence. I was a thousand shards of mind and body, a city of birds trembling in unison. The more I refused to listen, the easier it got – like breathing, it became part of the ambience of life, requiring no conscious effort. Life became something moved through like so many identical streets, sodium light and ugly cars, a uniformity. I grew comfortable with the sound of my screaming. It was, after all, in someone else's voice.

Eight thousand two hundred and forty-one I wore the right kind of shoes, but you didn't own the right kind of shoes. There were days we'd walk to the foothills of the Dublin Mountains, up around the Hell Fire Club. I'd joke about seeing ghosts, but you were practically haunting the place yourself. We'd look out over the city together. Poolbeg, the incinerator, the Spire, all the rugby pitches on the southside. Our awful home, its edges jagged like our own. I think you liked being away from everyone. It made your eyes kinder. You joked that if we got married, we could live on a boat. Then you emphasised: *if*. You wanted to be loved, but I think you needed a kind of love I wasn't able to give you. I was your first, but you weren't mine.

Eight thousand four hundred and forty A poster was on the wall, encouraging people to stop smoking, featuring a cartoon woman in a blue pantsuit, a website, a helpline. *Learn to breathe easier* was the slogan. My hands fiddled with a pair of in-ear headphones. I was sitting in the waiting room of a doctor's surgery in Dublin, but I did not smoke. I was there because I was at war with myself – but I wasn't, not really, because that would have been impossible. To be at war with myself would have meant certain defeat. All battles are lost until the arms are set down. The war is only won once it ceases to be a war. But I did not yet know any of this, so I waited to be called, walking, still, through the desert.

Eight thousand four hundred and sixty-six Of course, I also got pills over the internet. They arrived through the letterbox of a friend's house in a jiffy bag surrounded by white tape. There was a London postmark, and a handwritten address with IRISH REPUBLIC in big letters at the bottom. The block capitals made me think of the word REPENT. I sat on my bed and stared at it on my lap. It was small, but bigger than what was inside me. I didn't feel like you did. I didn't feel a connection to anything. I felt like invasive hands were running over the inside of my body, inspector's hands. I felt like I didn't belong to myself. I was still trying to figure out a purpose for myself and now I was given one without being asked. I was told: this is who you are. Why did I have to have an instinct, an intuition?

Eight thousand four hundred and seventy-four My friends called you a manchild. I stood up for you, though

I didn't disagree. My ma told me it's worse to have a mismatched relationship than none at all. You live and learn, she said, like you might say to someone who's been scammed. I suppose, if I was nicer, I'd tell you I always thought about us as parents, thought about what you would be like as a father, whether you would be kind or strict, what our kids would look like, whose hair, whose nose, but the truth is that the notion was so odd that it never crossed my mind. It would be like thinking about flying to the moon, or having two heads, or being a man. I've looked into the gold fillings of one-night stands and thought they'd be more plausible fathers than you.

Eight thousand four hundred and sixty-three We were drinking cups of tea, the colour of the ugly loafers you used to wear. My hands resting on the cold of a yellow and orange PVC tablecloth. I asked her what I was going to do, and she told me to shut up. 'Shuddup,' she said. We're going to get through this and then we'll worry about the next thing. One day at a time. I started wondering what she knows, what she has seen. I had reached an age where I started thinking about how much like her I was. I had started to see that she was once a young woman herself, and how much of myself was really just an echo of her. She said she was with me all the way. She kept saying that: all the way. All the way where?

Eight thousand four hundred and sixty-eight I told a man in a suit and he pretended not to hear me. He told me officially there was nothing he could do. The law was very clear, he said, and I told him I hadn't asked about the law. He said I should find someone else but made no recommendations. I told a woman in a green blouse and she advised me to take painkillers. That was all the advice I got, searching through faces, looking for an answer.

Eight thousand four hundred and sixty-nine The prison sentence was fourteen years, but I wasn't worried about that. What worried me is that I would die and no one would care. I didn't have an excuse. I didn't have a backstory. I wasn't important. I was bleeding within a few hours of the first tablet. My insides were rising and falling like the sun. Sometimes I felt like I was evaporating away. Other times I felt like my body was a cement mixer. Then there was clear liquid too. I spent the next twenty-four hours expelling myself from myself. Expelling you, I suppose. It was an efficient enough process.

Eight thousand four hundred and forty-nine We drank coffee, something with milk, and a barista's heart in the foam. We sat at a shaky metal table outside, a criss-cross texture, like a giant manhole cover. It was April and the weather was improving. I was abandoned again: first by me, then by you. You told me you felt the timing was wrong. How long do you want me to wait, I thought. You were so sensible and mature. You were perfect, and I was murdered by your perfection. I told you I was doing well. I thanked you for everything, the good times especially. I put a ten-euro note on the table and didn't talk to you again for seven years.

Eight thousand two hundred and twenty-two I was a flower, waiting to be picked. I was a misdeed, eager for correction.

Nine thousand three hundred and ninety-nine You know how it happens in life, that you meet someone and your mind plays a trick on you, and you think you know them already? They seem to fit a space in your life that was waiting for them. There was a woman in a coffee shop in Camden Town. It was half past four in the afternoon and starting to get dark. The indoor light was the colour of honey. She was sitting at a long table with USB chargers at the end, but her laptop was closed. She was reading a book when I went to talk to her. I interrupted her. I got in her way. I saw her and decided who she was going to be. And she wasn't you – she could hardly have been less you. She smiled at me and told me I was rude. I spent most of the next two years with her, with the danger and light and subversion of her. For the first time, it felt like I had let myself love who I loved.

Eight thousand two hundred and ninety-six I couldn't help what I loved. I was with a woman queueing for a table at a bar on Wicklow Street. Her smile danced passionately with blue and pink light. I talked to her and she listened to me. She told me of the music she enjoys, noisy and extroverted, like her. I told her of myself, but never could I shake the feeling I was lying, recounting an alibi. I'm being ridiculous, I thought. I am young and stupid. People always say that love feels like anxiety – I was clearly head over heels in it. This is what it's supposed to feel like, I thought. We are young.

Nine thousand four hundred and seventy-four There are memories so vivid they don't need photos. A reckless October afternoon at Kew Gardens. It was pouring with rain. It was mouldy, I said, and she didn't know what I meant. Ten minutes of bad weather, then twenty, and soon the whole day was gone. We skipped from tree to tree like they were huge umbrellas. Afterward, she and I sat in a pub while cups of tea steamed like saunas. We were drenched but we didn't care. She said we were drowned rats and then we spent ten minutes talking about what it would be like to be a guinea pig. We laughed at the look on the barman's face, the knowledge he wouldn't have served lads in our condition. It was so different to meet someone and feel like they understood, like walking under a different sky. The woman I sat with was a reader and a writer. Maybe I got the beauty of her words mixed up with other kinds of beauty. She read me a poem about the meaning of life – but aren't they all? It was like I had stepped out of myself. I was learning from my mistakes.

Eight thousand three hundred and three I bit down into a pair of lips and held on for dear life. I was vampiric. I wanted to make myself through you. Wouldn't that be something? To be a part of my victory. Please save me.

Eight thousand four hundred and fifty-nine I didn't know you. In hindsight, I didn't even want to know you. What a waste of us both.

Nine thousand five hundred and thirty-eight I waited for the right time and eventually it came. I told this woman things I never told you. The greatest despair, the worst things that had happened to me. He never saw me as the eldest daughter, not a domestic servant or a childminder. He would have liked a son, though he never said that in so many words. I never went through an adolescence with him so he'll always be a godlike childhood presence to me. He had mousey, curly hair and was short, only five-foot-seven, but he was huge to me. He died young, but then, I didn't think thirty-nine was young. I thought it was ancient. He had honourable green eyes and he worshipped Rory Gallagher as a deity. He talked of wet date nights with my ma at gigs in the National Stadium before I was born, everyone sat obediently in their seats but not wanting to be. He'd go on pilgrimages to Cork, to remember his hero, a man who also died prematurely.

Eight thousand five hundred and sixty-seven My finger slipped and a couple of years' worth of photos scrolled by, until I came to one of us on my phone. It was blurry and spoiled by too much light. We were standing next to a man dressed as Shrek – was it Halloween? Why weren't we dressed up? Who took this photo? The detail of the moment escaped me, but I could remember caring. I remembered the fun we had, the permission I gave myself to have it. I was certain that if the person in the costume was here, they would vouch for me. Perhaps the problem was that it was all just too important. An overload of significance can create a response indistinguishable from apathy. Too much need and pain from the surface looks like nothing at all. People drown in lakes more often than they drown in the sea. There is jeopardy in stillness.

Three thousand eight hundred and ninety-five He died the week before the October school holidays. The crying didn't start when he departed – it started when he arrived, when he came home from the hospital, nowhere left to go but home. It's funny how death can break your sense of context. It was Halloween that week. We didn't have decorations, but others did. It rained non-stop on the day of the funeral. No wind, rain falling straight down, white-noise weather, the saddest sort of weather, resigned. Our clothes and belongings dripped all over the floor of the church. They played 'I Fall Apart' and my grandad read a poem about falling leaves. I can't remember it. I've tried to find it but I've never been able to. I mentioned it to her in London and she didn't know it either. They sang the 'Chorus of the Hebrew Slaves' as they lowered him into the ground. Misery is such a circus – he'd have thought it was hilarious.

Nine thousand nine hundred and thirty-three There were three or four razor cuts on my knee, like bullet marks in the side of an old building. There was another on my wrist, and spots of fresh, puerile blood on a white towel. I wanted so desperately to be beautiful. There was and remained so much poison to be purged. I used to read stories people would write online about taking the pills for the first time. They would feel something akin to a parting of the clouds, like everything had become clear and suddenly they were at peace. That was all I really wanted: a special moment of catharsis, of self-actualising insight, me against the world, winning for once.

Ten thousand and eleven I cracked an egg open and it was mostly air, but there was also a question: can you be loved if you never tell anyone who you are? I had obviously never experienced unconditional love, because my life had been always conditional. I had made do without it. I had performed. I had played the necessary roles, functionally, like a piston in a car's engine, like the hand of a reliable clock. Perhaps that is why I fell in love with lies, why I cradle falsehoods and comfort objects and illusions of beauty filling in for the real thing. I have lied and I have been lied to.

Three thousand nine hundred and thirty-two What happened to her was pretty gradual. She took a lot of time off work, but no one had a problem with that, under the circumstances. Everyone was lovely about it – I think, after a while, she started to hate being asked how she was holding up. I didn't care. I liked having her home more. And then sometimes I would find empty bottles in the narrow space between the settee and the wall. School lunches would go unmade, but I tried to do the work myself, trying to master the unwound roll of cling film, the butter knife. Being a mother is a kind of magic too, or, at least, that's how I saw it back then. Now, it's just another kerb I keep tripping over. We'd get lifts from neighbours in the mornings, while she was still asleep, and we'd get home in the afternoon, and she'd still be in bed. She had taken to the bed, she had taken the drink, but most of all, she had taken to herself. No one could find her anymore. She was tired, we were told, by relatives. She'd had a long year.

Ten thousand six hundred and eighty-five I went to Amager – a day at the beach. My first summer in Copenhagen had begun and the referendum in Ireland had been a success. Northern Europe was baked by a heatwave, which moved across the landscape, from the courtyard of Dublin Castle to the Øresund strait. I didn't swim, obviously, but I sat with my thoughts on the white sand, on a towel with Lund University's crest on it, while the hours spilled behind me. It was like I had left a cult. I was humbled, but I was free. I had learned my capabilities, and I still had so much to unlearn. I got home that evening and found out that the white sand at Amager is artificial. Indeed, the whole island on which the beach is located is manmade. In Denmark, they call it 'Shit Island', because it was built on a landfill. I decided I could wear that as a title of nobility. A self-made wonder. A tranquil island of shit.

Three thousand nine hundred and thirty-five A few weeks after he died, we were brought to a park and asked to let off a balloon for him. We had to write a message for him. I wrote: *it's hard without you, but I'm being good.* I watched it climb through the clear blue air and thought about how little my feelings really mattered against the December wind. I didn't feel like I had communicated with him. I was too small and the balloon too small for that. The most productive thing I could do was be useful to my ma. My sister had only just started school the previous autumn, so I had to look after her, make sure she got to and from school, keep her fed and washed, tell jokes about the mushrooms growing in her ears like my dad used to. I was helping Ma out. I thought, if I made myself helpful, I would help her to get better.

Ten thousand and fifty-six A picture of my sister and I stood on a shelf in my old flat. It was an image of us as children, in a forest. The scale of the trees only made us look smaller. I framed it and put it up when I thought I was at peace with everything. I printed it at the university. But that was then. Reconciliation, such as it is, is jittering and hesitant. Is it wrong to say I came to wish my sister hated me? Maybe I envied the simplicity with which some people are discarded by their families. They don't end up with all this residue inside them. I didn't want to be an edge. I wanted to be a child again.

Ten thousand one hundred and fifty There was a pot on the floor, in pieces, tangled in the remains of a cactus bought months ago in a supermarket. I wanted to break more. I wanted to tip over the shelves. But no, I thought, no, they are not your property. Restrain yourself. Restrain yourself. Six months later, home again, my mother told me that failing me was one of the biggest regrets of her life. That she was sorry for not having done anything. Perhaps that should have been vindication. I could have bit her courtesy off and spat it at her. I could have refused to forgive her. I could have broken everything, furniture and family ties. I could have said things that could never be taken back. But I restrained myself then, too. Because, really, she had nothing to regret. Whatever anger was woven through me was always at the mercy of a shame that served as a reminder. You did this. You know you did this.

Three thousand nine hundred and sixty-nine The first week of the new century, still on holidays from school, our aunt brought us to the wax museum in town. It was full of old men, footballers none of us recognised, and puppets from the television. Caoimhe would run over to things and stand and inspect them, like she was at a proper art gallery, like she was making mental notes. I found the whole day strange. It was eerie. It was like we were being led around the edge of a world where things were happening that we couldn't understand. It was like our own lives were a museum, and we were standing behind glass. I felt like an animal being taken off to what might be a farm, but might not.

Ten thousand four hundred and seventy-four Life is a process by which illusions are lost. That is why bodies get smaller with age: they are less bloated with the theoretical. I moved from one apartment to another. I learned to live with my own diminished significance. I had thought, foolishly, that I would achieve inner peace while shocking and outraging everyone else, but the truth was the other way around. I lost something fundamental: an idea of life as a just thing; the sense of safety a child needs to put one foot in front of the other. The truth, it turned out, was that no one really cared what I did. It was as if I had died and gone without mourning.

Three thousand nine hundred and sixty-nine When we got home that day, we were told that Ma had gone into hospital. It was a psychiatric hospital, with big gates and empty grounds around it. I guessed it would take ten minutes to run from the door to the street, and you'd have to climb too. The best place for her, they said. She needs a holiday. We visited her a few times. We had to put on shoes to see her, but she didn't wear shoes for us. She was there for three months, and she was better afterwards, so much better that we never needed to talk about it again. But it changed things. Kids grow up believing their parents can do anything, and I suppose there's a hidden edge to that: when you realise they're not all-powerful, you see it as a reflection on yourself. You're in the big world, realising your power, and you never know what's your own responsibility and what's not.

Ten thousand four hundred and seventy-six Healing can only be seen in rear-view, so I lived my life assuming it had already started. He was a poison I wanted to purge from myself, but, the more I tried, the more I realised that it was my body that had produced the poison. We were simultaneously parasite and host. He broke me into so many pieces and then he tried slowly to solder me together again. Give him a hammer and a nail and he would do a very good line in hammering nails. Ask him what he wanted to do and he would look at you blankly. Perhaps that was the good in him. He never asked questions.

Four thousand and thirty-nine I didn't tell anyone in school what had happened. It was a secret I kept. I had been told that children aren't supposed to keep secrets, but this was a benign one. I was doing her a favour, doing everyone a favour. We were nomads in strange houses until well into the spring. Spare rooms, other children's toys, other families' habits. Other people are hard work, but they get easier when you do the work yourself. The blackout curtains would be closed and I would perform, I would sing and dance, All Saints and Britney Spears, and I would show that, despite everything, I was still here, and I still mattered. I helped everyone to feel better.

Nine thousand nine hundred and ninety-three I went to the national park at Söderåsen, a coniferous forest surrounding a lake. I wandered alone between trees and water and open space, knowing that soon I would no longer be able to. My all-alone body would be more vulnerable than before. My horizons would be that bit narrower. And maybe that was his gift to me. He was a wanderer. The world offered itself to him, and he let me go, and that is why I buried him in foreign soil.

Nine thousand five hundred and thirty-eight I told the woman in London everything. She comforted me, and then she left.

Ten thousand nine hundred and ninety-six, just about The average life contains more days than there are miles in the circumference of the earth. Twenty-four thousand nine hundred and one miles: sixty-eight years' worth of ground to cover. Life is not short – it is vast. A life is a celestial body, with populated and less-populated spots, with its own atmosphere, its own gravitational pull. *Life is short* is a lie for which there is ample evidence – people say it when they want you to buy something. But, if you live each day like it's your last, you are limited to the scale of a single, final day. A life lived in fear of missing out becomes a life with little to miss out on. Existence is a responsibility over which we totter, on which every compass-point seems to nudge us backwards. History is an experience shared incompletely, its yawning tensions a blessed trap, because, truly, we are nothing without them. They are the very ground beneath our feet.

Ten thousand nine hundred and ninety-six

Monday

06:55 The new week is nameless abundance, unbaptised, unsaveable. Perched like stood-up mermaids on a round rock ridden by bodies, on the cool side of a temperate continent in denial of its storm-port position, by a bitter sea that was once a cautious lake, in a country never quite as perfect as the happiness index made it seem, in a snub-nosed quarter of a gentrifying city, between walls which for too long stood to offcast the preceding and its consequents, Grace and I grow silently, fresh-hearted, into our shortcomings.

A mobile phone alarm wakes us, bleeps and cymbals and artificial acoustic guitar; a dawn chorus to which Dolly quickly adds her own voice.

We start again. The early morning carries a heavy weight – though the wash of rain can no longer be heard outside, dim light fills the room in a manner suggestive of submersion, adding a layer of depth and distance between us and beyond. There is the sense that tectonic floors have rearranged themselves in our absence and we are no longer upon them. Adrift, we are, everything is, at a life's-length remove from itself.

I half-dream half-think of home. My mother's regimentation. Ten past seven on weekday mornings, no later than half past eight at the weekend. 'Get cracking,' she used to say. Sometimes there were handclaps, sometimes Áine Lawlor's voice from a shower radio. That so many of her mothering days were replaceable didn't stop her seizing them. Now, though, I am without her and her mordant awakenings, and content to close my eyes and let the dawn crack first.

Grace is up and about before I've properly shaken off my sleep, an unseen noise in another room. Her flight departs in five hours, but she moves as if in a much greater hurry. It might be the thrill of escaping again. Really, it was the inevitability of our parting that obliged a nod to truth, the way the closing of a door can prise open a person – otherwise, we might have carried on pretending for ever.

Sitting on the couch, I hear her stuffing clothes into a plastic bag. 'D'you wanna help me pack, Dolly?' she says, in a squeaky voice. She still has belongings in the hotel room, so she'll need to go back there and check out before heading to the airport.

'Morning,' I call out. 'Do you need a hand?'

'No, don't worry, I'm on top of it,' she yells back.

I laugh to myself. I was never worried.

Then she comes to the door and smiles at me. Her face is dreamily awake and her hair dozily askew. 'Good morning. I'm not being rude. Just, like, you know,' she says, holding up a half-full carrier bag through which I can see a loose purple sock.

'No, I know you're not being rude,' I reply, but by the time I finish the sentence she's already gone again.

The sofa is strewn with thin strands of hair. I try to indulge a mystery, perhaps to blame the dog, but it's clearly all mine, too long and dark to be anyone else's. I'm leaving traces of myself everywhere, now, perhaps more than ever.

The air in the flat is stale, with sharp notes of old love. I open a window and put on some coffee for the two of us, something to trade words over, something to counteract the empty whiskey bottle that sat in front of us as we slept.

07:31 'I'll miss your coffee,' she says, sitting on the sofa. There is an audible slurp.

'That's all you'll miss?' I say, standing in the kitchen, putting the bottle into a bag of clear-glass recycling.

'I'll miss a few things. The coffee is one.'

'They take it very seriously over here. I suppose because in winter it's dark at three in the afternoon. They have to keep themselves awake somehow. I bring it home at Christmas. It beats my parents' jar of instant. I think I have a spare packet here if you want it.'

'I wasn't looking for a freebie.'

'No, but you've got one, so don't talk yourself out of it.'

'Have you ever got Dolly a Puppuccino?'

I inhale sharply. 'That sounds like it would loosen her bowels.'

'It's grand, it's only whipped cream in a little cup. Starbucks do them.'

I hastily put a dampened paper food-waste bag into something stronger. 'We have whipped cream in a little cup at home, don't we Dolly?'

And it's just that, nothing much, the soft-speaking of the lost and finding, words circulating like air, filling a space, an unexpected pocket of time.

We don't live together in the domestic sense, but here we are, together, living, overprepared and underready. There are so many families that brew between us: the stone-etch ones we retain indefinitely; the one we might plausibly have had together, ruinous for us both, and others still; the family of moments we had back then: the misunderstandings, the misplaced chivalry, the mistiming; the family of worries and hopes of which we are sturdily constructed; the family of conversations we might wish to have had, among ourselves, and with others, here and gone; the family of people we have been to each other. All of it appears now, not beautiful, but impossible not to love – and what could be more unequivocally familial than that? A person is always collective: you have to hold them severally.

While I organise rubbish, putting empty cardboard rice boxes and plastic apple bags into another bag, also plastic, I can hear her. I'm unable to see around the corner to find out what she's reacting to, if she has her phone out. Sometimes she laughs – not quite a laugh, really, just an 'mmm-hmm' chortle. She seems to be carrying on a quiet conversation with herself.

I go over and sit beside her, and she scoots over unnecessarily to make room for me, and then she starts babbling. 'I can't believe I did it. I can't believe I quit.'

'Yeah. Me neither.'

'I was so sick of everything. God, I feel so free. I have so much power over things now. And I know it won't be easy but I don't care. I'm supposed to be going in an aeroplane but I feel like I could fly myself home. I'm walking on air.'

'What are you going to do with yourself now?'

She pauses for a few seconds. 'Live. I'm going to live.' And we both laugh softly to ourselves, like she's said something silly, even though she hasn't.

I pick up the dog, who was standing in wait at my foot. 'Are you going to live in your mam's house?'

'For now. I mean, I don't have anywhere else. But I don't even care about that. I'm just sick of doing things because they have to be done and not getting what I want. What's the point?'

'It's like being in an abusive relationship with the world.'

'Yes! Fucking *yes*. I'm divorcing the world,' she says, with a cackle. She's seeing something I like to think I recognised a while ago: that the best things in life are temporary. If everything is random and unrelated to merit, if disease and sadness and lacking are inevitable anyway, why not succumb to it? Why worry about the maybes when you're being thrashed by the currentlies? So many people go through life taking a chance on everything but themselves.

'You're washing the world right out of your hair,' I say. 'Did you ever see that picture of Nicole Kidman after she divorced Tom Cruise?'

She laughs. 'Do I look like that?'

'Yeah, a bit.'

She smiles. 'It's funny the things that bring you close to people. It is, isn't it?'

I nod, though I don't know what she means.

'Like,' she continues, 'the things you did to cope with who you are. They're the things I fell in love with. It's not very romantic, but, when you think about it, it's the same for everyone.'

'It's so hard to ever really know anyone, and by the time we do it's too late for us not to love them.'

She laughs quietly. 'That's very true. You must not be as hungover as I am.'

Then we sit in silence for a few minutes, punctuated only by sups and the groaning engine of the odd car in the courtyard outside.

'I was just thinking,' I say to Grace, 'when we were dancing to the Saw Doctors here on Friday night, I thought that was it. I thought you had come over to put me back together again, that I would end up back in Ireland, where I thought I really belonged. But that's not what happened. If anything, I think you've convinced me I was right to leave.'

She smiles. 'If you ever end up in Ireland again, I'll look after you. As long as you have an air mattress.'

'I might hold you to that,' I say, and look at my phone. It is the first of April. Anything could be said; anything would be disbelieved.

08:36 A bag of glass recycling is left next to the door of the sitting room, ready to be brought down once Grace has left. Every so often it settles itself, uneasily, like it too cannot keep still.

We stand by the door, Grace keeping herself one step removed from the rituals of departure. 'Sorry last night didn't work out the way you planned,' she says.

'No. It's okay. I got what I wanted out of it.'

She smirks. 'Do you not have work today?'

'Bollocks, yes. Do you think they'll notice?'

'A woman in academia? Nah, you're invisible already.'

'Yeah. Thanks. I appreciate that, I think.'

She leans against the frame of the door. 'So, what do you do with yourself all day?'

I laugh divertedly, at the way it's taken us this long to get to such a perfunctory question. 'I teach a little bit. A module on Aid and Development, Tuesdays and Thursdays, so I haven't missed any. The students are funny, and generally not at my expense. The girls are nice to me. And the guys are . . . the guys are quiet.'

'I'm sure your students love you,' she says, pursing her lips. 'They're your babies.'

And I laugh again. Perhaps the faculty are my family, and the students might well be dolls around me. Growing up, I was always told to look out for things that seemed too good to be true. But how everything is: jobs are hobbies are families are love. Everything, from candles to careers, must be seen to plug an emotional gap. It's no way to live, this buck wild searching, but for now, it's the only way.

I used to think myself utterly fascinating, because there seemed no one in the world like me. The tensions within appeared utterly unique, and I came perilously close to giving in to the desire to carry them as prized possessions. The enduring danger of despair is that you can find yourself in it. Now, I know how alike I am, throwing stones in the ruins of someone else's life – left, as everyone is, with the responsibility of inventing a future out of found objects and tatty old scraps. It is not authenticity, nothing is, but it is real.

'Please do come home for my thirtieth,' Grace says. 'I'd love to see you there.'

I want to produce for her a clear answer, but the way is blocked by a thicket of questions, about her, about who we are to each other. 'I'll see what I can do,' I hear myself say.

'Okay,' she says, and walks out to put her shoes on. Dolly starts making noise, but by now we've learned to tune it out. 'And another thing,' she says, as she pulls a shoe on.

'Yeah?'

'Talk to Leyla.'

I feel myself becoming smaller in the presence of the remark. 'About what?' I ask.

'About anything. You need people like her in your life. She rocks.'

'Are you saying I should ask them out?'

She giggles and sticks out her tongue. 'I'm not saying anything. You're the one who said that.'

'But they think you're my girlfriend. How would I explain that?'

'Tell her . . . tell them the long-distance thing wasn't working out.' She stands and looks straight at me. 'There was just too much distance. Tell them we really loved each other a lot, but there was too much weird history between us. Tell them you needed a fresh start with someone who could love you for who you are. Someone who really understands you, without needing to be taught.'

It is an acid truth that sits between us. She is right, though neither of us want her to be. We have spent the night grieving, but only now is the death at the centre of it all truly visible. History wrote us into these roles, having to lose something twice to realise what we had really found. Loss speaks its own language, and only time coheres it.

I give her a smile of boxed-up heartache. 'You know, when you arrived on Thursday I texted my friend Ana about you.'

'You were talking about me behind my back?' she asks, in mock-outrage.

'Yeah. I was plotting. Ana said this was like something out of a film. And it really was, and now the film is over and the lights have come up and the floor is sticky.'

'And real life is back,' Grace says, finding the words to ground my sentence. 'It had a happy ending, though. The reason I came over was because I wanted to remember who I was when I was young and had all that freedom. And I guess what I learned was that I was hurting even then. And so were you. We had a lot in common, looking back.'

'Yeah. Yeah, we did,' I say, sniffing gracelessly. 'Listen, I'll keep in touch. And you know where to find me, but please call ahead next time.'

She laughs. And then we stand and stare at each other, at a conclusion both inevitable and so fiercely resisted. The door open, and the dog is anguished – everything is just as it was on Thursday night. Then Grace steps forward. 'I want to give you something.' She manoeuvres through her bag and hands over a familiar piece of paper. 'Here.'

It is the picture of Valerie sitting on her picnic blanket in London. 'Thanks,' I say, though I don't know how to interpret the gesture.

'I think she's better off here with you. I need to get rid of her, you know? I shouldn't be carrying her around with me all the time. Throw her in a bin. Set her on fire. Give her the send-off she deserves.'

And I guffaw, first because I don't know how to respond, and then because I realise that she understands after all, that the world is a pool of grief made bearable only by its being shared.

'We'll take good care of her,' I say, 'won't we Dolly?'

Grace smiles. 'Eat her with some fava beans, Dolly.'

We both laugh, and Grace steps forward to hug me, just as she did when she arrived on Thursday night, but this time we kiss, the end of the weekend more complex and unknowable than the beginning. Now her mouth tastes of filter coffee. I know her, and she knows me. I am known.

And then she is gone.

09:15 I am sitting on the arm of the sofa, looking out the window. In my hand, I hold the picture of Valerie, staring at it like it is tomorrow night's homework, something almost familiar but not yet fully comprehended. The background is cloudier than I remember it being yesterday. Then the image was polluted by my jealousy; only now can I see it for what it really is.

And it comes over me as a sudden ache within me. I hate this woman. This awful person, this collection of expletives, this person I've never met before, this woman who could be a stock photo model for all I know. I hate what she represents, feel myself hate her and feel that hatred shiver out of me, and then I am at ease. It is like a tight knot has loosened. I can move again.

For so long I have been like a child, so frightened of my capacity for love that I cannot bear to give any away. But now

I am burning furiously, from the inside out. I have learned to say yes and Grace has learned to say no, and though the words are different, the lesson is the same. It is by actions like these, the encounter not merely of love but ardent recognition, that we make each other legible, that we make each other bearable.

Yet Grace will now be walking through an airport, making her way to a gate, waiting for a plane that will take her back to a life that aspires to little more than continuing languish. I think of her thoughts. She will have extra time on the journey back, potentially fifteen more minutes, because the winds are west to east over northern Europe, so they are headwinds on the way to Ireland, as if to hold her back. She might think during that slack quarter-hour, as she approaches home's forcep embrace, of how existence has betrayed her. She may herself burn as she looks like a sea bird at the curves and bluffs of Ireland's east coast; at Bull Island, where we used to walk, coupled, but anonymous to one another; at the cold sea over which we used to gaze.

I wonder what it is I have created in her this weekend. She is the one that got away, now more than ever – I have no idea what comes next. She will need me, and I her, as we make with history, not peace, but a softer-hearted form of war.

10:07 The smell of it can't be romanticised. The gel is mostly alcohol, so it resembles slightly the experience of rubbing a cleansing disinfectant into myself.

Okay – perhaps it can be romanticised.

I sit on the bed, an outbreak of routine in a day at neither its beginning nor its end. I squeeze it toothpaste-like from the tube and rub it into the skin of my leg, following the instructions carefully. It covers the great expanse of my thigh, shimmering for thirty seconds or so, until it disappears into me, where it belongs.

Bodies have an intent that supersedes our own – it's just that we can never fully know what it is. The skin is, supposedly, for protection, yet the hormones find a way through the dead cells and the dermal layers. The alcohol in the gel acts as a kind of soap, breaking surface tension, denaturing membranes and aiding absorption. The chemicals are then stored in the subcutaneous fat, and from there distributed slowly through the body, like a healthsome intravenous drip beneath the skin.

And then the hormones have their own process – skin: thinner; nipples: thicker; eyes: bigger; crying: uglier. I am not altering the blueprint of my body – these things were always there, from the day I was born. They just required a certain mature and gentle coaxing, a habitual tensing of the muscle of self-knowledge.

Almost a thousand days have passed since I started doing this. Yet between varying changes in method, adjustments to dosage, forgotten doses, I couldn't possibly calculate how many times I have done it. It is not a particularly grand gesture. It has no real posterity. Like much that changes a life, it is merely a tweak to routine. To live is a choice that is made every day, without fanfare – and to be a woman is to focus on the small things of life, to view each day as a site of exploit, as beginning and end and everything else.

I think now of my mother, of the loneliness the two of us have spilled on one another, as a baptism. The times she would phone me and talk about her day, her work colleagues, the extended family, the neighbourhood, politics local and domestic, trying to fit me into an empty space. She had something to share, meekly in her words, and fiercely in her silences. Yet more pointed than any of that was the quiet that emerged when she realised I didn't care, and stopped calling me.

Loneliness can be a presence and an absence. It can be a sharp, agonising thing, a malnourishment, yet it may also amount to nothing less than a screaming presence that demands to be shared with the world. Loneliness can be a pathology, it can be a compulsion, but it is so often an unsurveyed site of possibility.

Once, I pushed people away, hacked at them like they were thorns around me. Having dismissed them all, perhaps I have learned in spite of everything that I am irredeemably one of them, one of the people. I too am a thorn, and now it is time to pierce a side.

I dry my hands on my bedsheet, where the gel leaves a residue that gently fades away. It is clean, after all. It leaves nothing essential behind.

I take out my phone and press her name, and wait for an Irish dial tone.

Acknowledgements

To Candida Lacey, Vicki Heath Silk, Vidisha Biswas and the rest of the team at Footnote Press, for giving me an opportunity I can only hope I have lived up to.

To my agent, Liv Maidment, and the team at the Madeleine Milburn Literary Agency, for an extraordinary amount of support and motivation. (Sorry about the teary emails.)

To Fiona Murphy for her words of encouragement when I was just starting out, and Danielle McLaughlin for, among other things, reassuring me that making a dog a major character wasn't a mad idea.

To Martin, Eleanor, Karolina, my writing group, the Madeleine Milburn mentorship and Penguin WriteNow group chats, and a small, impatient dog called Heidi on whom I became emotionally dependent during lockdown.

To Ireland's trans community. I am forever grateful for you and you deserve better.

(Side note: the Black trans girl Phoebe says she read about, who loved Fleetwood Mac, is based on a real-life letter in Jules Gill-Peterson's brilliant *Histories of the Transgender Child*.)

And, finally, to my family: my parents, my sisters, my brother, my niece, and everyone else. Σας αγαπώ όλους.

Most of this novel was written in my grandparents' house in County Wicklow, an act of artistic patronage they didn't quite realise they had signed up for. They both passed away in the months before it was finished. My grandfather was a noted wit and a talented yodeller, and my grandmother was a bravura dressmaker who loved Maeve Binchy. They'd both have found this book very strange. I miss them greatly.

About the author

Soula Emmanuel is a trans writer who was born in Dublin to an Irish mother and a Greek father. She attended university in Ireland and Sweden, graduating with a master's in demography which she likes to think inspired her interest in society's outliers. She has written for *IMAGE* magazine, Rogue Collective and the Project Arts Centre, and has had fiction published by *The Liminal Review*. She was longlisted for Penguin's WriteNow programme in 2020, took part in the Stinging Fly fiction summer school in 2021 and was a participant in the Madeleine Milburn Literary Agency's mentorship programme for 2021/22. She currently lives on Ireland's east coast.